P R

An Arro...

An IndieBound Bestseller
An NPR Best Book

★ "In lush prose, Pan retells both the Chinese legend of Chang'e and Houyi and Shakespeare's Romeo and Juliet. The seemingly ordinary setting of '1991, in Fairbridge, Where We Lay Our Scene' opens up to a world full of mystery and magic."
—*The Horn Book*, starred review

★ "This novel is a work of art." —*SLJ*, starred review

★ "Intricately woven tapestry of first love, intergenerational struggles, and the joys and heartaches of growing up."
—*The Bulletin*, starred review

"An effortless fusion of myth and realism, coming of age and fairy tale, this luminous love story rises on gossamer wings but cuts bone deep." —Melissa Albert, *New York Times* bestselling author of *The Hazel Wood*

"This story really comes alive through Emily X.R. Pan's prose. Every sentence feels imbued with an ethereal magic. The two protagonists bond as they discover their family's secrets, navigate their futures and seek to understand the mysterious forces that surround them." —NPR's *Books We Love*

"*An Arrow to the Moon* is a beautifully crafted blend of mythology and modern love story, full of stunning prose, characters who feel achingly real, and magic lurking just behind the ordinary. One of my new favorites!" —Hannah Whitten, *New York Times* bestselling author of *For the Wolf*

"A lyrical love story infused with Chinese mythology." —*Time* magazine

"A brilliant story that will have you lingering on every moment. Hunter and Luna will capture your heart." —B&N Reads

"Story that glows with ethereal magic." —NPR

"A lovely, lyrical exploration of how a poignant Chinese myth might play out in a contemporary setting." —*Kirkus Reviews*

"As anyone who read *The Astonishing Color of After* can tell you, Emily X.R. Pan's writing is, well, astonishing, and this story, pitched as Romeo and Juliet meets Houyi and Chang'e, solidifies that fact." —Buzzfeed

"Like Pan's debut, *An Arrow to the Moon* will blend romance, emotional storytelling, Chinese mythology and fantastical elements for an unforgettable combination." —*BookPage*

"A young adult novel that crafts a bittersweet narrative of love, family, and culture." —*The International Examiner*

"Expansive, third-person chapters—including some from the adults' perspectives—and snippets of lore create a contemporary telling with an otherworldly, age-old feel in this cleverly conceived novel." —*Publishers Weekly*

PRAISE FOR

The Astonishing Color of After:

A *New York Times* bestseller
An IndieBound bestseller
Bustle Best of YA Books
A *Paste Magazine* Best Young Adult Novel
Winner of the Walter Honor Award
Winner of the APALA Honor Award
A *Los Angeles Times* Award finalist

"Emily X.R. Pan's brilliantly crafted, harrowing first novel portrays the vast spectrum of love and grief with heart-wrenching beauty and candor. This is a very special book." —John Green, bestselling author of *The Fault in Our Stars* and *Turtles All the Way Down*

"Emily X.R. Pan utterly transported me to a world reminiscent of Isabel Allende. Haunting at every turn, this is a glorious debut." —Renée Ahdieh, bestselling author of *The Wrath and the Dawn*

"This beautiful, magical journey through grief made my heart take flight." —Holly Black, bestselling author of *The Cruel Prince* and *The Darkest Part of the Forest*

"An extraordinary debut from a fiercely talented writer." —Nova Ren Suma, bestselling author of *The Walls Around Us*

"Magic and mourning, love and loss, secrets kept and secrets revealed all illuminate Emily X.R. Pan's inventive and heart-wrenching debut. " —Gayle Forman, bestselling author of *If I Stay* and *I Was Here*

"Emily X.R. Pan beautifully depicts grief in all its complexities: the numbing sadness, the rage, the confusion, and, most hauntingly, the joy." —Bustle.com

"Through Leigh's emotional, illuminating first person narration, Emily X.R. Pan peels back the layers of her grief to expose the heart at the center. The result is a novel as lyrical as it is earnest." —Tor.com

An
Arrow
to the
Moon

Emily X.R. Pan

LITTLE, BROWN AND COMPANY
New York   Boston

Copyright © 2022 by Emily X.R. Pan

Cover art copyright © 2022 by David Curtis. Cover design by David Curtis and Sasha Illingworth. Cover copyright © 2022 by Hachette Book Group, Inc.

Little, Brown and Company
Hachette Book Group
1290 Avenue of the Americas, New York, NY 10104
Visit us at LBYR.com

Originally published in hardcover and ebook by Little, Brown and Company in April 2022
First Trade Paperback Edition: October 2023

Little, Brown and Company is a division of Hachette Book Group, Inc. The Little, Brown name and logo are trademarks of Hachette Book Group, Inc.

The publisher is not responsible for websites (or their content) that are not owned by the publisher.

Little, Brown and Company books may be purchased in bulk for business, educational, or promotional use. For information, please contact your local bookseller or the Hachette Book Group Special Markets Department at special.markets@hbgusa.com.

The Library of Congress cataloged the hardcover edition as follows:

Names: Pan, Emily X. R., author.
Title: An arrow to the moon / Emily X.R. Pan.
Description: First edition. | New York : Little, Brown and Company, 2022. | Audience: Ages 14 & up. | Summary: "A lyrical and magical novel about two teens who fall in love despite their families being caught in a bitter rivalry"— Provided by publisher.
Identifiers: LCCN 2021006084 | ISBN 9780316464055 (hardcover) | ISBN 9780316464048 (ebook) | ISBN 9780316428910 (ebook other)
Subjects: CYAC: Love—Fiction. | Families—Fiction. | Magic—Fiction. | Chinese Americans—Fiction.
Classification: LCC PZ7.1.P3573 Ar 2022 | DDC [Fic]—dc23
LC record available at https://lccn.loc.gov/2021006084

ISBNs: 978-0-316-46402-4 (pbk.), 978-0-316-46404-8 (ebook)

Printed in the United States of America

LSC-C

Printing 1, 2023

*In the process of writing this, I almost thought
I would never find my way out of the woods.
But I did—and so this book is for me.*

Once upon a time

There was a girl who lived on the moon as its guardian. She was its heart and its breath.

One day, standing on tiptoe to glimpse the boy who made the stars fly, she lost her footing and stumbled off the edge. Her plummet was like a stone displacing water. It shifted the universe off its axis.

Slowly, slowly, everything began to crack.

1974

XIYANG VILLAGE

The air smelled of overturned earth and impossible things. Birds dove in front of the sun like embering ash from a stick of incense. The farmer wiped the sweat from his brow and paused his work at the drill to take a swig of water. He spat aside the grass in his mouth and felt a shiver cross his skin: that distinct feeling of being watched.

The unblinking eyes stared at him from several paces away, low in the grass. The head of a man. Mud-colored. Preserved. Was it some kind of hungry ghost, making itself visible in order to bestow a request upon the living?

No. Neither a man nor a ghost. A sculpture? The farmer thought it was likely made of the same clay as the teapot that sat on his kitchen table. A nudge of his foot sent it rolling and revealed a shard of similar material half-buried in the ground.

"What are you doing?" another man called as he bent toward the land. "The well won't be over there."

"I found something," he replied. "Do you have a shovel?"

"What do you need a shovel for?"

The others came over to watch as the farmer dug and scraped. More hands and tools joined to scratch at the earth, and by the time the sun was treading just below the horizon, they'd pulled up a collection of broken terracotta pieces. Enough to fill a wheelbarrow. The men would take these to the nearest city to see what money could be gotten for them.

Someone called out, "Look!"

They all saw it: light shining from the very bottom of what they'd excavated. It burned brighter with each second, and the men held up palms to shield their eyes. The ground shook; one farmer shouted an earthquake warning.

By now the world was a quick-dimming gray. It was in this almost-night that they watched the silvery light rise into the sky—a star falling in reverse—until it disappeared from sight and none of the farmers could be sure the phenomenon had been real.

The star arced through the skies. It cracked in half as it fell back down to the other side of the globe. One piece landed first; the other tumbled for a longer stretch.

In those moments, two children were born and given their names.

Hunter Yee.

Luna Chang.

1991

IN FAIRBRIDGE,
WHERE WE LAY OUR SCENE

Luna Chang

Luna Chang was about to make a bad decision.

The door of the walkout basement yawned wide, and the older kids were already pouring into the night. Guppies who'd been flushed down the toilet, now finding their freedom.

"What are you doing?" Luna said to no one specific.

"There's a guy the next house over who's a senior at Fairbridge High—he's throwing a party," said one girl.

"Like, a real party?" said Luna.

"Yeah." The girl hesitated. "Our shoes are upstairs, though."

As if in response, a saxophone intro blared from above, followed by some auntie's microphone-enhanced vibrato. Luna hated these things. Her mother and father liked getting together with the other Mandarin-speaking members of their very white community—which, good for them. What she didn't get was why they had to drag her along.

While the parents wailed out Chinese oldies on the sound system upstairs, all the kids—aged four through eighteen—were relegated to the basement. This was where the youngest ones wreaked havoc and broke the cue sticks of the miniature billiards set. Where the teenagers were sullen-faced and sighing, and the oldest ones pretended not to have heard about one another's SAT scores from their parents. Luna used to have Roxy for company...but Roxy was away at college now.

"We're celebrating the Mid-Autumn Festival," her father had said when Luna didn't want to go. He'd opened his face wide with exaggerated cheer. "There will be so many different types of mooncakes!"

And then he was wrong. There was only one kind—red bean—and they didn't even have salted egg yolks in them. This party sucked.

Luna could stay here in this corner of this random auntie's house, watching awkward middle schoolers work at loops of string for cat's cradle. Listening to the occasional exchange of jokes that weren't particularly funny. Idly wondering about the people she didn't recognize and probably would never see again.

Or she could do something different.

Her heart drummed in her ears. She was not a rule breaker.

"We don't need shoes," Luna said as she stood up.

Most of the teens had already gone. Only the youngest kids were left.

"I'm telling," said a little boy, pouting. He looked fearful of the open door, the wind gusting through. He was the one who had snapped all the cue sticks in his fists.

"No, you're not," said one of the older guys, his tone nasty.

The kid deflated.

Luna ran over the prickly grass, shivering in her T-shirt and jeans, the late September wind whipping at her ponytail.

In a few blinks she was across to the other yard, stepping beneath the back deck and through a new door into a crowded basement. The air was thick with the smell of cigarettes and maybe something more.

Music thrummed in the bones of the house. If not for a group of people drunkenly singing along to "Losing My Religion," she would not have been able to pick out the song behind all the chatter. This was the kind of party you saw in movies, or heard about after the fact, through the gossip chain. It was not the kind of party where Luna ever found herself. She wasn't even allowed to attend school dances.

Maybe this was a bad idea. Should she go back?

Directly ahead of her was a couch with just enough space left for one.

"If you sit here you have to play," said a red-haired girl she didn't know.

"Play what?" said Luna.

"Seven Minutes in Heaven." The girl grinned mischievously.

Luna had never played it before but knew the gist of the game. There was a flutter in her gut. She was seventeen years old and had never been kissed. She'd never had the opportunity, especially given her parents' *no dating* rule.

And really, Luna was curious to do a lot more than kissing.

The girl leaned over to explain. "Each person takes turns spinning that bottle, and whoever it ends up pointing to—"

"Go, already!" someone shouted.

The boy being nudged was sitting on the floor, shaking his head. Luna was pretty sure he'd also come from the basement of the other house—he was one of the kids she'd never seen before tonight.

"I'm just watching," he said.

Someone with pale skin and the world's baggiest jeans stood up. "Nope, you're playing, and I'm spinning for you."

The empty Coke bottle was sent turning like a spoke in a wheel. Luna thought she felt a droplet hit her knee; the bottle was probably newly emptied. The glass swept around and around, trapping the light and colors of a nearby lava lamp, drawing circles on the low table.

The bottle began to lag and teeter, then rolled to a stop. As if summoned by her gaze, it pointed directly at Luna.

The group howled with delight, and the girl who'd made her join was pulling at Luna's wrist, getting her to stand. Her pulse shifted like gears changing.

Luna could have resisted, if she'd wanted to. She could have bowed out—peer pressure was a thing that didn't really work on her.

But a feeling rolled up like a current: Here was a kind of adventure.

Hunter Yee

Hunter Yee hadn't meant to join the game, but here he was, being shoved into a random room in a stranger's house. The door slammed shut behind him, and it was like a bell jar dropped down. Noise disappeared, sucked away in one gulp.

He looked around at the modern art adorning the gray walls. Large bed pristinely made and stacked with pillows. Small dresser in the corner. All of it dimly lit by two lamps.

And there was the girl the bottle had chosen. She faced away from him, watching creatures in a bright fish tank as they swept and darted from one side to the other.

Well, this was weird.

Hunter tried the doorknob. Whoever was on the other side was holding it tight. They gave a hard knock as if to admonish him.

He stuck his hands into his pockets and headed for the tank. It would probably be a good idea to speak. His palms were

sweating. Why was he so nervous when he didn't have any inten-
tion of actually *doing* anything?

"Cool fish," he said, then winced. *Cool fish?*

The girl didn't respond. Didn't even acknowledge that he'd
spoken. Hunter hadn't gotten a good look at her face back when
the bottle had been spinning. But her hair was so dark, and the
way her ponytail hung…he was guessing she was East Asian.
She definitely didn't go to Stewart.

She was wearing a T-shirt and jeans and her feet were bare.
That was a clue—the lack of shoes. Hunter wondered if she'd
hopped over from next door, same as him.

That was when he noticed the fish were following the girl.
She held her fingers up to the tank, and wherever she moved,
they moved. The water pulled gently from side to side until she
dropped her arm.

"Whoa," said Hunter, stepping forward to give it a try. The
fish scattered before he got his hand halfway up.

"How'd you do it?" he said.

She shook her head. "No idea. I've never seen that before."

Her reflection watched him in the glass of the tank, dark eyes
locking on his. For a moment, he forgot to breathe.

She turned so that their gazes met through nothing but air.
Raised her index finger up in front of his face, moved her hand
from side to side.

"Guess my trick only works on the fish," she said.

Hunter found himself huffing a laugh.

The girl smiled, and he felt as if a weight slipped off him. Her ponytail had gotten swept around in front. She smelled like fresh laundry and something sweet. Maybe honey.

"So," she said. "Have you done this before?"

"Done what?" His knees were oddly weak.

"Wandered into a random house for a game of Seven Minutes in Heaven with a fish-controlling girl?"

His eyes dropped to her lips.

What he knew about Seven Minutes in Heaven—or rather what he guessed, based on the conversations he'd overheard in the Stewart cafeteria: It was supposed to be spent lip-locked, maybe shedding a few items of clothing. It was supposed to go by in a hot, sweaty blink.

Several things happened in the next breath:

Someone called, "Time's up!" The door swung open and cacophony spilled into the bedroom.

Luna spun to look and her knuckles grazed Hunter's arm by accident. Light bloomed where their skin met.

The floor rumbled and tilted, and in some other part of the house, people started screaming.

Hunter heard the words "It's an earthquake!"

The girl disappeared out the door and into the crowd before Hunter could stop her. Noise came rushing back into his ears like a blast of wind.

Luna Chang

Luna ran through the house, dodging inebriated bodies and dangerously angled SOLO cups. Picture frames rattled against the walls. The ground was still shaking when she burst out of that basement and into the night.

It felt almost like a punishment for what she'd done. She never broke the rules like this. Not that there had been any spoken restriction—just the implicit understanding that her parents expected her to stay put, that they would be furious if they knew where she'd been.

She made it back to the other basement just in time.

"Luna!" her mother was calling from the top of the stairs. "We're going home!"

The rumbling had stopped, but her parents were too nervous to stay.

"That didn't feel like a normal earthquake to me," said her dad. "Not like the ones in Taiwan."

"Aiya, look at your feet!" her mother exclaimed. "And what

is that smell?" She checked that nobody was within range before whispering to Luna, "How is their basement *so* dirty?"

In the car, her parents gossiped about the families in attendance at the party, and Luna tried to quell the guilt thrumming in her veins. What on earth had come over her? She couldn't believe she'd snuck out like that. It was miraculous that her parents hadn't noticed she was gone. She pressed the end of her ponytail to her nose—it smelled like cigarette smoke. She would dive into the shower the moment she got home.

Laughter from the front of the car helped to settle her pulse. Some joke or other exchanged between her parents; she'd missed it. Luna watched how her dad gazed lovingly at her mother until the light turned green.

She exhaled. The days would pass, and this one night would be nothing but a memory glittering in the back of her mind. She tapped a finger against her knee—the same finger that had drawn the fish back and forth in that water. How strange it had been. How right it had felt.

And that boy—something about him felt very right, too.

She wasn't sure what had prompted her to behave the way she did. There'd been this unfamiliar boldness. Like someone had reached inside and turned her volume way up. She blushed and shivered to think of the minutes spent in that room. His eyes had been inky pools. His mouth looked soft. She'd very nearly leaned in and kissed him, because why not? That was the whole point of the game, wasn't it?

What had given her pause was the feeling that they were being pulled toward each other, as magnetic and bizarre as those

15

fish following her fingers. And when the door burst open on them: that point of contact for the sliver of a second. Her skin against his, and the spark between.

No, not a spark. Something bigger that made her hold her breath. She remembered the way it glowed before snuffing out.

Then there was the floor tipping and shuddering—she might have stayed longer if that hadn't happened.

Luna couldn't help wondering: Would she see him again?

Hunter Yee

Would he see her again? For the rest of the night, he would replay that moment of her disappearing, his mind wheeling around the regret of not getting her name. He'd thought that maybe he would find her back in the other basement…but then the house was in uproar, and his parents were looking for him, already mad. And his little brother was quiet in that way that indicated he was tremendously upset. Hunter guessed that it was because he had left Cody behind to go to the party.

It was hard to sleep. Hunter stared up at the ceiling, thinking of the exact shape of the girl's dark ponytail and her soft-looking lips. The way she had taken that awkward moment and somehow burst it open, like touching her finger to a bubble.

The next morning was hell. The thing was: Hunter was a wayward star, shooting in the wrong direction.

Stay out of trouble, his mother said, time and again.

He tried, for the most part. But it was hard to fix a crooked arrow, forever veering from the intended path. The times when things went mostly right, his parents still had a way of finding fault in everything he did.

So he wouldn't bother telling them that he had gotten himself kicked out of Stewart on purpose. In their eyes, that would probably be even worse. There was no scenario in which they would pause and listen enough to understand. They would think whatever they wanted.

Their voices floated high above him:

...irresponsible...

...waste...

...disrespectful...

...disgrace...

The words were misfires, launched at the wrong angle. They couldn't pierce him.

Hunter's parents believed this dark little kitchen, where they stood now, to be the most insulated part of the house. This was where all the yelling ever happened, where their raised voices were least likely to be heard from outside. Even irrationally angry, they were cautious.

The Stewart School had called, of course, making them aware that when Hunter applied for college and needed the academic transcripts, the details of his record would be forwarded along as well—with strong emphasis on the descriptions of his various misdemeanors.

He rolled his eyes. It could have been so much worse. But his parents only cared that Hunter was, yet again, a screwup. Why couldn't he be the eldest son they'd hoped for? Didn't he understand that he put them in a terrible position?

Hunter bit back his response: *They* were the ones who had pissed off some random dude they refused to talk about. *They* had gotten *themselves* into their terrible position, and Hunter and Cody were the ones suffering the collateral damage.

There was nothing to do but stand there like a cold pillar of stone and let his parents shout until their throats were sore. His little brother was nowhere to be seen. Hunter bet that Cody was huddled beneath the blanket fort in the corner of their shared bedroom, eyes squeezed shut, listening through the wall.

"If this ruins us, that'll be your burden to bear for the rest of your life." Hunter's father was panting now, he'd gotten himself so worked up.

"How would this ruin us?" said Hunter. He'd almost blurted: *How would this ruin* you?—but caught himself just in time.

"People will hear about your antics," said his dad. "They'll ask questions. 'Who is this Hunter Yee? Who is his family?' Not only do you bring us *shame*—" And here he spat the word, then paused to take a big breath. "Not only do you cause us to lose face, but if someone discovers where we are? If the right person finds us? Do you think that all these years we've been so cautious just for fun?"

Hunter knew what his father was turning red trying to say, and he would have been lying if he didn't admit that the thought sent a cold trickle down his spine. But Hunter was also tired of this, of the constant paranoia. Sick of how everything went back to that same fear.

His mother shook her head, her small frame wilting as she did so. "He understands. Now that he's going to a new school, he'll start fresh." She turned to speak to him directly. "You'll be better, right? No more trouble. Remember that anything you do affects others' perceptions of Chinese people."

She sounded exhausted.

"We're disappointed, Hunter," his dad said. "This is not the behavior I expect from a son of mine. If you keep this up... maybe you won't be. Not anymore."

His mother gasped.

"What's *that* supposed to mean?" said Hunter.

"You want to be a criminal? You want to be a failure? Do you know how often you make your mama cry? When we speak to you, erbianfeng. Do you even hear what we say? If you don't want to be part of this family? Fine."

"No, Dawei," said his mother, determined to be his mouth-piece. "Hunter will try. He will be better."

His dad turned away. "We'll see."

"We can ask Zhang Taitai to pick him up and drop him off—"

"I'm perfectly capable of taking the bus, you know," Hunter said loudly.

But his father was already out of the kitchen, and his mom shot him a look telling him to accept it.

Great. He would be escorted to and from school by a babysitter.

Hunter retreated to his room and found his brother exactly where he'd guessed, under the fort with a worn sheet over his head. Hunter crawled along the floor, squeezing between the wall and bed frame until he made it to the socked feet peeking out.

"Hey, Cody."

Cody pulled the sheet off, and it rubbed a crackle of static into his dark hair, made the strands stand up.

"Sorry for all the shouting," said Hunter.

Cody rubbed at his eyes. "Why are they always so mad?"

Hunter searched for a pocket of truth big enough to hide the lie. "That's just how grown-ups are."

"But you're almost a grown-up. And you're not mad."

Hunter laughed, but it was without mirth. "Sure I am." He was mad all the time. In fact, he was furious. Sometimes he lay awake deep into the night, unable to understand how his parents made their decisions. He wound the rage tight like a string around his finger, wondering what it would take to finally cut off the circulation.

Sometimes he thought it would be best if he just left. He was certain that he could survive on his own, and he'd been saving up money all these years in case it really came to that.

But he couldn't abandon his little brother. That was what kept him tethered here.

"When I grow up, I'm never going to be mad," said Cody.

"That's a good aspiration," Hunter replied. "I should try to be like you."

Cody crossed his arms. "I'll *never* be mad like that."

Luna Chang

There was a firefly on her hand as she reached for her tea. She blinked and it was gone.

Luna paused, waiting for any other hint of movement. Things had been weird for the last week. Ever since the night of the party.

"Everything okay?" her father asked.

The owner of Fortune Garden came over to their table bearing three platters, and Luna was saved from having to respond.

"Here are the dishes I told you about. Bitter melon, oyster omelet, and fried sauce noodles."

"Mary, these look wonderful," Luna's mother exclaimed. "So impressive!"

"A sneak peek for my favorite regulars." Mary grinned. "You have to be honest about the flavors. I'm still tweaking the recipes before they go on the menu."

"Delicious," said Luna's dad, his mouth already full. "The pork fat really makes a difference."

Mary gave the noodles an extra stir. "When you go to Taiwan this year I might ask you to bring back some spices for me."

They'd been speaking in Mandarin to help Luna practice, but now her parents switched back to Taiwanese to wax poetic about the merits of dry soybean paste. She took it as permission to let her mind wander.

The question was: Why were there suddenly fireflies everywhere? Sometimes the flicker of a light as she was tying up her hair. Sometimes pressed against her window. They were appearing at all hours of the day—weren't they supposed to come out only at night? Wasn't it too cold for them now? She'd pointed one out to her dad the other day when it was especially chilly, and he'd simply shrugged, made some comment about how perhaps a species of them had evolved.

She felt like once upon a time she'd known why the fireflies were important. What had she forgotten?

"Luna, you're graduating this year, aren't you," said Mary, jolting her from her thoughts. "Have you decided which schools you're applying to? All the Ivies, I bet."

"Her first choice is Stanford," Luna's father supplied, beaming.

Mary produced a thumbs-up sign that was almost cartoonish. She said in English, "Shoot for the moon, and even if you miss, you'll land among the stars." Switching back to Taiwanese: "But we all know you'll make it to the moon."

Luna worked to keep a pleasant look on her face. She took a second helping of noodles as a way to busy her hands and mouth.

Her dad's eyes lit up. "Have you heard the story of how she came to be named Luna?"

"No, tell me!"

"She wasn't supposed to come for another two weeks," said Luna's mom. "I had just seen the doctor that morning."

"I was impatient," her father added. "I wanted to hold her already."

"That night, we ate dumplings for dinner. Hsueh-Ting made them—he's a great cook."

"I believe it," said Mary. "You hear how he critiques my recipes?"

"I looked up through the window and saw a bright light falling." Whenever Luna's mom told this story, her voice thickened. "I thought it was the moon at first. Then I thought it was a shooting star."

"But it was more elegant than that," said Luna's father. "The way it moved—a shooting star is a scratch across the sky. This was like a flower blooming as it fell. It touched down at the same time that Meihua's water broke."

Her mother beamed. "So I decided to name her Luna, and she was exactly the blessing we believed her to be."

Luna was embarrassed. Sometimes when her parents told this story it felt sweet and fizzy, and she grinned along to the silly dramatization.

Today it made her restless. She was sick of staring at college applications, brainstorming for asinine essay topics. Her parents' expectations had become a paperweight, and she was meant to hold still, neatly flattened.

"I'm going to the bathroom," she announced, standing up.

"Wait," said her father, pointing at her, "do you want to order anything else? Dessert?"

"I'm full." A couple steps away she realized she hadn't thanked Mary, but they'd already moved on to a new conversation.

"Did you hear what happened after that earthquake the other day?" Mary was saying. "It's terrifying—they found a crack in the ground...."

The restroom was cold; Luna welcomed the shock of it. Beneath fluorescent lights, she washed her hands and scowled at herself in the mirror. Her usual ponytail pulled her black hair tight against her scalp, but the shorter bits had sprung free. A few pimples dotted her forehead. Had that boy at the party noticed them? She fought the urge to run the pad of her finger over the bumps.

Senior year of high school was meant to be some important milestone; next fall would be the start of college. For some people, that was exciting, but for Luna, based on her parents' expectations... it would really just be more of the same.

She worked hard at everything she did, of course. She was "meticulous and high-achieving," as her teachers wrote in the comments section of her report cards beneath the column of As.

Really, she wanted... something different. She wanted to be the type of person who took charge of her own life and went off on epic journeys. Someone who did daring, unexpected things. Why couldn't some mage appear, like in the fantasy stories—a sorcerer summoning her to become her true self?

The future her parents envisioned for her did not include

mold-breaking adventures. It involved desks, maybe corner offices, and stifling clothing. Papers and numbers and all manner of mind-numbing elements that brought in the kind of paycheck that offered stability. She was meant to fly from the nest in pursuit of this.

She knew the things that were expected of her. The clear path forward. Her parents just wanted the best outcome, and it was wise to trust them.

If only she wanted the same things. To go to Stanford. To live that perfect life. She wished she even *knew* what she wanted.

There was a restlessness between her ribs, itching and pulling at her heart. A feeling that she was meant to do much more.

She and Roxy had gone to see *Dead Poets Society* a couple years ago, and afterward that quote from Robin Williams's character had echoed endlessly in Luna's head: "Make your lives extraordinary."

Extraordinary. She liked the sound of that.

Turning to leave, she noticed a painting hanging on the wall next to the sink. It showed a firefly sitting in the palm of a dark, open hand. Her breath snagged. What the hell did the fireflies mean?

Outside the restroom, she could see her parents gathering their things up to leave, pausing to chat with someone they recognized. She waited for them beside a line of wide fish tanks that smelled like the raw section of a supermarket—more functional than decorative. The creatures inside the murky glass were storm-colored and silvery, slow-moving, the length of her forearm. They looked numb, like creatures who didn't know how to want.

Luna found herself remembering the brightly colored fish at the party. The turns they'd made, trailing her finger. She raised her hand, an experiment.

Like the needle on a compass, the fish pivoted. They moved in unison, swooping to the left, veering back to the right. She was a conductor and this was her silent orchestra.

Roxy would never believe this. Who would? Nobody.

Except for that boy with the inky eyes.

Luna dropped her arm and the fish scattered, and it was as if she had summoned him with her thoughts: That exact pair of eyes blinked at her from the other side of the tank, setting off her heart. Was it really him?

She shifted, and so did he. For every step she took, he followed. He sucked in his cheeks and made fish lips, and Luna laughed. They shuffled to the end of the tanks, emerging from behind glass and water into air, into nothing. Before she could think of anything witty to say, his gaze jerked toward the counter, where voices were climbing in angry Mandarin.

"It only says fifteen percent off. There's no date on it."

The man behind the desk looked tired. "My apologies, there was an expiration listed on the page you cut this from."

"What page? This was a loose flyer!"

Mary appeared then, her face stony in a way Luna had never seen. "Is there a problem here?" She glanced at the flyer. "We'll honor the discount this one time."

Only then did Luna notice the tense set of the boy's shoulders, his slight cringe when the customer grunted.

"That's the total? After the discount?"

"Yes, sir."

More grumbling as the man dug through his wallet for cash. His fingers grew frantic as he thumbed through the folds. Change spilled, rolling off the desk and clattering to the floor.

"How much is it, Dad?" said the boy.

Luna saw then how similar their faces were. Nose wide like a lion's, square jaw, eyebrows that went scattered and sparse at their tails.

"Dad?" said the boy. He stepped up to the counter, and Luna felt alone and exposed beside the fish tanks. She watched him pull neatly folded bills from his back pocket and slide them under his father's elbow.

"What are you doing?" the man spat.

"It should be more than enough," the boy said apologetically.

His father turned to leave, not even bothering to count the bills, and the boy followed. Luna wished he would glance her way one more time.

Mary let out a derisive huff as Luna's parents reached the counter.

"Did I hear someone arguing with you?" her mother asked. "Who was that?"

"Who else? The Yees."

"David Yee was here?" Luna's father was surprised. "I didn't see him."

Luna's heart was a timpani in her ears. That boy—now she knew who he was. The eldest son of that family her parents despised. Hunter Yee.

Hunter Yee

Cold air sliced through his chest and roared in his ears. His father fumed silently as they crossed the parking lot to where the rest of their family waited in the car. Hunter tried not to cough; it would provoke more anger. There hadn't been tightness in his lungs like this in years. He yanked open the door and sat down behind the driver's seat.

His mother looked from Hunter to his dad and back again, measuring their expressions. She cleared her throat. "Cody, can you please go get my scarf from the trunk?"

And there it was. Always easier for them to scream at Hunter when they could pretend he was the only one in earshot. His little brother unbuckled the seat belt and slid out, hesitating for just a moment before nudging the door shut.

They listened to the pop of the trunk, the creak of it yawning open.

His dad twisted around. "Did you *steal* that money?"

Hunter recoiled as his mother gasped.

"No," he replied, "of course not!"

"We came here to celebrate your ma," his father hissed. "It was supposed to be a good day. And what do you do? You *humiliate* us."

"I swear I didn't steal it," he said. "It was given—I mean. I found it."

They didn't believe him, of course. His parents launched into their usual scathing roar, and as their voices rose, Hunter sank inward, stilled his breath. Narrowed the focus. He brought himself into the tension of a bow's string, the muscles drawing an arrow back.

This—pretending he was alone in his place with only the trees and the sky and his bow and arrows—was his only way of steadying himself.

A thump snapped the three of them out of the moment. His father opened the door. "Cody, what is taking so long?"

"Sorry," came the small voice, distant and muffled. "Be right there."

Smog of silence, dense and uncomfortable. It settled between them and stayed. Cody returned to his seat, thrusting the knit scarf over the center console and into his mother's lap. Hunter thought he glimpsed a bit of a shine on his brother's fingers, but Cody brushed his hands and there was nothing to see.

Their father put the car into reverse and jerked at the wheel, as if the whole family needed to be reminded of his anger.

"David," his mom began to say. "You should slow—"

The car jolted. They all looked toward the collision. It had come from behind.

Through the two windshields, Hunter found himself locking eyes with the girl from the fish tanks. From the party. Wisps of hair had wormed free of her ponytail and were slanted across her face. She didn't blink.

His mother groaned in dismay.

A man who was most likely the girl's father stepped out from the driver's seat of the other car. He scowled as he examined the back of his vehicle, and then offered a cursory glance at the Yee family's trunk.

Hunter's dad cranked down the window and stuck his head out into the crisp air. His face was unreadable.

The man shrugged. "There's nothing."

Hunter watched his dad shift into drive and scrape away without another backward glance. The trunk had popped open behind them and there was a sea-like noise of wind pulling and pushing at the lid.

"It wasn't me," Cody blurted quickly.

"I know it wasn't you," their father said through gritted teeth, pulling over onto the shoulder of the highway. "It broke yesterday morning. Hunter—"

"Yep, I've got it." Hunter jumped out to slam the trunk a few times, until the lid finally stuck.

They were pulling up to their house when his mother spoke again. "We should have stayed back there."

"I have nothing to say to him," his father replied.

"But in case their car *is* damaged—"

"He knows where my office is."

Hunter listened to his mother's long, restrained sigh. "Why is it always that family?"

"What family?" said Cody.

"The Changs," she said, fidgeting with her scarf.

As in Dr. Chang—his father's nemesis. Hunter blinked. That meant the girl with the ponytail was Luna Chang.

Hsueh-Ting Chang

Luna's father

Hsueh-Ting Chang watched David Yee pull his ugly car out of the Fortune Garden parking lot. The wheels passed over a bit of uneven ground, and something tumbled from the trunk. It rolled to a stop at Hsueh-Ting's feet. A carved stone, white and hexagonal. Small enough that he could wrap his fingers all the way around, heavy enough that he would be conscious of the thing sitting in his pocket.

It smelled old. It *felt* old.

There was that same thrill that he remembered from his very first trip out in the field. The electric knowledge that those points of contact between the stone and his body were the closest any human could get to time traveling.

Hsueh-Ting pocketed the hexagon. He would examine it later.

Luna Chang

Nobody had warned Luna that Hunter Yee was transferring to Fairbridge High School. When she realized who he was, she'd resolved to never speak to him again. It should have been so easy. Outside of her father's work obligations, her parents had largely managed to avoid that family all these years. If Luna and Hunter had ever been in the same place at the same time before the night of that party, she couldn't remember it.

But now he was in her orbit all day, one of them a moth, the other a flame. She wasn't sure who was which.

On his first day at FHS she'd nearly crashed into him as she raced from French to Lit.

And during social studies, Hunter walked into her classroom by mistake. As he hurried back out, Joyce Chen wiggled her eyebrows at Luna and said, "Looks like our demographic has increased by fifty percent."

Then in the cafeteria an empty root beer can had fallen off

her tray, and he'd been the one to pick it up and launch it—in a perfect arc—into a trash can that was impossibly far away.

Then it had turned out they were in the same AP Chem period, and after a brief introduction Hunter was seated at the one lab table that had an open chair—which was, of course, beside Luna. She'd spent the whole period trying not to look at him.

And now, gym.

She stood in the very back, retying her ponytail, before her team thinned out enough that there were no bodies to shield her. This was the worst. How lucky that Hunter Yee was here to witness this final slice of her hell.

Today it was dodgeball. The phys ed teachers called it Bombardment, as if fancying up the name made it any better. Under Ms. Rissi's watchful eye, Luna moved from side to side to offer the illusion of participating. She picked up the occasional ball and pretended to look for an opening...before rolling it to someone actually invested in the game. The very definition of a team player.

Now that Roxy had graduated, gym class had a way of punctuating Luna's loneliness more than anything else. It wasn't that she didn't get along with other people; she was pretty well liked. It was that all her life she'd felt this invisible separation. As if she stood on one side of a wall of glass, and everyone else on the other—even Roxy, who had grown close to her out of sheer proximity, thanks to their parents being good friends.

A ball slammed into the bleachers inches away from Luna's elbow, jolting her back into the game. She wished it had gotten her. Most of her team was out. Only three of them remained, hanging toward the back.

A ball sailed past.

Two people left. Luna and that smart girl with dark brown skin, Vanessa.

On the other side there was just one person: Hunter Yee. Luna hadn't been paying attention enough to notice how well her team was doing.

Hunter scooped up ammo until his arms were full before heading for the halfway line that divided the gym. He started with Vanessa, pegging her ankle. She yelped, kicking the ball away—though that didn't change the fact that she was tagged out.

Now it was just Luna.

"Go, Hunter!" someone shouted.

He stood across from her, staring her down. One ball in his right hand, poised for throwing. He let the others fall. They bounced, and the sound reverberated through the gym. He gave her an apologetic look.

She raised her eyebrows. His confidence made her want to prove him wrong.

Luna picked up the nearest ball and closed the distance until there were maybe a couple yards between them. She waited, daring him with her eyes. He didn't move.

"Come on already," Ms. Rissi called. She had the whistle in her teeth, ready to be blown.

Luna transferred the ball to her right hand, exposing her body.

He took the opening and made his throw, but she sidestepped just in time. It nearly grazed the hairs on her arm.

"*Ooooh*," the other students chorused.

Hunter bent to grab more ammo, and she aimed for his knee, gave it her best throw. The ball lobbed through the air, arcing slightly. It seemed to glow, like a rare full moon spotted in a still-lit sky. As he straightened up, the ball landed against his toe.

Rissi blew the whistle. Luna's team had won.

Hunter Yee

"*Can't believe the* new kid got taken out by *Luna*," some guy was saying in the locker room. "It's too hilarious."

Well, that sounded unfair. Why *not* Luna?

The strange thing, though, was that Hunter prided himself on his aim. For as long as he'd lived in Fairbridge, he'd had a *gift*. No matter what he did, if it was about making something go from point A to point B, it came to him with a certain ease. Scoring a goal on the soccer field. Tossing the spare car keys onto the hook by the door. It didn't require training—he practiced only because it brought him into a comforting trance.

Sometimes he envisioned the precise trajectory, and it seemed his mind alone could direct the object in question. But even when he didn't give it much thought, simply let the instinct travel down his arm: His aim was always true.

Other people didn't know this. No one would believe him if he told them he'd never missed a shot until now. His arm had moved the wrong way at the last second, thrown the ball too far to the left.

Not that it actually bothered him. And not that he cared about the eye-roll-inducing hoots from the people in the locker room.

He just wanted to hear Luna's voice again, to learn the cadences of her sentences. He wanted to look into her face and understand what it was that tugged him in her direction.

Cody Yee

Cody Yee woke up on his birthday thinking about how he was supposed to feel excited, like other kids did. Every year his classmate Harrison spent days boasting about the toys he'd received. His golden-haired mother would come to their classroom to pass out buttercream-frosted cupcakes she'd baked herself.

When was it that Cody's family would get to live the way Harrison's did? They were so loud and full of joy and very, very blond. The birthday parties at that big blue house were legendary. And the Monday after, all the kids buzzed about who took home which prize, who had gotten cake smashed in their hair. Cody was never able to go. His mother said they couldn't afford to buy a gift, so it was better to stay home.

"Besides," she would say, "you don't want to get too close to anyone."

"Everybody else has friends," he had tried telling her.

"You have us. You have your brother. We are your *best* friends. You can trust us more than anybody."

As Cody brushed his teeth he could hear Hunter talking in a low voice about a special dinner, and their mother replying that things were tight this year and Cody would understand.

"Happy birthday!" his mother exclaimed with an exaggerated smile as he emerged for breakfast. "Baba will be home later."

Hunter nudged his shoulder. "When you're done eating we'll go on an adventure."

The sky was a dusty blue, the air unusually warm. In the part of the neighborhood with all the nice houses, people had set up tables in open garages or spread blankets on their lawns and laid out things for sale.

"We're getting you a present," Hunter said. "You get to pick."

From house to house they went, and Cody carefully evaluated the stuff he saw. A mancala board where half the glass pieces had been replaced with pennies. A squeaky, wobbling globe that mapped the constellations. A music box with a dancing figure; he didn't like the tune.

A crystal vase, cut with facets that trapped the sunlight— he'd really wanted that one, but Hunter wasn't able to bargain the price down.

It was at the house after that, as Cody sat in a broken rocking chair surveying the tables, that he saw a wooden sculpture of a rabbit with brass ears, just big enough for him to hug. He'd always liked rabbits.

Cody stood to go look more closely, but before he reached

the table, he saw a cage on a picnic blanket that housed a *real* rabbit, tiny and white, nibbling on a stalk of celery. The cage was at the end of a row of cast-iron pans, picture frames, an old Polaroid camera, a set of porcelain dishes.

"Is the rabbit for sale?" he called out to the woman whose house it was, in a voice that rang loud and clear, nothing like his usual whisper. His boldness startled even him, and he saw his brother turn toward him in surprise. Cody was not in the habit of speaking to strangers.

The woman gave him an appraising look. "You think you could take good care of her? A bunny isn't just some toy. She's a living being, same as you and me. You have to be committed."

"I would take the *best* care of her," Cody declared fiercely.

She nodded slowly. "Then you can have her."

"How much?" Hunter asked.

Cody had begged for a pet, but his parents always found a million reasons to say no. He wondered, gut sinking, if his brother was going to decide the rabbit was too expensive.

"Free," said the woman. "I have some pellets and hay for her—you can take those, too. I'm selling the house and I need everything gone."

As they lugged the cage home, Hunter asked, "What'll you name her?"

"Jadey," said Cody.

"Where did that come from?"

"I don't know. It just popped into my head." He watched her through the metal bars. She was quiet, tucked into a little box in the far corner with her nose poking out. "Are Baba and Mama going to be mad?"

Hunter shrugged. "Who cares? I'm the one they'll be angry at. Nothing new."

Cody found himself smiling. It was the best birthday ever.

Luna Chang

Luna needed to practice making herself comfortable in the rigid seat shaped from her parents' wants, so Saturday was spent blasting through a couple more college application essays. She worked on a yellow notepad at the kitchen table, because in her room and left to her own devices, her mind would wander.

Here, out in the open, her parents hovered over her and beamed. This turned out to be almost equally distracting.

"We're so proud of you," her father said in English, which always made things a hundred times more awkward. It was as if he couldn't express those things in Taiwanese or Mandarin.

"Your top choices will want you," her mother added. "Yiding hui."

But Luna didn't really have any top choices. It was more about the schools for which her parents lusted, the well-known names that filled their eyes with starlight. Her father was so enamored with the idea of Stanford that he'd forgotten to ask if

Luna actually wanted to go there. She'd send that one in just to humor him.

Luna felt like she *should* care more—the way Roxy had cared, spending all that time looking up schools and statistics and applying to nineteen of them, gunning for those merit scholarships.

Luna sighed. The moment senior year had begun, there'd been a specific type of energy in the halls and classrooms. Everybody was keenly aware that this was the last year, that next fall everything would be different. Everyone would be on their way toward their destiny or whatever. What was hers supposed to be?

"When you finish your Stanford essay," said her dad, "I can give you notes to help make it better."

"Thanks," she said, trying not to sound sarcastic. She rubbed her eyes. "I think I need to take a break for now."

As she set down her pen, her father stood up and zoomed past her. He grabbed the tub of rolled oats out of the cabinet.

"I know what we should do." He wiggled his eyebrows.

"It's almost dinnertime," Luna's mother protested.

"We'll just go until the sun's gone," her dad said.

Luna grinned. Maybe other seniors in high school didn't want to hang out with their parents this way, but it was one of her favorite things.

He drove them to the university where he taught, and parked the car beside the lake. The geese were spread out along the edge of the water. When Luna and her parents emerged into the crisp air, the birds perked up and began to make their way over.

She threw the first handful, trying her best to scatter the oats in a wide arc across the grass.

"Don't get too close," her mother nagged.

"I know," said Luna. Sometimes the geese were mean. She took another step forward anyway.

The water rippled with pink sky. A breeze pressed against her windbreaker and combed through her hair. It smelled earthy.

Luna loved simple moments like these. Watching the geese peck at the oats. Standing here before the lake and the flaming sunset with her parents. She didn't want to leave for college. Didn't want things to change. She just wanted to stay here in this moment.

"We haven't done this in forever," Luna said, fighting the tightness in her throat. "This was a good idea, Dad."

"Of course it was. All my ideas are good ideas."

She angled herself away so that only the water and the sky could see her sadness. Her eyes blurred. The lake turned black and lost its reflection, hollowing out into emptiness. Was that movement out there in that darkness? She swore she saw some kind of figure made of shadows—

"What is that?" Luna took a step back. "What's happened to the lake?"

"What are you talking about?" said her mother.

She blinked, and everything went back to normal. "Never mind...just a trick of the light, I guess."

When they left, she glanced over her shoulder one more time to be sure. The water caught the glitter of the first star overhead. It winked at her.

The next morning, Luna found herself setting up to teach a Chinese knotting workshop to kids at the Fairbridge Chinese Language School. Her parents had said it was a thing she should do—that it would look good on her college applications.

She passed out strands of thick nylon string and handouts she'd made for anyone who wanted a visual. A quick head count showed that she was missing one student.

"Um, we can go ahead and get started. You can call me Luna."

"We don't have to call you 'Teacher'?" said one of the kids.

"Or speak Chinese?" said another.

She smiled. "No. 'Luna' is fine. English is fine in here. So! We're making a tiny human today. This is what it'll look like." She held up her example, showing the loops for arms, the macramé body, and string dangling down with beads for feet. "We start with a loop...."

It was a chatty bunch of kids, and they picked up the knotting techniques quickly. Luna snipped a few stretches of blue and green threads for herself. They were thicker than the cord of her headphones, smooth and silky between her fingers. In the light they gleamed like treasure washed up on the beach. Maybe that was why she often found herself wanting to knot little sea creatures.

Over, under, around, and through. There was always a clear

pattern, a correct way to do a knot. The string traveling with precision. Tug by tug, colors assembling themselves into shapes.

She wished the questions in her life were this easy. Where to go for college. What to choose for her major. What career to pursue. How would each of those knots add up to become the life she wanted? What kind of life *did* she want?

Luna tied off her butterfly and dug through her bag for matches. This was her favorite step—burning the ends of the nylon to finish the piece and make sure the fibers wouldn't come apart. She watched the material begin to melt and pressed it against the table like she was making a thumbprint cookie. It cooled instantly, turning to a smooth and plasticky surface that sealed in the ends.

She was halfway into another creature—this time a large owl, made from thick rope—when she realized the workshop was nearly over and her last student was still missing. Luna was scanning her roster for the one name she hadn't ticked off when the door opened to reveal a small, shy-looking boy. And behind him—

Hunter Yee stopped short just inside the room and blinked at her. She stared back, determined to ignore the fluttering between her ribs.

He cleared his throat. "Sorry to interrupt. My brother, Cody, keeps getting lost. I believe he's signed up to be here."

She tried to shape her mouth into a normal smile. "Well. Cody! Nice to meet you. My name is Luna. Come on in."

Cody glanced up at his older brother.

"You can come in, too, Hunter." It was the first time she'd said his name aloud, and the syllables were a jolt of electricity on her tongue. Was her face turning red?

The brothers sat down in the back just as the bell rang.

"Oh." Luna cleared her throat. "Well, that's it, everybody. If you're done, I'll fix up the ends of the strings for you. Otherwise, you can ask your parents to help you with that—the instructions are on the sheet."

Luna grabbed new pieces of string and made her way over to Cody, who looked devastated. "This is pretty easy," she said to the kid, trying to pretend his brother wasn't there. "In fact, I bet you can figure out the whole thing. But I'll show you how to get started."

She looped a yellow thread into position and tugged the blue around to form the first bump. Cody stared at her hands, but she could feel Hunter's eyes on her face.

"You want to give that a try?" Luna passed the threads over to Cody.

He didn't speak, but he caught on fast, little fingers separating the strands, already looping the knots with certainty.

"There you go," said Luna. Out of the corner of her eye she noticed a bracelet around Hunter's wrist, made from a thin red cord in one of her favorite knotting styles. It looked worn, like someone had crafted it long ago. She wondered if he'd made it himself.

Cody let out a noise that sounded like a question, holding his work up for her to see.

"That's exactly right," she said. "I can already tell, Cody: You're going to be a pro at this."

She couldn't help it then—her glance rose up to meet Hunter's. His eyes were sharp, gleaming in a way she couldn't quite read.

"Thank you," he said.

Hunter Yee

"I like her," said Cody as he buckled his seat belt.

Hunter knew who his brother was talking about, of course. He cleared his throat. "Good."

"Do *you* like her?"

The keys jangled and dropped. Hunter groped for them in the shadows beneath his knees.

"You do," said his little brother. "I can tell."

"Well," said Hunter, and left it at that. He didn't want to think about how his parents would react to learn that both their sons were admirers of the Changs' daughter.

He'd promised his mom that he would lie low for this one last year, stay out of trouble to the extent that he could control. But it wasn't like he could do anything about the fact that he shared three periods with Luna at school.

Cody pushed in the *West Side Story* cassette tape and fiddled with the volume.

Hunter had heard all the songs a million times, but it was

his favorite when his brother sang along like this, loud and glee-ful. When it was just the two of them in this car, and the windows were rolled up, they could be as noisy as they liked. They didn't have to worry about their conversations being overheard, didn't have to worry about whether they were drawing dangerous attention.

They were nearly back at the house when Cody turned down the music. "Do we have to go home right now?" he asked.

Hunter checked the time. Dinner wouldn't be for a couple hours, and he was pretty sure their father didn't need the car at all today. It was so rare that they got to drive anywhere on their own. "We don't *have* to. Why?"

"Is the bow still in the shed?" his brother asked. "Can we go? Please?"

As if he would ever say no. "Okay."

The fast way was blocked off by orange cones, probably because of the cracked ground everyone was talking about. Other drivers looked annoyed by the detour, but Hunter didn't mind. Here on these long stretches of road, winding between trees, going five miles an hour over the speed limit—just low enough that he wouldn't get pulled over—there was a sense of freedom and peace that was impossible to come by in their little townhouse. Nobody was potentially going to break down a door and threaten them. Out here, they could just be themselves.

He drove to the thickest part of the Fairbridge woods. He'd been drawn to the place ever since they first moved here—maybe because of the branches that beckoned, or the whispers against the forest floor. He'd gone into the trees to chase the rushing creek, to watch tadpoles dart through the water.

Thirty or so paces into the woods, at the edge of a wide clearing, he'd found the run-down shed. The first time Hunter flung open that door it had been too dark to see anything but the gaping mouth of a space waiting to swallow him. The second time, with watery morning light pouring over his shoulders, he saw a bow and a quiver of arrows sitting in the corner. He didn't touch them, but whenever he came back and looked, they were still there, wearing a thick blanket of dust. After a few months, he decided the bow and the arrows were meant to be his.

For the last seven years he'd been returning to that shed, stepping into the silence to think, to breathe. To launch arrows into the trunks of the trees with closed eyes, listening for the thud of their landing.

Now Hunter nudged the car off the road and onto a grassy patch of land. He parked by a giant tree that was split in half all the way down the trunk. This was where a smooth stretch of earth made for the quickest entrance to his clearing.

Cody ran a few paces ahead, hopping over exposed roots. "You know why it's called Lightning Creek?"

"Why?"

"Because one day a long time ago, there was a thunderstorm, and lightning struck right here. It made a big groove shaped like a snake across all of Fairbridge, and the storm filled it with rainwater, and it turned into a creek."

"Wow," said Hunter. "Where'd you hear that?"

"Miss Jordan told us. She was a teenager when the storm happened."

The bow was much too big for Cody, but he didn't ever care. Mostly he just wanted to hold it in his hands, feel the thrum of it as he released an arrow with Hunter's help. It was always the same. They came out here to be among the tall grass and the chirping birds. Cody would try a few times, and then he just wanted to sit in the grass and watch Hunter.

One after another, Hunter's shots landed in the gray trunks, in the branches that bent at tricky angles, always exactly where he intended. Each time he nocked an arrow, he slowed his breath, searched for the moment between two heartbeats when all was quiet and the world went still. He relished the vibrations that rang through the bow, tremoring in his fingers. The satisfying *shushttt* each time he found his mark.

Even with eyes closed he struck every target. He knew the exact path an arrow would travel, how the wind would push it, the way it would arc and fall. The instinct came as naturally as his inhales and exhales.

Occasionally, Hunter paused to make a funny face at Cody, who beamed up at him with adoring eyes, as though Hunter was the one who'd strung the stars in the sky. Sometimes he worried that his younger brother admired him a little too much. Hopefully he wasn't setting some kind of awful example.

At the same time, he wished that Cody would stop allowing himself to be steamrolled by the overwhelming rule of their parents. It would be nice if just a little of Hunter's rebelliousness transferred over, for Cody's sake.

He thought of Luna again. The gentleness she'd had with his brother. There'd been none of the impatience that so commonly flared up in educators when Cody went all quiet. The teachers at the public school—all of them white—assumed he didn't speak English. The teachers at the Chinese school assumed he was unintelligent. But they were wrong—Cody was probably the cleverest member of the Yee family.

Time passed like this until the sky turned the color of fire. Together, they plucked all the arrows from the trees and returned the equipment to the shed before making their way back to their father's car, back to the place they called home.

That night Hunter woke up to the ghostly whistles of two owls mating. The first time he'd ever heard the sound, he had nearly jumped out of his skin, certain someone was pulling a prank. Now it reminded him of the owl that Luna had been weaving with her deft hands as he and Cody walked out of her classroom. He thought of the brown, gleaming rope. The way she twined it around her index finger. The focus with which she slid each knot into place.

Luna Chang

Her mother filled the table with freshly steamed zongzi, sautéed greens, tomato scrambled eggs, a platter of savory taro cakes. Luna grabbed the chili sauce.

Coming back into the dining room, she saw her father holding a satin-wrapped box tied with a ribbon. "Meihua. This is for you."

"Weishenme?" said Luna's mom. "I don't need this."

"It's a gift," her father replied.

At that, her mother looked up, mouth in the sweet shape of a vague smile. It was a bottle of perfume, the glass faceted to look like a gemstone.

He pulled the top off. "Try it. See if you like the smell."

Luna's mom tentatively spritzed her wrist. "It's...salty."

"I like it," said Luna. Her mother passed her the bottle and Luna held it to her nose. The scent made her think of beach air and smoke from a fire pit, flower petals curling against a bed of still-warm ashes. She *did* like it.

"Well," said her father. "Good."

Her mom was silent, fingers busy fighting with the string that tied the zongzi leaves around the rice.

Luna dashed back into the kitchen, and when she returned with the scissors looped over her fingers, she found that her father had worked free two of the knots.

Her parents looked so sweet like that, side by side, her dad's face full of concentration, her mom watching over his shoulder. Luna loved these beats that served as reminders of what it meant to be a family. Her mother had always been weird about presents, but it was clear the gesture meant more than she let on.

"The scissors are more efficient," her mom said, taking them from Luna, breaking the spell. The zongzi strings fell limp, *snip, snip*, and then it was time to sit down and eat.

Her mother had already begun ranting. "Today there was a parent visiting to check out the school for her kids. She suggested cutting zhuyin fuhao from the curriculum—we would need new textbooks! What's next? Teach simplified characters instead of traditional?"

"Kaiwanxiao," said her dad. "That would be cultural destruction. It's been bad enough with all the changes those Guomindang supporters are trying to make."

Luna heard her mom sniff. "They told me today that I won't be heading the committee for Lunar New Year."

"What?" her father exclaimed. "But you did it the last five years!"

She sighed. "Fanshi you yi de, bi you yi shi. At least I won't have to worry about coordinating anything while we're in Taiwan."

"Who is going to do it instead?"

"I don't know. They offered it to Yvonne Yee, who turned it down." Her mom's face was stormy. "Can you believe it? That family is everywhere—we can't escape them. Their youngest son is my student this year."

The mention of the Yees turned Luna's thoughts to the look on Hunter's face in gym when she'd tagged him out. Then in that workshop, how tender he'd been with his little brother.

The air thrummed when he was around. She thought of his shiny black hair, the way it sometimes stood up from his head. His angular jaw, his eyes dark but warm. Luna imagined seeing him at school and having an excuse to start up a conversation.

There was a word for these kinds of thoughts. Daydreaming. She was momentarily dizzy, then embarrassed.

She sipped at her tea and tried to return to the conversation happening at the table.

"Well," Luna's father, ever the diplomat, was saying, "he's lucky to have such a good teacher. He'll learn a lot from you this year—I'm sure of it."

Her mom scoffed. "I doubt any of the Yees are capable of learning anything. He doesn't look like the studious type, either. Just as bad as his older brother. Did you hear how that Hunter got kicked out of Stewart Prep? He lost his scholarship."

Luna's dad made a noise that was half disbelief and half contempt.

Her mom continued. "I have seen so many students just like Cody Yee. I can tell from the first day how lazy they are, and unwilling to learn."

It had never before occurred to Luna to doubt such sweeping statements, but in that moment the lens through which she saw her mother began to fracture.

"Cody was in my workshop today," Luna said slowly. "I think he's a special kid."

Her mother turned the color of the sauce poured over their ba-wan. "Nobody in that family is *special*," she spat.

"Don't talk about things you don't understand, Luna," said her father. His face hardened, his voice went uncharacteristically sharp.

Luna tried to swallow a mouthful of rice that had gone tough and dry. The grains clawed at her throat.

Meihua Chang

Luna's mother

Meihua sank down on the edge of the bed and ran her knuckles over her aching eyebrows. She was still tense from teaching. Why did she encounter the Yees around every corner she turned?

On her way out she'd seen the two sons in Luna's workshop room, the last ones to leave. Through the cracked door, Meihua had glimpsed her daughter's warm goodbye.

And worse: the way Luna had been defensive about the younger brother at dinner.

Meihua shook her head. She would have another conversation with Luna to emphasize just how important it was to maintain their distance from the Yees.

She remembered the first time she met that family. Removing her shoes in the Zhangs' foyer while David and Yvonne smiled shyly, their sullen-faced child holding the hideous dumplings that were their contribution to the potluck.

Meihua had been so prepared to like them. Over plates of

mifen and water spinach, David and Yvonne softly explained how they'd recently moved to Fairbridge and hoped to stay for a while. They wanted some stability for their son and their second child, who was on the way. Meihua had looked with surprise at Yvonne's belly then, the roundness hidden beneath her loose dress.

"Gongxi ah!" Meihua had said warmly, meaning it. A new child was a lucky thing. She and Hsueh-Ting had tried to conceive again after Luna, but it wasn't meant to be. And anyway, their one daughter was enough of a handful with her condition. Meihua remembered noting with gladness that she held not even a kernel of jealousy for David and Yvonne's good fortune.

Then came the awkward discovery: Hsueh-Ting and David were interviewing for the same job. They were professors with similar experience, coveting that tenure-track position. Everyone laughed at the coincidence, but Meihua saw how Hsueh-Ting had gone rigid.

They needed this job. Luna was constantly sick, had missed so much school it was unclear whether she would advance to the fourth grade. They needed health insurance. She had viruses and infections, unexplained swelling, so many fevers. Nothing helped except, strangely, the light of the moon.

When Meihua set her daughter out on a lawn chair below the night sky, Luna's temperature would finally begin to drop. She breathed easier. "Mama," she would call, and point out shapes she traced in the stars with her tiny thumb.

Weeks after the potluck, Hsueh-Ting got the job. Their relief was overwhelming.

61

The next time Meihua encountered the Yees, they were icy. She tried to start up a conversation, but Yvonne turned away as if nobody had spoken. The tension grew from there. David and Yvonne had brought some kind of poison to this pool in which they all swam. From that point on, the Changs did what they could to avoid that family. And vice versa—there seemed to be a tacit agreement that they would not attend the same social gatherings. But these days something had changed, tipping their orbits so that they collided again and again.

Now Hsueh-Ting stepped out of the bathroom, toweling off his hair.

"What are you doing, sitting there?" His tone was innocent, but she couldn't help feeling accused of something.

"Nothing," Meihua answered. She stood and began to swing her arms from side to side, letting her hands knock against her body. Her daily exercise. "You should do this, too," she said to her husband, because it was what she always said, though by now the statement was a habit with no real meaning.

"Mmm." Hsueh-Ting nodded, as he always did, and pulled open a drawer to hunt for fresh socks.

Cody Yee

Cody had been watching his brother closely for his entire life. It took him a while, but at some point he noticed that Hunter never missed a shot. Hunter could ball up a piece of trash and aim for the garbage can from an impossible distance, and it would arc perfectly through the air. Never mind the lightness of it, or even the fact that it should have been pushed to the side by air churning from a heavy fan.

Sometimes, after his brother had left the room, Cody would attempt to make the same throw. It never got anywhere close.

He longed to be like Hunter. Confident and bold. Perfect aim even through closed eyes. Strong enough to wield a bow and arrow like they weighed nothing. Unafraid.

That last one especially. Because Cody was *so* afraid. Everything made him nervous. Loud voices. The unease that hummed in his parents' conversations. The parts of the house where the lights stayed off when the sun went down, so that neighbors wouldn't be inclined to look toward their windows.

His parents' worry became his worry, as if by breathing the same air, he absorbed their stress. He wondered if his family would ever have enough money. If they would ever be able to stop hiding.

He wondered if he would ever know what they were hiding from.

All he knew was that it had to do with a man they'd been trying to escape since before Cody was born.

His fear was a jacket glued to his skin, impossible to shed. It was all that people saw: his timidity. They thought he didn't understand things, that he was slow to learn. People outside his family didn't know that he was reading a few grade levels ahead, that he had an excellent memory and understood far more than they could guess. Teachers made many assumptions about him; so did his classmates.

Maybe some of it was because he looked different from the majority of them, with their pinkish skin and freckles and eyes that were blue or light brown or maybe even green. But for the most part, he was pretty sure it was because they could see that he was so afraid.

"Are you scared, too, Jadey?" He touched his nose to the rabbit's head. It comforted him to speak aloud to her.

If only he weren't nervous about anything. If only he had the courage that Hunter was always reminding him to keep tucked in close, like a secret treasure. Hunter made it sound so easy. *Just pretend you're brave. It takes practice. Then one day, it won't be pretend anymore.*

But Cody wasn't sure how to do even that. As far as he could tell, bravery was a trait he had been born without.

Someone had told him long ago that shooting stars granted wishes, and so he tried to keep his head craned up toward the sky whenever night fell. He had yet to see something that might count as a shooting star. But he was ready to wish on anything.

Hunter Yee

Hunter sighed into the night as he rolled the trash bin down to its designated spot. He paused at the curb to stare at the row of townhouses. The one his family lived in was on the very end, the faded yellow paint turned a sickly shade by all the mold. Number seven, Belladonna Court. From here he could see how the house sagged on the side where the row ended, its skeleton tired and hunching. The path to the door uneven like a set of crooked teeth.

They'd moved into this house when Hunter was starting the fourth grade, and back then his parents had called it *a temporary solution.*

Now, eight years later, Hunter had stopped asking when they were finally going to move. The rent on the place had gone up only once, and they still hadn't received the phone call they'd been bracing for since the day they arrived. Clearly, his parents believed it to be an adequate hiding spot. Here, they had turned themselves into a needle in a haystack.

There was the telltale rustle, a finger of wind grazing the earth near his ankles. Hunter held himself still, waiting, his every muscle tense with curiosity. If he tried to look at it straight on, it would sneak away. This phenomenon had been happening for years now. He didn't remember when it started.

The rustling stilled and silence returned, and *then* he looked. There they were. Two crisp twenty-dollar bills waiting beside his heel. He bent under the guise of retying his shoe so that he could fold up the money and tuck it inside his sock. As soon as he had a moment alone, it would go into the box that held his escape funds.

Hunter made his way back to the dark and stuffy house. He longed to open a window, but his parents didn't ever allow such a thing. Too easy for voices to be heard, for curious eyes to find a mark. Better to keep the latches locked, the heavy curtains down.

The moment the front door swung shut behind him, he knew something was off. His father could be heard from the kitchen, uttering a quiet string of Mandarin that came too fast and urgent for Hunter to catch.

The main hall of their tiny house ran right past the open doorway to the kitchen. It was impossible to reach his room without encountering his parents. They were forever on alert. The creak of a floorboard, a branch softly tapping the outside of the house—every little thing made his parents pause, gather their breath tight in their lungs, wait to see what would happen.

Hunter had learned their behavior. He tiptoed everywhere and seized up at the slightest noise. Home was not a place for relaxing. It was a caution zone.

He slid his shoes off. The wood beneath his socked feet let out its low complaint, and the voices in the kitchen instantly halted.

"It's me," he said. "I was just taking out the trash."

He gave up on being quiet and slunk into the kitchen, where his dad leaned against the fridge, tie discarded in a pile on the counter, and his mother hunched in the center of the room, hands wrapped around her elbows.

"What took you so long?" his mom asked.

"What do you mean? I went out and came right back."

"You took longer than usual," she said, on edge.

"What's wrong?" said Hunter.

"Nothing," replied his father, at the same time that his mother said, "We received a call."

A call. The most innocuous word—but for them, the most sinister. Hunter's heart began to pound. Was this, after all these years, the moment they'd been bracing themselves for? Had they been found?

"From an unknown number," his father added.

Hunter looked from one parent to the other. "So...that could be nothing, right?"

"Right," said his dad.

"Or it could be *something*." Hunter's mother sighed. "Nobody in Taiwan would ever believe that a professor's family would have to live this way."

"Don't tell them," his father replied sharply.

"Of course not." Hunter's mother reached for the kettle, which held water that must have been boiled hours earlier. She poured it nearly to the top of a jar that had once been a gift of strawberry jam, and set the glass inside the microwave to reheat.

Hunter could feel the edges of the bills itching his skin where they poked at his ankle. His mind dove for his room, for the small duffel shoved into the corner at the back of his dark closet. If things got desperate enough, at least he had that.

His father leaned to peek around the edges of the curtains. The paranoia was infectious. The three of them stood there in silence until the microwave beeped.

"Hunter, you need to work harder." His mother took a sip of her water and set the jar down. "Now that you don't have your scholarship—"

"Ma, I know."

"It's going to be harder to get into top universities." She sighed. "Stewart had such a good reputation."

He was sick of hearing it. How he had thrown away this opportunity. How he was an embarrassment to his family, especially now that there was an official mark on his record. How they couldn't afford shit, and he'd given up his best chance at amounting to anything.

"I have to go do homework," he said.

In their bedroom, Cody was sprawled on the floor, petting Jadey. Hunter wasn't in the mood to speak, so before his brother could say anything, he threw himself down on the bed and closed his eyes. His fingers curled, nails pressing against the flesh of his palms. He longed for the day that he wouldn't have to live in this house anymore.

Hsueh-Ting Chang

Luna's father

Perhaps it was because of the crushed-velvet clouds soaking up all the moon. Perhaps it was because the air was oddly thick, every breath gluey through his nostrils. Hsueh-Ting couldn't sleep.

He crept down the stairs to the kitchen and slid open the drawer that held keys and twist ties and other miscellaneous things. The white hexagon was all the way at the back. He wanted to wrap his fingers around it.

There was a weight to the thing, and a warmth—no, more than that. A vibration. It smelled old. *Old* old, he knew with an instinct he'd first developed in grad school, like a pig hunting truffles. Was it an artifact?

How the *hell* had David Yee gotten his hands on this?

Then his mind was spinning, remembering Yee's latest publication, the one making waves across the field. Hsueh-Ting's breath hitched in his throat when he thought of those claims.

The suggestion that Qinshihuang's imperial alchemists *had*

possibly managed to develop certain elixirs even before the supposed burning of books and burying of scholars. The idea that the emperor had in his possession not only the famous Heshibi, but other pieces of precious stone considered to be additional Mandates of Heaven or divine talismans of protection.

Hsueh-Ting had been astounded; the paper read like a work of fiction. He'd had trouble tracking down a good quarter of the listed sources, and many of the other citations were vague. *This* was the work of an academic hoping for tenure?

But people were taking it seriously. Quiet, awkward Yee, who had no real friends among their colleagues—at least none that anyone saw—was suddenly popular. He was being invited to special lunches and to speak at conferences. Other research teams were attempting to connect with him. And he was conniving enough to pretend to be bashful over it all.

Hsueh-Ting was no stranger to acquiring artifacts via unconventional routes...but nothing that had come into his hands had ever held such potential. And look how hard he worked. Meihua was right. The Yees *were* taking everything: her stature within the community, his reputation as the department's lead researcher.

He wanted David Yee gone once and for all. He wanted his promotion. Hsueh-Ting hadn't even told his wife that he was trying for it; he didn't want Meihua to get her hopes up. Or, more accurately, he didn't want to face her disappointment. There was too much of that already. When he got the promotion, it would be a dazzling surprise for her. He wanted to see Meihua smile like the sun, the way she used to. He wanted to be able to pay for

Luna to go to Stanford. He wanted her to graduate without student loans. How proud and free she would be.

Was this hexagonal thing the subject of Yee's next paper?

Hsueh-Ting considered the possibilities. Maybe he could use this in his *own* research. He held it up and a faceted edge seemed to trap some faraway light. The stone glowed.

A sound from another part of the house made him jump. He shut the drawer, brain already churning with ideas.

First thing in the morning, he would get to work.

Luna Chang

Luna jolted awake with a gasp. She'd been having a dream that she was floating above treetops and fireflies were winking all around her. There was a taste like honey and cream on her tongue.

What had woken her so abruptly? Her body felt different; she was intensely aware of a hollowness at her center.

She...hungered. For lack of a better word.

It wasn't food that she craved but something unnameable. Her heart, too, stumbled in agreement. Palpitations. An aching emptiness in her stomach. Veins prickling and skin slicked with cold sweat.

But she wasn't feverish, and she didn't feel *sick*, exactly.

Dots of light flickering at the edge of her window drew her out of bed. It was only when she swept the curtains aside that she saw them: her fireflies, crowded up against the glass. Never before had she seen them like this, a little throng of soldiers flashing their lanterns.

Luna reached with fast fingers to undo the latch, to slide the pane up. But it was cold and stuck, and her every movement startled away another handful of the lightning bugs. When she finally got the window open, only a few remained.

They winked at her, one by one, before leaping away into the hidden-moon night.

Rodney Wong

It was extremely late—or extremely early, depending on one's preferences. Neither of those were unusual times for Rodney Wong's phone to be ringing, as his was the kind of work that seeped well into the unholy hours.

It was, however, an *inconvenient* time for such an interruption. He stood in a tiny, water-damaged San Francisco basement, idly flicking a small knife open and shut, open and shut. Building up the anticipation was important.

The man strapped to the table in front of him was gasping, though nobody had done anything to affect his air supply. It was purely nerves, Wong observed with amusement. All he'd had to do was make the suggestion of a sharpened blade wedging between the tip of a nail and the soft skin of the finger, and his subject had spiraled into a full-blown panic.

Extracting information should be easy with this one—if the guy didn't pass out first.

That ringing, however. Each blare cut apart his carefully

wrought silence. Wong could see the man's breaths slowing, the taut muscles in his arms beginning to loosen. Perhaps he thought he was being rescued.

At this point they would have to start over again anyway. Wong swallowed a noise of frustration and went to answer the phone, which sat on bare concrete in the southwest corner. Its coiled cable was badly stretched and knotted, thanks to being thrown across the room a few too many times. What better way to end a rage-inducing call? Anyway, he would get a new phone when this one died.

"Yes?" he answered gruffly.

A voice he hadn't heard in quite some time began to speak, and the words that came through the line were like magic. Wong's mood flipped. His mind was spinning. Questions, ideas, plans all began to take shape. He would have to book a flight, figure out a car. He would go alone for this one.

When he hung up, he flicked open his knife with gusto and sliced away the bonds that held his subject to the table.

"You're free to go," said Wong. He didn't have to do this, but he was feeling generous. He was feeling downright jovial.

"What?" The man sat up. "Who was that on the phone? Was it—did they call for me?"

"No one cares about you." Wong grinned. "It was somebody with something far more valuable than what you have to offer me."

He'd been waiting eight years for that call.

Luna Chang

Luna's head was lit up with thoughts of fireflies when Joyce Chen, who sat one seat ahead, turned around. Luna could feel those eyes on her as she noted the social studies assignment in her homework planner. Self-conscious, she slowed down to neaten her handwriting. Ever since their first year of high school, Joyce had always been the other Asian girl in the grade, but somehow they'd never had a class together until now. She was one of those people Luna had always longed to befriend.

"Hey," said Joyce.

Luna straightened. "Hey. What's up?"

"Have you talked to the new guy?" Joyce asked.

"Hunter Yee?" Luna said, and her cheeks went hot.

"Yeah. Him."

"Not really."

Joyce leaned in closer and dropped her voice. "I heard he pulled a ton of shit at Stewart before he got kicked out."

"Like what?"

"People say a couple years ago he set off the fire alarm to sabotage final exams. There was no proof of it, so he never got in trouble—but everyone knows it was him. And apparently, right before a pep rally, he knocked all the bleachers down like dominoes."

Luna blinked. "Whoa."

"Yeah. I heard it from my cousin who goes to Stewart. That dude's got an intense reputation."

The bell rang for the period to start. Joyce turned back around, and Luna was left with a feeling like a stone sinking inside her. Her parents were right. Of course they were. Hunter was a person that she should stay away from, as best she could.

Luna had told her parents she was staying after school for an assignment. She felt guilty for the lie, but it wasn't like she was out peddling drugs. And she *had* done all her homework first. She'd claimed an empty table at the back of the library, and now she took her time setting up the stack of books so there was a nook to hide her candy. You weren't allowed to eat in the library, but, well, how was anyone supposed to get anything done on an empty stomach?

This was her fourth visit to the reference section in two weeks. Yes, there were more important things to be doing— like her college application essays—but Luna had developed an obsession. She needed to search out everything she could about lightning bugs. Hovering over dusty tomes, she'd read about how their life spans were incredibly short—a matter of weeks.

She learned that they were called Lampyridae, and there were so many different species. Some emitted different colors, or blinked their lights at different speeds. But no description she found matched the fireflies that had begun appearing around her.

Without paying close attention, anyone might think they were all the same. But *her* fireflies, the ones that could withstand the cold, had a specific look to them. Long and slender, darker than she'd ever seen, and on their backs a silvery diamond, almost a star.

She paused. Had there been a light in her periphery just now?

No. Her brain was making things up.

Luna took a bite of her chocolate and flipped through the index of one book. It was infuriating that she couldn't search for the *opposite* of a characteristic. Why was it that if she looked up hibernation, there wasn't a subsection talking about species that *didn't* hibernate?

Science said that fireflies liked the summer humidity. But hers had stayed out even with the rapidly dropping temperatures. She didn't know how they survived the cold. The more she thought about it, the more she wasn't even sure she could really call them fireflies, or lightning bugs, or Lampyridae... because their uncanny survival abilities made it seem like they should be considered a species all their own.

Luna flipped to a section in the book on cannibalism. Fireflies sometimes ate each other—that had been fascinating to learn. She couldn't imagine hers doing such a thing. They functioned as a pack, as a family. They were so careful in how they moved around each other—yet another defining characteristic that separated them from the Lampyridae she'd read about. Their basic instincts were totally different.

Luna began to read about praying mantises and spiders, about the cannibalistic rituals they had...until she realized she wasn't reading anymore. She was daydreaming again. Distracted with thinking about Hunter Yee. His sideways grin. His elbow accidentally bumping hers during Chem.

She blinked hard, shaking her head. What was wrong with her? Especially knowing how terrible his parents were—that whole "apple not falling far from the tree" thing. Then hearing the stuff Joyce had said...

Not to mention the reaction her own parents would have. She could just see the looks of disgust on their faces.

The PA system came on then, announcing that the late buses had arrived. Luna gathered up the books and returned them to the shelves.

Hunter Yee

Hunter had gotten his first detention at Fairbridge High School, thanks to the wind following him to class and knocking over the teacher's podium. Papers had gone flying; a pencil cracked in two; the blackboard eraser landed against someone's shoulder. Of course it had happened when he crossed the room to grab a tissue, while everyone else was bent over a pop quiz and nobody saw that he had in fact touched nothing. Wrong place, wrong time. He was the only logical target for the blame.

It was not the best impression to make. But he'd learned to grit his teeth and deal with the punishment so it would be over that much faster. That was his general life philosophy: swallow the unfairness, count down the days until he could escape.

Nobody could pick him up at four o'clock, which meant taking the late bus home. His dad was furious, but Hunter was glad for the change. Most seniors took their own cars to school or caught rides with friends, but he simply longed for the day when he could commute without a chaperone.

Taking the bus would be a breath of freedom.

He sat against the south wall right below the clock and spent the hour listening to its slow ticks. The rhythm reminded him of the last time he'd sat somewhere counting the minutes until his freedom. He'd still been wearing his Stewart uniform then, staring down at his brown loafers and jiggling his knee as he waited for the discovery to be made, for his name to be called over the PA system, summoning him to the main office. That felt both like it was yesterday and like it was a lifetime ago.

When at last detention was over, it had grown so frigid outside that his exhales turned to white puffs. The cold stung his throat and tightened his chest. He wanted to cough but tried to swallow the feeling away. Why was it getting so bad again?

The last time he'd taken a yellow school bus was years ago. How weird to jog along the line of them now, searching for the right number in the window. He wasn't supposed to be running in the cold like this, and already he could feel the pressure against his ribs and the air scraping the back of his mouth.

That one, right there. Number eighty-eight.

He climbed the steps just in time and the driver folded the door shut behind him. The bus was moving before he even sat down. At least it was warm in here.

The sound had changed; he paused to assess.

The vehicle looked empty. There were no heads poking up. Hunter dumped his backpack into a two-seater—

And then he saw her, sitting directly behind the seat he'd chosen, a textbook open against her knees. Luna Chang looked up at him, her face registering the same surprise.

Luna Chang

The world was gray and frozen, and shadows moved in places they didn't belong. Luna fixed her gaze out the window to stop from staring at Hunter Yee.

Had he lived in her neighborhood all this time? In the weeks since he'd started at Fairbridge, she'd never seen him take the bus. What were the chances that they were the only two people on board?

She wondered about his terrible reputation. It was incongruent with what she'd seen for herself.

The bus swerved and lurched. Its wheels found ice instead of road. They went skidding; the outside spun. The front of the vehicle dropped and slammed before tipping to the right.

They crunched and ground to a stop. What the hell was going on? Luna gripped the back of the seat in front of her so hard that her skin was straining over her knuckles.

The driver was cursing. Finally, the woman stood up and turned around, bracing herself with one bent leg against the front passenger seat. "The radio system is down."

"What does that mean?" Luna asked.

"You two stay. I'm gonna get help. Can't have the bus running without me here, but I'll close it up to keep some heat in." The driver opened the door and a blast of cold air tunneled down the length of the bus. It took a moment for her to maneuver out. She pushed at the door, but it refused to shut all the way.

From inside it was hard to see what had happened. Luna gave up trying to look and zipped her coat to her chin before crossing her arms. She was already starting to shiver. Air whistled against the side of the bus. She leaned on her backpack—at least it was warmer than the window.

She was hyperaware of Hunter sitting on the other side of that seat back, of every movement he made, each inhale he took. He wheezed, breathing heavily. The wind rattled the windows. She hoped the driver would be back soon.

Hunter began to cough. At first a small, throat-clearing type of sound. But it grew louder. Soon it turned violent and hacking.

Something clattered to the floor, skidded under Luna's seat. Hunter knelt down in the aisle to search. He seemed unable to speak, but it was obvious that whatever he'd dropped, he urgently needed. Luna bent to retrieve the item: a cylindrical thing made of green plastic.

He seized it from her, trembling, and shook it hard before clamping his lips around the tube and spraying stuff into his mouth. Medicine, Luna realized. An inhaler—though she'd never seen one up close. She'd heard people talk about asthma. Was this an attack? In between breaths she could hear the chattering of his teeth. His cough wasn't getting any better.

"Do you need help?" She pressed her way to the aisle.

He was shaking so much she couldn't tell if he was nodding.

"What do you need?"

He opened his mouth but no words came out. He gasped for air.

"I think we need to get you somewhere warm," she heard herself say. "Somewhere with a phone? Where we can call someone?"

Hunter tried to stand, but his legs gave out and he fell backward.

"Let me help you," said Luna, grasping his hands of ice, pulling him up.

This angle made everything awkward, made it tricky to find her footing. A strong gale knocked at them and the wheels rolled forward, tipping the vehicle more. Luna fell against Hunter, back into his seat. She nearly bumped his nose, and her body was on top of his, and she worried about crushing him when he already couldn't breathe.

The wind vanished—the quiet so sudden her ears rang. Hunter was no longer coughing. Their faces were inches apart, and his ragged exhales puffed against her chin.

"Are you okay?"

He nodded, looking exhausted.

Luna became extremely aware of her own breath. What had she eaten for lunch? Plus, they were making a *lot* of contact, legs tangled, his knees between both of hers. Mortified, she started to pull back, tried to get herself upright once more—

Hunter's coughs returned. He clutched his chest, and Luna

understood that he was in pain. She scrambled to get up faster, to find a way to help him, and ended up slipping and falling on top of him again.

The coughs stopped.

"I think—" Hunter's voice was scratchy, and he paused so suddenly she wondered if it was getting worse.

"What?" said Luna. "What do you need?"

"I think your breath—um. I think it helps me breathe," he said.

"It does?" she said, bewildered. Was that a thing? Didn't she mostly exhale carbon dioxide? Didn't he need . . . oxygen?

He looked embarrassed. But she noticed, too, how when her face was close to his the color returned to his cheeks.

"Okay," said Luna. "But maybe we should . . . try to sit up?"

They managed to rearrange themselves in the two-seater. When Luna was farther from him for too many minutes, his wheezing returned.

"Here." She tipped his head down onto her shoulder and kept her face turned toward his, hoping it was close enough for her breath to reach him.

Hunter had mostly recovered by the time the driver came back, having procured another bus. They slid clumsily down the steps and out the door and leapt the rest of the way over a breakage in the ground. The road had split, and in that gap was where the wheel had gotten stuck. It was too dark to see much more than that.

Police lights swirled behind them as their new bus drove away. This time they were in a three-seater so Hunter could slump down, and Luna breathed in his direction for the ride home, chattering nonstop to keep up the flow. She talked about classmates, and teachers, and a recent scandal to do with Homecoming. When she exhausted all that, she began to tell him stories.

"Once upon a time there was a monkey named Sun Wukong," Luna said, her voice a hum. "He was born from an ancient, magical stone."

Hunter made a face.

She paused. "What?"

"I think I've heard this story before. What is it called again?"

"*Journey to the West*," Luna told him. "I was obsessed with it when I was little. Should I stop?"

He shook his head and started wheezing again. Luna could feel the jolts of his coughs where his body leaned against hers. She held back from reaching out her hand. What could she do to soothe him?

"That's what you get for interrupting," she said, feigning grumpiness. "Now, are you going to listen or not?"

The bus rumbled on as she continued recounting what she remembered of the legend. Yellow tides from the streetlamps poured through the windows and shrank away again. With each sweep of light, Luna studied a new section of his face. The furtive darting of his eyes. His lips slightly parted to take in air. She leaned closer under the guise of offering more breath.

Her stop came before his. "Will you be okay?" she asked.

He nodded. "Thank you."

Down on the sidewalk, she turned back to look, searching the windows for the seat they'd shared. There he was, face pressed to the glass, watching. She held his gaze until the bus rounded the corner. A couple fireflies winked beside her.

For the rest of the night, Luna wondered at the strange new feeling that had wormed its way into her chest.

Yvonne Yee

Hunter's mother

Yvonne Yee stood in the unlit room at the front of the house, watching through a sliver between the curtains as her son walked up the steps. She heaved a sigh of relief. He was late getting home, but he hadn't disappeared. He hadn't been kidnapped for ransom or blackmail.

David, of course, would swear that it was his precious stone that was keeping them safe. That silly thing he kept hidden in the trunk of the car and spoke of with an unhealthy obsession. She didn't know when her husband had become so superstitious. She *wanted* to believe in it—who wouldn't? But her protective and mothering instincts were stronger than any hope she might place in a supposedly divine object.

This was the problem with children: They never fully understood the danger that was waiting around the corner.

Her skin prickled in a way that warned of trouble coming. When would Huang figure out where they'd gone? Would he send someone to enact his punishment and collect payment, or would he come himself? Yvonne shivered. She could only hope they had hidden themselves well enough.

Hunter knew more about it than he let on. She and her husband had tried, as any parents would, to shield their sons, but he'd figured out most of it. Even so, the knowledge didn't sober him the way she thought it should. Why did he insist on wading through so much mischief when time and again they emphasized their need to stay invisible?

Children. When would they understand?

Hunter Yee

The cold had shoved its icy fist down his throat and taken hold of his ribs, pulling so hard he thought his bones might break. Hunter had never had an attack like that. Like he'd swallowed the arctic and the winds had stolen his breath. Like his entire body might freeze and shatter.

He *hated* the cold.

And then Luna: She'd swooped in with magic between her teeth, warm exhales that—bizarrely—allowed him to breathe.

The whole ride, he'd leaned against her while she told him stories. School gossip. Fables and fairy tales. Limericks, even. Her voice little more than a whisper. It stuck in his head long after she was gone.

The short walk from the bus stop to his front door had been enough to set the cold tightening his chest once more, and by the time he let himself in, he was coughing again.

His mother shouted at him for worrying her. His father refused to believe that the bus had gotten stuck in a crack—*the* crack that everyone had been talking about—until Hunter challenged them to call the school and verify it, all the while trying not to cough up a lung.

"Where's your inhaler?" his mother demanded, seizing another opportunity to be angry.

"I used it already," Hunter told her wearily. "But it's expired, remember? Who knows if it even works anymore."

"It works," she said.

He tried not to roll his eyes. What could be done, anyway? Precious money wasted on a trip to the hospital?

When he was little, doctors had been thoroughly baffled by his condition. Inhalers hadn't worked back then, either, expired or not. The only thing that had helped was an unusual concoction his parents fed him years ago. Dried herbs cooked into a soup. They'd sent the tightness away, eased his breaths. He'd thought himself mostly healed...until now.

"Do you have more of that medicine?" he asked.

"What medicine?"

"You know. That soup stuff you made when we first moved here."

"I don't know what you're talking about," his mother said sharply. "The only medicine is the inhaler."

Who knew why she felt the need to rewrite history. Hunter didn't bother replying. He skipped dinner and crawled into bed. After hours of wheezing and hacking, he turned to his little brother.

"Hey," he said between coughs. "Will you help me do an experiment?"

Cody set Jadey down, latched her cage shut, and crawled onto the bed.

"Can you try breathing on me?" said Hunter. "I think it might make this go away for a little while."

His brother settled beside him, leaning forehead to forehead, and Cody offered a steady stream of breath. Hunter could smell the garlic from dinner, but he didn't mind.

Minutes passed; it didn't do what he hoped. The tightness remained.

"Thanks, buddy," said Hunter, pulling away, tired of the experiment.

"Did it work?" said Cody.

"Yeah," Hunter lied.

It was Luna, as he'd suspected. She was who he needed.

There was one stroke of luck: Zhang Ayi had called to say that she was finally getting her hip replacement and would have to stop driving Hunter to and from school. His parents could think of no other solution but for him to take the bus.

He practically jogged to his stop, not even caring how the morning air sliced at his lungs. He'd seen kids huddling there at that intersection, backpacks dripping off their shoulders, thermoses in their hands. Now he was one of them. Sort of.

Nobody spoke to him as he joined the group; a few people angled away. He didn't care. What freedom, to commute to and from school without supervision. It was like he'd broken out of jail.

When the bus arrived, Hunter was the last to get on, and there were only a couple of empty seats left. He plopped down into the first one he saw and closed his eyes. Three stops later, he became aware of someone standing beside him.

"Oh, hi." It was Luna.

He blinked up at her, feeling the urge to apologize.

"*Sit down already!*" the bus driver called from the front.

"Is she talking to you?" said Hunter.

"Yes," said Luna. "This is my seat."

"It's a two-seater," he said. "So . . . there's room for both of us, right?"

She waited as he grabbed his backpack and slid toward the window, where a draft of cold air snaked its way in. He couldn't help letting out a cough.

"Are you feeling all right?" she asked.

"Yes," he said. Between the gray morning light and the quiet of a bus full of kids who were tired and dreading the start of the school day . . . he was embarrassed all over again. He couldn't ask for her breath. Not right now.

But she shifted closer. The air from her exhales reached him enough to offer the tiniest bit of relief, and he was grateful.

Luna Chang

Luna was so distracted by Hunter that she almost didn't notice the driver taking a detour. They drove past a line of orange cones blocking the road where their late bus had gotten stuck. The crevice looked huge in the morning light. Had it grown bigger? Was that possible?

"Whoa," she said. "Look."

Something twinkled, hovering above the crack in the ground. Another tiny light just beside it.

Fireflies.

"Weird," said Hunter.

That was the extent of their conversation before reaching school.

All day Luna carried a secret kernel of emotion tucked behind her sternum—a feeling she didn't quite understand, wrapped up in a newfound shyness. Each time she saw Hunter, her heart changed rhythm. First, it was in the hallway between third and fourth periods.

"Hi," he said, looking indecisive about the greeting.

"Hi," she returned. She wanted to be clever and memorable, but before she could think of anything to say, he was gone.

She saw him again right before lunch, when he was switching binders at his locker. A firefly flashed its lantern beside his ear, then disappeared.

There was a specific instinct that had made her so bold during that game of Seven Minutes in Heaven—it was that same feeling now, hooking its finger around a muscle somewhere south of her throat, nudging her forward.

Luna reached him just as he slammed the locker shut. "Hey. Uh. How are you doing with your—is it asthma?"

Hunter blinked at her. "That's what doctors thought it was at first. But then they weren't so convinced."

"Is it any better now?"

"I'm not sure, honestly. But thanks."

Somehow they ended up walking side by side, and as they entered the cafeteria, Hunter pointed his thumb toward an empty table in the corner.

"Wanna sit here?" he said.

"Sure." She tried to sound casual, and not like she was speaking over the volume of her pulse in her ears. Like it was no big deal that she was eating with the son of her parents' nemeses. No big deal that Luna actually thought he was a pretty all right sort of guy.

They'd both brought sandwiches from home: Hunter's in a worn lunch cooler with a stain on one side, and Luna's in a brown bag, which suddenly occurred to her as being terribly wasteful.

They laid out their food and she began to panic about the lack of conversation until Hunter said, "Here." He broke apart a giant cookie, set half on a napkin, and slid it over to Luna.

"Oh, wow, thanks."

"There are, like, three dozen of these in our freezer just because they were on sale. It's my mom's survival instinct." He paused, looking embarrassed.

Luna worried the quiet would return. "You don't really strike me as the Stewart type." The words were out before she could stop herself.

He laughed. "Wow. You're pretty blunt, aren't you?"

"Sorry," she said.

"Don't be," Hunter told her. "It's refreshing. And you're right. I'm not the Stewart type."

That first lunch was filled with starts and stops and awkward silences. But the day after that, Luna found herself going down the same hallway, walking alongside Hunter, pulling out the same chair in the cafeteria.

"Déjà vu," she joked.

The next week, as she finished her sandwich, Hunter shyly pulled a tangle of bright red yarn from his backpack. "I was hoping you could teach me how to make a bracelet like this." He pointed to the one on his wrist.

"You didn't make that yourself?" she said.

He shook his head. "My mom made it. Years ago."

How sweet that he'd worn it all this time. Luna had never seen him without it.

"Cody wants one," Hunter continued. "He keeps asking me

when he'll get a bracelet of his own. I offered to cut this one off and give it to him, but he wouldn't let me."

"I can show you how to do it," said Luna. "It's a pretty simple knot. But we'll use the real stuff, not yarn."

The next day, she brought in a coil of her favorite maroon cord. It was thin and tough, the kind used for knotting small ornaments and charms. She pulled her chair close to Hunter and showed him how to set it up, how to weave the lines from one side to the other. It was a fast knot and she figured he would finish it on his own. But he brought it out at lunch again the next day so they could work on it together.

Luna helped him tie it off and trim the threads. She leaned far under the table so the teachers wouldn't see her lighter, and sealed the ends.

"Whoa," said Hunter, looking at the way the nylon had melted into itself.

"I know," said Luna. "That's my favorite part. It closes itself off, and the ends won't unravel."

"Cody's going to love it." Hunter grinned.

Over the next few weeks they settled into a new rhythm. They were too tired during the morning bus ride to talk much, but their silence had grown companionable rather than awkward. Lunchtime conversation evolved into a comfortable back-and-forth. In gym they partnered up for volleyball drills, spotted each other in the weight room, held the timer for each other's sprints.

She marveled at the transformation of her days. She didn't feel so lonely anymore. Though Luna had once detested gym, it was now a high note. Each afternoon, she hurried to change her clothes and retie her ponytail so that she could get out of the locker room and over to the bleachers where students waited for the final bell to release them back into the world. Hunter was always there by the time she emerged. She spent those last few minutes chatting with him, or tapping his sneakers with the toes of her shoes and shuffling from side to side to escape his returned taps—a silly game of tag that they'd invented without quite meaning to.

In fact, the phrase *without quite meaning to* served well to capture the essence of their new friendship. The thought made her glow.

Hunter Yee

"*What are you* so smiley about?" said Luna as she plopped down. The bus lurched forward and Hunter caught her backpack before it hit the floor.

"Just in a good mood for no reason. What are *you* so grumpy about?" In truth, there was a reason. He'd realized pretty quickly that his moods were directly proportional to how much he got to see Luna.

She sighed. "My dad's been up my ass about college apps for, like, no reason. I already sent in six of them."

"That's annoying," said Hunter. He hadn't even looked at college applications. There was a stack of pamphlets that had come in the mail and was gathering dust underneath his bed. He couldn't be bothered.

She closed her eyes. "We were up until two in the morning editing this one essay together. He just wouldn't *stop*. There are still two months until the deadline!"

"What if you messed with him and, like, wrote fake essays about random other things?"

Luna snorted. "That's too much effort. Besides, what would I write about?"

Hunter shrugged. "The history of mayonnaise. Why *Beauty and the Beast* is a terrible movie."

"You didn't like *Beauty and the Beast*?"

"Didn't see it," he said. "I don't really go to the movies. I just think the premise is inherently flawed. Girl falls in love with furry monster guy? Why is Disney so obsessed with bestiality? Also, isn't he holding her captive?"

She laughed. "One movie equals obsession?"

"More than one! *The Little Mermaid* is about a fish-girl—who, let's face it, is essentially just a fish—who falls in love with a human."

"But in both those cases everyone ends up human, thanks to magic."

He shrugged. "The magic is bullshit. Deus ex machina."

Luna laughed again, and he drank in the sound of it. "I think *you* should be the one writing those essays."

"*The Truth of Fairy Tales: A Meditation on Bullshit*. I'll get some kind of award for it."

"You say bullshit.... Other people say romantic."

He rolled his eyes.

"But I agree with you," said Luna, surprising him. "Fairy tales make it sound like everything in life is designed to fall into place. There's always a perfect fix. You just have to walk in the right direction, drink the right potions, fall in love with the right person..."

"And bingo," he finished. "Happily ever after."

"Sounds like propaganda, when you think about it," she added, and Hunter couldn't help noticing how the sideways sun lit her hair in a blazing red. The bus rounded the corner, and her ponytail returned to its silky black. "The way they put that at the end of everything? Maybe the truth is happily *never* after."

He raised his eyebrows. "Sounds like you've got a pretty good handle on the topic. So you write that, and I'll write about... I know. Aliens."

Luna looked amused. "Like UFOs?"

"Not so much UFOs, but more the question of whether some things here on Earth are not what they seem."

"So you've got a hypothesis," she said.

"I don't know what to think, really. But have you ever felt like something about the world was... *weird*? That something was off, or I guess just... different, according to the rules we know?"

Luna was silent for a long beat, and he tried to think of what he could say to make her laugh again.

Finally, she said, "I have, actually. I've felt like that a lot."

"Well," he said, shrugging, "maybe it's aliens. Or, you know. Maybe it's that Disney magic."

Luna Chang

The fireflies. That strange hunger. Both of them her constant companions these days.

Little lights hovered at the edges of her vision. The back of her throat tickled with the unsettling feeling that she needed to swallow. When she paid closer attention to it, her stomach rumbled, but no food or drink satisfied the craving.

There was also an unspecified oddness to the world around her. Sometimes in her periphery a tree melted or a building appeared to tilt. But when she turned to face them head-on, everything was normal.

Luna also caught herself daydreaming far more than she wanted to admit. She'd begun collecting certain memories without quite realizing, and sometimes in the middle of the most mundane things—doing homework, pouring milk over her cereal—one would bubble up to the surface.

Like the memory of Hunter kneeling carefully on her sneakers and capping his hands over her knees to hold her in place for sit-ups. How he'd said, "Tell me if I'm squishing your toes too hard," with real concern in his voice. How each time she folded forward, she found herself looking at the soft mountains of his knuckles and focusing on the warmth of his palms through her sweatpants. She hoped her knees weren't clammy. Was that a thing?

How when it was Hunter's turn to do the sit-ups, tendrils of his hair that were heavy with perspiration flapped down into his eyes, and she could feel the rocking of his entire body with each repetition.

Occasionally, she remembered how her first encounter with Hunter had been in that random bedroom, for that game of Seven Minutes in Heaven, and she had the desire to wriggle, to shake away an unidentifiable feeling that made her warm and ticklish.

What would have happened, she wondered, if she'd gone ahead and kissed him?

Rodney Wong

Wong sat behind the wheel of a black sedan, entering the town called Fairbridge. *How quaintly named,* he thought. He turned down a quiet street that led him to a suburb full of houses in neutral tones. There were driveways and rock gardens and white picket fences. Occasionally, he glimpsed a backyard with a swing set or a trampoline.

It was not the kind of place he would have expected them to be—if they were indeed here. He'd pictured them running from one concrete jungle to another, burying themselves away somewhere densely populated, where it would be easy to disappear.

Then again, maybe they'd counted on him guessing that. Tricky. They always had been unpredictable.

He'd flown in well ahead of his first scheduled obligation. He liked to have time to do his due diligence, get the lay of the land. Working outside the bounds of other people's expectations was one way of keeping a step ahead.

Beneath his seat was the cold metal of a small gun, tucked

within easy reach. If he slid his heel back, he could feel the tap of its handle against his shoe. It was comforting just to picture it there. Not for protection or anything. No, he was the biggest threat around.

Wong had been doing this work for almost thirty years. He once heard someone speculate that he'd become who he was as a result of some evil done to him as a child. The notion made him laugh. How desperately people clung to their ideas of right and wrong. How horrified they would be to learn: He wasn't all that different from them.

He was just doing what he needed in order to survive—some things more unpleasant than others. But any task became tolerable over time.

Wong slowed to a stop and rolled down his windows to smell the town.

The air was cold and gray and prickly in his lungs. It was full of scents he didn't know. And maybe some he did.

It was full of promise.

He had no idea where they'd put themselves, but he knew they were here. And he was going to find them.

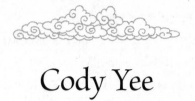

Cody Yee

The wind was in some kind of mood, whipping at the already torn screen behind the glass. There was always wind around, no matter the time of year. Cody was tired of how it scraped at his skin. He hated the way it sometimes howled, keening like a hurt animal.

It was as if his thought encouraged it: A new, whistling gust made him shiver. He stood to go cram a towel into the edge of the sill, and the window slid open.

This made no sense—Cody had learned about gravity in school. How on earth could the wind have pushed the glass *up*?

It breathed its ice into the room, plucking at his clothes. It roared against his brother's loose-leaf papers, tore them from the homework binder. Slammed the closet door wide open. Sent the shredded newspaper in Jadey's cage flying everywhere.

Cody shouted, as if that would quiet the gales. He jumped to get his fingers hooked around the top edge of the windowpane, and pulled down as hard as he could.

Instantaneous silence. His ears rang.

Hunter was not going to be happy about the mess. The thing was, though, when Cody told him it was the wind, Hunter was going to believe it. He always believed Cody. It was part of what made him such a good brother.

Cody began collecting the trash, and that was when he saw what the wind had revealed. In Jadey's cage, where the bits of newspaper had been swept aside, was an old-looking book. Probably small enough to fit in his mother's purse. The faded cover depicted a round moon, a black-haired lady floating near it in a billowy dress, and a little white rabbit.

There was no title, and the pages were blank. He flipped front to back, back to front, front to back again.

He set the book down and it flopped open to the middle. Now there were words in it.

Houyi was the God of Archery, and his aim was always true. When he drew an arrow, he could tell—by the scent of the wind and the rays of the sun—how to angle his shot, how to time his release. He never missed, for archery was his breath and his life, and his divinity.

Cody thought of Hunter in the woods, focusing on the tree trunks, closing his eyes because he didn't even need to look.

Could this be telling the story of his brother?

Cody looked down at the pages. They were blank once more. That couldn't be right. Where had the text gone?

He turned one page, and another, and then he was flipping

quickly, his movements frantic. He wanted to read the words again. How could they just disappear like that? Front to back and back to front. Blank, blank, blank. He shut the cover and held it tight to his chest.

There was something about this book. Would there be more words later? Part of him wanted to show this find to his brother...but Hunter had been special all his life. Maybe this book had appeared because it was Cody's turn to hold a bit of magic.

He decided: He was meant to keep this to himself.

David Yee

Hunter's father

David Yee stood in the parking lot closest to the university library, where the blacktop had split, a zigzagging crack that appeared overnight. It wasn't like other cracks, where one could reach a stick in and poke the bottom. If he peered straight down into it, he almost thought he could see a way to the center of the earth. That darkness made him shiver with wanting, with a hunger for success.

Even after all the cards this life had dealt him, he was still ambitious. He would turn things around.

Tomorrow he would meet with the dean. If he could get tenured, they could be free of their debts in two years. Was it too good to hope for? First, he would gather the rest of the money. After that…well. All these years later, he still wasn't sure of the best course of action. Reach out and offer up payment, interest included?

And what if he said that they'd been forced to make a sale? That his family had been desperate for money, and there was nothing left for them to give back aside from the cash?

When all that was settled, he would finally apply for a credit card. What freedom it would be to make purchases out in the open without worrying that they left a record of his location. He could begin to save for a house. The thought of owning property...he ached for it. He wanted that stability for Yvonne, for Hunter and Cody. He wanted them to live the American Dream.

All their plans and hopes had been halted, but that would soon be fixed. He swore it. His family did not deserve to be punished for what he had done.

The memory of that pivotal evening glared in his mind like the high beams of a car. One impulsive mistake tipping all the dominoes. He'd been sitting in that drafty office tucked away in the corner of the noisy restaurant owned by the vice president of the tong. It smelled like the toilets back there, which helped make it a good spot where one was unlikely to be overheard.

Unless, of course, someone was due for a meeting and had been told to wait in a seat just beside the closet where the phone was. Huang probably didn't realize that even through the door, David could just make out the conversation about the panacea, how it would fetch a high price. Did it work? Of course it did. There were more, too, he said. An entire collection of things. But among them, the easiest sale would be the panacea.

A cure-all. David had immediately thought of his son Hunter, wheezing and coughing, looking miserable and inches away from death as he shivered inside layers of blankets. Hunter, who baffled doctors with his condition. Wasn't he exactly the type of patient who should be given a panacea?

There'd been Huang's briefcase, open on the main desk. The

round wooden box inside, an old and precious-looking thing. A hunch made David pry off the lid and have a look.

He remembered returning home to that dark and moldy San Francisco apartment, shaking, unable to explain to his wife what he had done. Beautiful and brilliant Yubing, belly swollen with their second child, heart swollen with fear.

"We have to pack," David had told her. "We have to get on a plane tonight."

She'd stared at him with the widest eyes, paused in the middle of stirring a pot on the stove.

"No," she'd said, in the smallest voice. "No no *no*. Why?"

He didn't need her to remind him that her mentor and advisor were both here, that the plan was for her to pick things up right where she'd left off after she gave birth to their second child.

That evening marked his biggest failure as a husband, as a father. What had gotten into him? Yet his knuckles had tightened around the handles of the bag where he'd hidden his acquisition. Already, he was unwilling to let it go.

David shook his head to clear the memory. It clung to him like smoke from a heap of burning trash. He would never be rid of the smell.

Luna Chang

Her period came and brought with it the wrenching waves of nausea, the bone-tearing ache. It wasn't usually so bad at the very start. Luna couldn't help feeling like she was being punished.

She tossed and turned all night, sticky with sweat, the pain-killers doing nothing. Curling into a ball was unbearable. Lengthening her body hurt just as much. She wished she could crawl out of her skin, escape somewhere. Or at least be knocked out into oblivion. When she did manage to slumber, it was a cursed half sleep, and she woke each time a fresh surge rolled over her.

What she needed was more medicine. There was a temporary break in the cramps. She seized the opportunity and made her way down the stairs. Feeling like a ghost, she traced the walls with her hands. The first kitchen cabinet on the left was where the ibuprofen lived.

As she opened the door, a firefly lit up between the shelves. Luna rubbed her eyes. The lightning bug drifted past her shoulder. She turned to follow and saw the glittering mass outside the window. An uncountable number of lightning bugs hovering over the back deck.

She slung on a heavy coat and tucked her feet into her mother's flannel slippers. Slid open the door, and the wind made her insides clench, bringing back the nausea—

There they were, twinkles rising to greet her. Fireflies were gathering below her navel, pressing close as if she, too, sparked with light, and they recognized her as one of their own.

Was she dreaming? There was a tug, and warmth, then release. Her breath came easier, as if bonds around her organs had been cut free. The ache diminished. The fireflies had taken her cramps away.

"Thank you," said Luna.

They danced around her face, close enough that she could hear the soft and sibilant brush of their wings against air. They didn't move like anything she'd ever seen—moths, or bees, or the regular lightning bugs that came out in the summer. She'd never known any fireflies to make sound. Sometimes they fluttered erratically; other times they were steady as little drums. The wingbeats sounded like whispers.

"Are you trying to say something?" she asked.

One of them paused on her wrist. She cupped her other hand to it. Between her fingers there was a small flash of light, a flutter. She didn't mean any harm, just wanted to look at it up close. She held her catch like the most fragile filament.

Back inside, she walked over to the upside-down water glasses in the drying rack, ready to grab one for the firefly. She lifted her hand away.

There was nothing there.

Light winked in her periphery, down by a drawer. Without understanding the instinct, Luna opened the drawer and found a white stone cut in the shape of a hexagon.

It made her hungrier than ever. The surface gleamed like hard candy that would dissolve on the tongue. What was that silvery garden scent, so faint and tantalizing? She held the stone up to the moonlight, and then brightness exploded around her. Luna jumped, her elbow sent a folder flying, and her father's papers ended up strewn across the tiles.

"What are you doing?" Her dad was standing in the entrance to the kitchen, a finger glued to the light switch.

She felt embarrassed and caught. "Um...I must have been... sleepwalking."

He stared at her, his expression unreadable. "Did you fall? Are you okay?"

"Yeah. I'm fine, just..."

"You have school in a few hours. You should go back to bed."

She nodded and let him help her gather the pages. He followed her up the stairs.

"Wait," said Luna. "I left a thing."

"What thing?" her dad said.

"A...stone. I think I might have left it on the kitchen floor. I didn't put it away."

On the landing he turned. "I didn't see a stone. You must have dreamed that."

She stared at him for long enough to become aware of the clock ticking away the seconds. It had been real...hadn't it?

Luna woke before her alarm went off. She could tell by the still-ness of the house that her parents were asleep. She went down to the kitchen, to the drawer where she remembered discovering that white hexagon.

It hadn't been a dream. She was certain of that.

She looked and looked, but the stone was nowhere to be found.

Rodney Wong

Rodney Wong strode into the main office of Fairbridge High School wearing his most glittering smile. He let his cheeks wrinkle the edges of his eyes. He'd been told it was charming.

"I'm so sorry to bother you...Ms. Hart." He made sure to dial up his British accent. "I'm a bit of a mess these days and can't find my daughter's copy of the directory. Do you have an extra one I could have?"

The young woman had pinkish skin emphasized by the white of her fluffy turtleneck. She thumbed aside a rogue strand of mousy hair. "We ran out, sorry."

"Or simply one to borrow," said Wong. "I'm working out a carpool situation."

For the quickest second her eyes flicked in the direction of a tiered organizer on the counter. She cleared her throat. "I don't think we've met. What did you say your daughter's name is?"

He was saved from answering by the ringing of a phone.

"Sorry," she said, looking not the least bit apologetic. "I have to go get that."

She disappeared into a back room, and Wong wondered for a millisecond whether she was a fool or she just didn't care.

He found the directory on the second shelf of the organizer and flipped to the list of names. He hunted through the *L*s first. The wife had always been the clever one. He had a hunch that they would have all changed their names to hers. There was one student named Mark Lee. Was it a possibility? He bookmarked it in his mind and continued tracing his finger down the rows until he arrived at *Yee, Hunter*.

Yes, Hunter. That was what they'd called the boy. And a slight change to the surname—enough to deter Wong's efforts to locate them all these years. He committed the address and phone number to memory.

"I see you've found it," the woman said dryly, returning to her desk.

"Ah, yes. Thanks very much." He shut the directory. "I got exactly what I needed."

Yvonne Yee

Hunter's mother

Yvonne was deep in her element as she leaned against the kitchen counter with her papers, penciling in edits. She'd drafted a new analysis based on the latest Qin tomb findings. Dawei had written something different, but he was wrong. At least by now, after all these years, he knew to defer to her on these things.

Her youngest son slid into the kitchen on his socked feet and stood on his toes to reach for one of the granola bars she'd bought in bulk from the discount store. She handed it to him so he wouldn't fall. Then she noticed it.

"Cody. Where did you get that bracelet?"

It was deep red, the knots tightly done. It looked new.

"Hunter made it for me," he chirped, and skated out of the kitchen once more.

She gulped down a few breaths, trying to slow the racing of her heart.

The memory was sharp in her mind: The red cord stained with dirt and smelling ancient, wound so tightly around the little cake of dried herbs. How she'd cooked them and Hunter had thrown a tantrum—coughing the whole while—as she commanded him to drink the soup, roots and all. Afterward, how she'd been unable to discard that thread. Because it felt important.

So she'd made it into that bracelet, focusing with each careful knot on her hope that it would keep Hunter safe. Keep him healthy and hidden. She willed it so.

She'd tied it such that it could be adjusted as he grew and his bones thickened. All these years later, it felt almost silly. Still, it reassured her to see him wearing it.

Now Cody had one, too. Except his was not made from an ancient cord imbued with prayers and the properties of an impossible medicine. His was only a facsimile. It wouldn't protect anyone.

The thought chilled her.

Hunter Yee

Hunter and Luna had just sat down at their lunch table when the fire alarm went off. Lights blinked an obnoxious red, and teachers herded students toward the cafeteria doors. He checked to make sure he was not being blamed for the alarm—force of habit. Tremendous relief as he confirmed that nobody was looking his way. He had no interest in getting expelled a second time.

Luna groaned. "I'm *starving*. Why didn't I get something more portable than soup? Why couldn't they have warned us we were going to have a drill?"

"Here," said Hunter, holding out his lunch bag. "You can have my sandwich. I'm actually not hungry."

"I don't understand you," said Luna as they filed out with everyone else. "I'm *always* hungry."

His teeth were already beginning to chatter from the December air, but it was bearable. At least this would probably last only a few minutes. He wished he had his coat and scarf.

Luna was halfway into the sandwich when Hunter stumbled. It was the wind by his ankles—he usually heard it coming first. But Luna was beside him, and her presence always muted the air hissing in his ears.

"You okay?" she asked with her mouth full.

"Yeah," he said, trying to keep his gaze fixed in place, which happened to be on a spot near Luna's elbow.

"What are you looking at?" she said.

"Just—hold on a second." He craned his ears to listen for the rustling, to hear when it ended.

It was impossible to tell. He heard only the conversations of students and teachers, the sound of Luna peeling open the Velcro of his lunch bag. Hunter counted to ten, then let himself look.

There they were, multiple bills. Twenties, fifties, even a crisp hundred. They were sprinkled around him obtrusively. Hunter bent down—he needed to gather them quickly, before anyone else saw.

"*Whoa*," said Luna.

Wind raged forth, and the money went sweeping around the corner of the school.

Hunter cursed and went racing after the cash. There was too much here to just leave it. He swung around to the other side of the brick building and threw himself after the bills. They tumbled across the grass, always just out of reach. He wasn't paying attention to where he was going, and that was how he ended up tripping over an exposed root and falling off an edge.

Luna Chang

Luna heard the shrill blast of a whistle—a teacher waving, calling all the students back. When she turned around, Hunter was gone. The drill was over and classes were resuming. Where the hell was he?

It had grown frigid, in the way that sank through skin and muscle and deep into the bones. Luna traced the brick, following the walkway until she'd circled the entire school, passing both the faculty and senior parking lots.

She found nothing. No sign of Hunter anywhere.

Luna exhaled over her fingers; they were so cold they ached. She went back around to the gym side of the building, toward the soccer field and the track. The wind whistled and scraped at her.

A single lightning bug appeared in her periphery. It skated so close that Luna blinked to keep it out of her eyes. She hesitated for a fraction of a second before following it across the field, away from the school. Her feet carried her past the soccer goals and into the trees. Into the same wood that snaked its way through the rest of Fairbridge.

There were more fireflies now. They slowed for Luna to catch up. She toed her way around uneven ground and over roots. She briefly leaned on a tree and her hand came away sticky. Her fingers glistened as if she'd spilled ink. It was from the trunk, the crevices full of some slow-dripping resin, bleeding black. She'd never seen anything like it.

No time to think about that right now. Luna kept her eyes trained on her lightning bugs, following them to the edge of a cliff.

Except that made no sense.

There wasn't supposed to be a cliff here. In the sixth grade there'd been a class field trip through these very trees to learn about ecosystems. She'd walked this ground before, and she'd been back a few times since. This was all wrong.

Luna cautiously stepped to where the land dropped away. It was like a scene out of a nightmare. As if a giant had cracked open the earth with a pickaxe, then reached in to pry the gap wide. She could see rocks embedded in the dirt, the tangles of roots peeking out.

Someone groaned from below.

"Hunter," she said, peering over the edge. It was like gazing from a high balcony.

His body looked like a fallen doll, small and fragile. The wind picked up again and Luna wondered how he could stand to be so cold. Was he too injured to move?

"Can you hear me? Hunter?"

He struggled to blink his eyes open.

Luna looked for a safe way down but could see none. What she *did* see was the tiniest finger of water trickling past him. She tried to think. If the map in her brain was right, then it had to be coming from Lightning Creek. The ground must have split right to where the water flowed.

If she couldn't reach him from here, maybe she could go to the creek and follow the water to where Hunter had fallen.

"I'll be right there," she said, hoping it wasn't a lie.

The creek led her through trees and between hills, winding this way and that. By the time Luna was scooping him up in her arms, the midday sun was completely obscured by clouds. He was heavy, but the weight was manageable. She was stronger than she'd thought.

Hunter began coughing, a terrible squawk that hacked at his lungs.

She did the only thing she knew to do. She bent her face to his, and breathed.

Hunter's eyes closed. He gulped in her exhales like a starved animal, and at last, the wheezing subsided.

He let out half a cough and winced. "Here you are, saving me again."

Luna stroked his hair. "When it's my turn, you can save me."

Hunter Yee

If not for the way his entire body ached, Hunter would have believed the previous day's events to be a dream.

He remembered the fall. Dropping until he hit the bottom and broken branches were digging into his ribs. Believing that nobody would ever find him.

Hunter remembered how the sky had been the color of stone as he lay there, chest bursting with pain, breaths sticking in his throat. Darkness wrapped around him. He was lost and cold and there was nothing that he could see.

He'd heard his name after a while, like an echo at first, then a question. It wasn't the wind this time but a person. Luna at the top of the cliff, looking down at him. He thought she was wearing a gauzy white dress, one that billowed around her in the wind, sleeves draping like bells.

But he blinked and she was just in her sweater and jeans. Then she left, and as he watched her retreat, his vision sharpened. The thought of her abandoning him was terrifying. He tried to call out to her, tongue lifting to shape her name, but no sound came out.

The clouds and the trees blurred together. The fog returned.

Luna was breathing on him, the honey sweetness of her exhales renewing him. She'd half carried, half dragged him back to familiar ground. He remembered the flicker of lights guiding them the whole way. Little stars.

He'd refused to go to the nurse's office, and so she'd snuck him into an empty classroom, gathering his arm over her shoulders to help him walk. Wrapping her own arm around his torso to offer support. Everything in his body was hurting, but he'd homed in on the distinct feeling of her fingers against his ribs.

She'd waited beside him until it was time to head to the buses.

"Luna Chang, cutting class? Has hell frozen over?"

She crossed her arms. "You're making a joke. That must mean you're feeling better."

Hunter remembered taking the bus home and going straight to his bed. Lying there, ribs aching, noticing how his red bracelet looked frayed—it must have gotten snagged when he fell. The sounds of his parents coming home and turning on the television, and the voice of a news anchor talking about a giant crack running through Fairbridge. He remembered the squeak of the door that came later, and Cody crawling onto the bed, putting the fluffy white rabbit in the crook of Hunter's arm. He could feel her warmth, her fur shifting as she inhaled and exhaled, and it was this rhythm that lulled him into true sleep.

Now, as he walked to the bus stop, his every step jostled his body, made him feel each bruise, each cut, as if it were being freshly received. He reminded himself he was lucky not to have broken anything.

For so many years, he'd thought of the wind as his ally—mischievous, perhaps, but still a friend who offered support in the form of company and dollar bills. But now he wasn't so sure anymore. What did the wind want? Why was it so unpredictable?

What a waste of a stunt. He hadn't even gotten the money.

His breath made clouds and the ice ate into his chest. He nudged the zipper of his coat higher, wishing for a hat over his ears.

Hunter imagined himself freezing into a block of ice, shattering and dissolving, blowing apart like the seed head of a dandelion. The breeze would carry him out of Fairbridge, out of this state, out of the country. It would send him to the sea, to the North and South Poles, to the sky.

Luna Chang

The image of Hunter crumpled there like a piece of winter debris was etched into her mind. It startled her into awareness. The thought of him hurt, dying, disappearing...it scorched her.

She had feelings for him, and she couldn't pretend otherwise. If her parents could see what went on inside her head, they would be furious and disgusted. She was expressly forbidden from dating and wasn't supposed to engage with any boys outside of school-work. They expected her to detest the Yees, even sweet little Cody.

But Luna couldn't help herself. Her thoughts of Hunter were delicate, silken things. She let them weave their web around her, sank into their embrace.

She drifted sloth-like through the early hours, feeling that time was viscous. It had stretched and distorted so that she couldn't quite track its passing.

When she stepped onto the bus, Hunter was slumped against the window, looking just as small and fragile as he had the day before.

"It was on the news," she said, "how the ground is broken. There's a line running through the whole town."

"A crack." Hunter nodded. "I heard."

"That's what you fell into," said Luna.

He gripped his left wrist, thumb massaging some injury under the coat.

"Let me see," she said.

He allowed her to tug at his puffy sleeve, pushing the layers up to reveal the fresh bruise, the scraped skin. She nudged his red bracelet out of the way and traced the edges of the injury. He sucked in a breath and she paused, afraid of hurting him.

"Don't stop," he said, so quiet she almost missed it beneath the rumble of the bus.

Luna circled the lattice of scratches covering his palm. Drew an oval around the contusion on his arm. Heat bloomed in the tips of her fingers, and she painted that golden warmth into his skin.

On an impulse, she leaned down to kiss the tender brown and indigo. There was electricity between her lips and his skin, a spark as she made contact.

The bus lurched to a stop and all around them were the sounds of students rising from their seats and swinging heavy backpacks onto their shoulders. They had arrived at school.

For the next few hours Luna was beyond distracted. She conjugated everything wrong during her oral quiz in French. She forgot to write down the Lit homework. In social studies she failed to hear a single word being said until everyone began shifting their desks around.

"Earth to Luna," said Joyce. "Do you want to be partners?"

"Sure," she replied. "For what?"

Joyce gave her a funny look and tapped the sheet of paper on the desk. "This project?"

Luna looked down at the newly distributed handout. "Oh. Yeah."

"*Someone's* got their head in the clouds," Joyce teased.

"So." Luna cleared her throat. "I guess we need to pick a topic."

"Too bad *hunter*-gatherers isn't an option," said Joyce.

Luna's cheeks went hot, and she thought of their conversation about Hunter's reputation back at Stewart.

"He actually seems like a nice guy," Joyce said, reading her mind.

Calc was the slowest to pass. Luna watched the graphs being drawn on the board and tried her hardest to concentrate.... Her focus dissolved. The lines morphed into the shapes of her kisses printed on Hunter's skin. Sketch upon sketch of that strange magic.

Hunter Yee

He swam through the morning in a daze, replaying those intoxicating moments on the bus with Luna.

Under his sleeve, the bruise was changing. It had started out brown and indigo, with hints of a nasty yellow.

Now it was blue. Not a normal bruise color. Blue like something electric. Like a wildflower beneath a full moon. It had stopped hurting and the scabs on his palm were falling away, the skin underneath fresh and unmarred.

Luna's kiss had worked some sort of magic, warming him when he couldn't stop shivering. He felt it even now, like she'd given him the halo of a flame.

At lunch he walked into the cafeteria and the volume changed. There was Luna, already at their table. Hunter took the seat beside her.

Her eyes flicked up to meet his and flicked away just as quickly.

"Do you know what you did?" he asked.

Luna looked worried. "What do you mean?"

Hunter pulled his sleeve back. "Look." By now his palm was entirely healed, the flesh soft and new. The discoloration on his wrist had shrunken down to the size of a coin.

"*I* didn't do that," she said.

"You did."

She shook her head.

He had an idea. A question. "Let me see your hand."

Luna hesitated at first, then reached over. He draped her knuckles over his index finger, held them under his thumb.

There was the fire beneath her skin. His own hand absorbed it, going feverishly warm.

"Do you feel that?" he said.

Luna nodded.

"Why does that happen?"

"I don't know," she breathed.

He turned her palm up so that he could see the pale inside of her arm, where there was a map of blue veins. His finger slid toward her elbow, tracing the longest of the streams. Luna shivered but didn't pull away.

He bent to look more closely, as if he might divine the future from the creases in her wrist. "Is this okay?"

She nodded.

Before he could lose his nerve, he brushed his mouth against the base of her palm. There was a spark. His lips buzzed and heat swept through his body.

Luna sucked in a breath and drew back, examining the spot where he'd made contact. This time it was her turn to say, "Look."

He saw the indigo print of his lips on her flesh, a tentative bloom.

"I'm so sorry," he said, bewildered.

"No, don't be."

Hunter sat back in his chair, face hot and head spinning. "Does it hurt?"

"It doesn't. It's just... weird."

He wondered if this was what a hickey was. But he'd heard the guys in the locker room laughing about their marks, about the girls who were wilder than they'd expected. Hunter had surreptitiously glanced their way to see, and the tracks on their necks looked more like mild burns, not like the bluish flower on Luna's palm.

"It's kind of a conversation," she said.

He looked up. "What?"

"Like a dialogue between our bodies." She made a big show of pulling her sandwich out of her brown bag, perhaps feeling embarrassed.

He thought about the strangeness of it all. She'd kissed his skin and taken away the bruise. He'd returned the kiss, only to cause the opposite.

Hunter pulled out his own lunch and their conversation turned. They'd begun inventing fairy tales about the people who worked the lunch line. Luna was crafting a decidedly *un*-Disney narrative about a haunted hairnet that tormented its wearer.

Hunter played along, chiming in with details like how the hair-net made you crave mermaid flesh... but it was hard to focus.

What did her bruise mean?

Just before the bell rang, he saw Luna angling her palm beneath the fluorescent light, a tiny smile at the edges of her lips.

Luna Chang

Luna curled her fingers into the mark, petals unfurling on the pillowy flesh beneath her thumb. There had been a warm glow when he kissed her, like putting her hand in a patch of summer sun.

She wanted to know what it would feel like if they touched lips to lips.

Hunter was leaning against the bleachers on the opposite side of the gymnasium. His hair was growing long, and a strand of it flopped down into his eyes. She was about to cross the room to him, but he looked up and a new shyness rooted her in place.

Ms. Rissi blew the whistle, and the shrill pitch released Luna from her trance. The class counted off to divide into four groups, and Luna ended up on a team far away from Hunter. They were playing a game that involved shooting balls into hoops without it being actual basketball.

Luna's attempts were half-hearted. She was too distracted.

The place on her palm where Hunter had pressed his lips was still hot.

"Nice, Luna!" someone on her team called.

Her ball must have sailed through the hoop.

On the other side of the gym there was whooping and cheering. The boys took turns clapping Hunter on the back.

"Come on, Luna. You get to go again, since you made that one!"

This time she watched herself miss, the ball careening past the backboard.

When she glanced in his direction again, Hunter was staring right at her. The ball was between his tented fingers, as if held there magnetically. He tossed it backward, over his head, not even turning to watch its trajectory. Everything stilled as it arced through the air and into the hoop, the gym momentarily noiseless but for the swish of the net.

His group roared in celebration.

The next morning, Luna drove her mother's car to school. She was sad to miss Hunter on the bus, but she found him at his locker and playfully poked his shoulder.

"Hey," she said.

His eyes lit up. "Oh, hey. I thought maybe you were sick."

"No, my mom had me take her car. She wants me to get more practice driving before they leave me alone with it while they go to Taiwan. I've barely driven since I got my license."

"Oh, cool," he said, sounding disappointed.

Luna made herself say it before she lost her nerve: "Are you free after school?"

He dropped one of his textbooks and bent to dig it out from the back of his locker. "Um. For what?"

She shrugged and tried her hardest to look normal. "To hang out."

It took an era for him to respond. "Let me think. Um."

"I mean, don't worry if you can't," she rushed to say in a fast breath.

"Actually—there's some conference thing at Cody's school. So my parents won't be home until late. So, yes."

Her heart fluttered. "Okay. We'll go somewhere."

The day dragged by slower than anything in the history of the universe. Gym ended a few minutes earlier than usual, and she was jittery with impatience for the final bell to ring. Hunter leaned against the bleachers, smiling in that open and sincere way he had.

There was an acorn on the floor that must've gotten tracked in from outside. Luna toed it harder than she meant to, and it shot off like a hockey puck, producing a *thump* as it smacked the side of Hunter's shoe.

"Hey!" He nudged the acorn around to the front of his foot and kicked it back in her direction.

Luna was already laughing in anticipation of the impact, but the acorn swerved away from her. "Ha!"

Hunter looked puzzled.

"What?" she asked.

"That shouldn't have been a miss," he told her.

This made her laugh again. "Cocky, are we?"

"No, really. That was weird."

Luna arched an eyebrow. "You missed the first time you tried to throw a dodgeball at me, remember?"

"That's true," he said. But he was frowning.

In the distant corner of the gym, a sophomore kicked something and knocked over the basket holding jerseys.

"You better pick those up, Andrew," called Ms. Rissi.

"She needs a story," said Hunter. So far they'd given tales to the lunch ladies, the librarian, their AP Chem teacher, and the vice principal.

"Rissi?" said Luna. "Let's see. By day, she's a strict phys ed teacher exercising unruly hordes of students. But under the cover of night, she ventures out into the woods of Fairbridge to help save endangered magical hounds who have lost their way."

"How does she save them?" said Hunter.

"She lures them to her with her fiddle, playing a tune that only they recognize."

He grinned. "Sounds pretty badass."

The bell rang. They slung on their backpacks and rushed into the hall, toward freedom.

Hunter Yee

Hunter marveled at all that had changed. His first thought every morning used to be a reminder to himself that one day he would escape this life. Now that he had met Luna, it didn't feel so urgent. Things were bearable . . . maybe even on their way to being *good*. Was it possible that getting himself kicked out of Stewart was the best thing he had ever done?

"So is your mom just stranded at home without a car?" he asked as they crossed the senior parking lot.

"What?" She blinked. "Oh, no. This is her old car. I mean, it's technically going to be mine on my birthday."

"Wow," he said. The red Volkswagen looked newer than anything he'd ever seen his parents drive. "When's your birthday?"

She clicked her seat belt in place. "March."

"When? I was born March twenty-ninth."

"No way! Me too."

"Wait." He huffed a laugh in disbelief. "Really? We were born the same day?" He held back his other thoughts: That maybe it meant something. Maybe they were destined to meet.

He needed to stop having ridiculous ideas like that. It was a coincidence, nothing more.

"That's so wild." She turned the key, and the radio started blasting "Let's Talk About Sex" at full volume. Luna jammed her finger into the off button and Hunter's face went hot.

She cleared her throat. "Where should we go?"

"I get to decide?" His heart was working double time, embarrassingly loud. Was it his imagination or was she now trying to avoid looking at him?

"Yup."

"Okay. Then... we're going to a secret place."

How surreal this was. Luna Chang sitting beside him, the two of them separated by only the center console. Technically they sat closer together than this on the bus—but that was completely different. Here they were enveloped in their own private space. All the rest of the world might as well have melted away.

With Luna turning down the rush of noise in his ears, he could hear so clearly: the hum of the engine, tires crunching over rocks. Her inhales and exhales. The shifting of her foot against the pedals.

He gave her directions to his favorite spot. Luna turned off the main road and rolled to a stop by the split tree.

She peered out the window. "We're actually not far from where we live. You know these are the same woods that go through the whole town?"

"Yeah. I usually walk. This is where I come to hear myself think."

He showed her the way into the trees. Above them, empty branches reached toward each other, forming gray networks like giant blood vessels.

"It's beautiful in here," Luna said.

The ground shushed and crackled beneath their feet. It was cold out, but Hunter barely felt it. He was exhilarated. He was nervous.

They followed the gurgle of the creek until they saw it tunneling between mud and rocks and tangles of roots.

Luna made ripples with the toes of her shoes. "This creek runs through the trees behind my house, too. Sometimes in the summer I come to watch the tadpoles."

He liked that there might have been a moment when he'd knelt here, scooping at things that swam through the murk—while at the same time she crouched on a different part of the muddy bank, dipping her fingers into the same water. Maybe the creek had carried her breath along its surface until it reached him, and he'd unwittingly breathed it in.

Luna held a hand toward the surface and the water reached right back. A wave splashed her arm. She was shrieking and laughing, jumping away and trying to shake the wetness off. She bent to wipe the rest of it on her pants, and her coat rode up enough to reveal a strip of milky skin. Hunter couldn't look away.

He led her toward his clearing, and as they drew near he tried to see it through Luna's eyes: The tree stumps, marked from where the arrows had bitten into the wood. The paper plates on which he'd drawn concentric circles were soiled and misshapen.

"What are these?" she asked.

He shrugged. "Sometimes I come out here to practice archery."

"Wait, really? Do you have, like, a bow?"

Hunter brought her around a cluster of trees to the shed with its gray and splintery wood, and threw open the door.

"Here it is." He held out his bow, pictured his arms circling her, adjusting her posture with his fingers over her knuckles.

"Whoa. This is a lot heavier than I thought it would be."

Hunter smiled. "You're holding it upside down."

"Oh!" She looked sheepish. "I thought it would be, like, carved wood or something."

"What, like Robin Hood?"

She smiled back. "Yeah. So . . . are you any good?"

He shrugged. "I never miss."

Luna slid her hand right up against the bow grip.

"There you go." Only then did he realize just how close they were standing. He could smell her shampoo. He thought of the bruise her lips had lifted from his skin, the bloom of indigo he had left on her palm. That spark of heat when they'd made contact.

Hunter was the shy one, afraid to look so directly at what he wanted. It was Luna who leaned in close enough that their noses were about to touch. It was Luna who angled her head and brought her mouth to his.

He'd worried he would be bad at kissing, but she made it feel easy. There was that electricity, and a sense of this being absolutely *right*. The smell of her soft skin was intoxicating, sent a pooling warmth down into his body.

They paused only to breathe, foreheads together and noses grazing. Her eyes were so dark he could just barely see the edges of her pupils. A wave of vertigo: He was falling into them, spinning and tumbling.

Hunter would have been content to stand here forever, with only the sounds of their lips, where time could stop and it didn't matter that light was draining from the sky and the temperature was dropping.

Luna pulled back to look at him. Her smile cracked him apart. "I half thought we were going to leave bruises on each other."

He studied her face. "I guess we canceled each other out."

There were no blooms on Luna's mouth, but her skin glowed. Her eyes turned playful and she brought his fingers to her lips. She kissed his thumb. His knuckles. They watched the color emerge on his skin, the way a droplet of water might slowly seep and spread through paper. He offered kisses of his own to the back of her hand, saw the same trail of indigo appearing.

"Does it hurt?" he asked, just to be sure.

She shook her head.

Somewhere nearby a child screamed. He shivered.

"What was that?" said Luna.

Hunter didn't have an answer, but he took back his bow. His feet were already moving toward the sound. Other voices began shouting.

"Did someone fall in?" Luna called from behind.

They were running now, and up ahead there was rushing water. Which was completely wrong.

This was not where the creek was supposed to flow. A map of

Fairbridge would show the blue line curving through the section of trees far behind them—nowhere near here.

Hunter stopped short at the edge of the ground and looked down. The earth was jagged, freshly broken. The water moved in uncharacteristically violent, crashing spurts.

Another scream. He spotted the color that didn't belong: A pink coat. Dark and messy pigtails bobbed to the surface, then churned under once more. The waves were too high and too fast.

On the other side of the water, adults raced after the girl. Hunter and Luna followed.

The child was moving farther and farther away, and the light was quickly fading. Hunter squinted to be sure he was seeing right: Several yards ahead there was a fallen tree, and in just a few seconds the girl would be thrown past it. The trunk was giant. Maybe it would be enough.

His bow was already raised. Hunter planted his feet, set the arrow in place—

"What are you doing?" someone on the opposite bank screamed.

There was no time to consider how it might look to anyone else. He blew out a deep breath and held still. In the gap between heartbeats, he loosed the arrow.

Not a moment too soon, because then whoever it was across the water pegged him with a rock. The surprise of it sent him stumbling, and Hunter landed hard on his shoulder. He craned his neck to look up and check, though he already knew.

His arrow had pierced the hood of the girl's coat. She was safely secured to the unmoving trunk. The adults were already working to pull her out.

"Oh my god, did you see that?" someone was saying.

"Avery," a woman cried. She looked out across the water at Hunter as she hugged the girl tight. "Thank you. Thank you so much. You saved her life."

Hunter held her gaze. What a marvel, the fierceness a mother had for her child. He absorbed it like a sponge, feeling, for a fraction of a second, like maybe he'd once experienced that kind of love. He realized there were tears on his own face, too.

"Who are you?" the woman asked. "What's your name?"

They had lingered too long. Hunter turned without answering and grabbed Luna's hand. Together, they ran.

Luna Chang

Their fingers pulled apart, and it became a race. She laughed as she nearly lost her footing and cut in front of Hunter when he veered to avoid crashing into a stump.

When she reached the car, she whirled to catch him by the arms and sent them spinning. She was deliriously happy. It was dark now, but stars pricked through the curtain of night.

"Why did we run away?" she asked. "You saved that kid's life."

He shook his head. "It's complicated. I don't want them to know my name."

"But why?" she said.

"What if some journalist writes an article? Someone could, I don't know, take a picture of me and put it on a local news channel."

"So you're afraid of the attention?"

"Not *afraid*," he said, so defensive she wasn't convinced.

"You did a good thing," Luna said. "I guess if I were that mom, I would want to know who I needed to thank."

"I just—I said it's complicated."

She unlocked the car and slid into her seat, feeling uncertain.

"I'm sorry," Hunter said, holding her door open. "It's this thing with my parents. It's hard to explain."

The day had been perfect. She didn't want to end it on a bad note. "Okay."

"Are you mad?" he said.

"No. I'm not mad. I just want to understand."

He nodded. "Give me some time to figure out how to explain."

Luna arrived home so late that dinner was cold on the table, untouched. Her parents were furious. She had the excuse ready: She'd lost track of time working on an after-school project, then took a wrong turn while trying to avoid traffic and ended up totally confused about the route home.

Her parents thought it was unforgivable that she hadn't used the phone in the school's main office to call them, and she made herself look properly shamefaced and guilty, relieved that they bought into her lies.

Sprawled on her bed and staring up at her ceiling, she thought about Hunter's secret place in the woods, and his shyness as he'd led her into the clearing. The way the wind pushed at his hair. The smell of him as they kissed.

And seeing that little girl churning in the icy water, how something had come over him. Luna had been baffled when he lifted the bow. His arrow had cut through the air with an accuracy that felt mathematical and superhuman.

Then Hunter had gotten knocked over, and only then did she realize how it must have looked to strangers. She'd trusted him implicitly, but those other people—or at least the man who threw the rock—must have thought Hunter was making some sick game out of it.

It took a long time afterward before her brain was able to process what she'd seen. Hunter's arrow had so precisely pinned the girl to the log by the fabric of her hood. There had been no hesitation; he must have known he would succeed.

She was bowled over by the thought. In the woods, when he mentioned archery, he'd been so—

Humble wasn't the right word. Matter-of-fact? Nonchalant. It had been a simple statement: *I never miss*. He'd said it the way he might have said, *I eat breakfast in the morning.*

The drive home had been quiet as she mulled over his reaction, the paranoia that had spurred him to race away mere seconds after the incident with the little girl. Luna had felt him watching her from the passenger seat, worrying. He needed proof that she wasn't upset.

When he was about to get out of the car, she said to him, "Your aim is ridiculous."

The sound of his laugh echoed in her ears now, warming her to the core.

Cody Yee

Hunter was different somehow. Cody still hadn't figured out the what or why of it.

Was it a coincidence that their parents had also been especially tense recently? The anger in the house was a constant roar, as if someone had forgotten to turn off its faucet.

He understood that they were always hiding, but nobody would explain why. Once, his father told him that everyone's lives were like this. "You have to be careful in order to survive."

Cody thought that other kids his age were really good at pretending they didn't have to be careful. Either that or they just didn't care about the things their parents told them. They weren't xiaoshun and considerate enough, as his mother praised of him.

Though he wasn't sure that he really *was* xiaoshun. He was pretty certain he was just scared. It was exhausting, being so constantly terrified.

Worst of all, he didn't know what he was scared *of.* He just knew—based on the darkness that swelled in their house, the slippery whispers he heard from down the hall when his parents thought they were being quiet—that something lurked out of sight.

Something that could make their lives go very wrong at any moment, without warning.

Cody wished Hunter would speak openly with him instead of trying to be a shield. Things needed to be fixed, and it was infuriating that he couldn't help because nobody would tell him anything.

On the nights he couldn't sleep, he crawled deep under his quilt. There in the darkness he lit the camping flashlight that Hunter had given him a couple years ago and used it to read.

His special book felt like a friend. It was heavier than it seemed it should be, and always warm like a mug of hot chocolate. Every time Cody looked inside, the words were different.

One early morning he turned to a random page and watched the ink spill out sentences that shaped a story about a girl called Chang'e.

Chang'e worked in the emperor's palace in the heavens. Each morning, she sat up in her bed of rose petals, put on a billowy dress, and gathered her hair behind her head with a silk ribbon, all in preparation for the day's assignments.

It was a position of great honor, to be asked to decorate the imperial chambers. To pluck jewel-like fruits for the emperor's family, gather flowers and herbs for the great hall. In the heavens, the air always smelled of night-blooming jasmine.

On one side there lived the suns, and on the other side the stars—the bright and winking eyes of beloved ancestors.

It was the luckiest place in the universe that anyone could be. Yet Chang'e had the impertinence, the audacity, to wish for a different life. She was tired of the unmarred skies, the perfect peaches, the tasks given to her. She longed for a life of her own imperfect choices. She longed to see and hear the storms that stayed away from the palace.

Chang'e wanted to know what it was like to have the warmth sometimes disappear, to have days when the world was ice.

Some call it an accident; others say it happened on purpose:

One day, as Chang'e carried a tray of flowers and tea through the imperial gardens, her sandal caught on a step and she lost her balance. Her tray toppled, and the emperor's most beloved glass teapot shattered. It had been a gift from a celestial being rumored to be his former lover. It was irreplaceable.

The emperor banished Chang'e. And so she left the palace and went to live on the earth among ordinary mortals.

Yvonne Yee

Hunter's mother

Sometimes when Yvonne watched her eldest son—scowling over homework, or gently tending to his brother—she experienced a wave of dizziness, as if she were teetering off some ledge and falling through time. Her vision went murky and she saw Hunter as the frail, gray infant in the crook of her elbow. She remembered the scalding forehead against her arm, the gurgle that warned of mucus clogging the airway. His every cough fracturing her heart. All she'd wanted was for him to be better, be healthy.

When she fell deeper into the past, what she saw was herself. The young academic with her hair in a bun, absorbed in the meditative clacks of typewriter keys. She still had that work, at least—the questions that ribboned through history. Her attempt to examine and answer them. Even if she had to do it tucked away, hidden.

Sometimes she opened the dented file cabinet that sat in

the corner of the bedroom and lovingly ran her fingers over the stacks of papers. *By David Yee.*

How she missed her career. How she ached to have her own office in which to sit and type. A collection of publications with her own byline on the front of each one. A life that she controlled.

Yvonne closed her eyes to imagine her name in print.

The letters blurred and took on new shapes, a waking nightmare: A man named Huang picking up a copy of a journal, recognizing her name. Finding her affiliated university. He would track down her family, pin them with their debt.

She let her exhale drop like an anchor and slammed the drawer shut.

Rodney Wong

Fairbridge was broken. Literally.

Wong had never seen anything like it, the land freshly split like dry, damaged skin. Cracked and seeping.

There'd apparently been an incident back in late September, right as the full moon peaked—coincidentally the date of the Mid-Autumn Festival—that some people prematurely declared an earthquake. But that was quickly proven by seismologists not to be the case, and it was, even now, an unexplained phenomenon. In the library, flipping through the recent newspapers, he learned that there'd been an initial wave of panic following that first major crack. It turned out all the new fractures showing up in the ground were connected to that earliest one. But nothing dire had come of it, and the township was working on fixing things. There were complaints being filed here and there, but for the most part people had accepted the inconvenience.

Traffic cones blocked off sections of roads, and metal plat-forms served as temporary bridges. By now everyone had grown used to driving around the breakages, learning new routes. One day Wong had stopped by a place called Fudge Shack for a hot cider, and when he asked the cashier about the cracks, she shrugged and rolled her eyes, called it *sort of annoying*, and gave him his receipt.

He wondered if none of the Fairbridge residents sensed what bled out from those dark crevices. Did it have a name, this stuff that smelled like pocket change and rose up to fill him with equal parts dread and inspiration?

It was exhilarating to stand at the edge and breathe it in, peering down at where the roots and layers of rock and soil pulled apart. The hair-raising tension it evoked. He relished that discomfort—it reminded him of the initial shock of jumping into a pool. The body beginning to acclimate. The hum of energy as muscles activated.

In the distance a car turned onto his road. He ducked back into the driver's seat and slammed the door shut, then pulled off the shoulder before anyone could get a good look at his face. The chances were slim, but he didn't want to be recognized. Not yet.

Wong turned down another route and raced ahead. He was getting the lay of the land. Fairbridge wasn't all that big, and now that he was here he had learned many things. Where the Yee family lived. Where their eldest son attended school.

He would hold on to those cards for now. It was time to strategize. First, he would have his possessions returned. Then he would enact his punishment. He would take Hunter Yee away forever.

Luna Chang

Luna's father was practically bouncing, he was so joyful. The evening felt celebratory, though there was nothing significant about it, other than that they were counting this as their holiday meal before her parents flew to Taiwan. Regardless, seeing her father happy made *her* happy.

The weather had turned gray and ominous, wind slapping at their clothing when they stepped outside, but a little thing like that wouldn't stop them from driving to Giuseppe's, the local Italian joint—and the only place her parents ever wanted to go that wasn't Fortune Garden.

Her dad unfolded the cloth napkin in the bread basket and gestured for Luna to dig in. "Eat all the breadsticks you want. We can always order more." His favorite joke. The breadsticks were unlimited, as was any soup.

Luna's mother's trick was to fill up on minestrone and get her actual entrée boxed up for later. It was forever embarrassing, the way she tried so hard to max out every dollar. It wasn't like they were struggling with money.

"What an amazing time it is for you, Luna," said her father. "Can you believe that soon you'll be a college student?"

"If I get in somewhere," said Luna. The subject dampened her mood.

"Your top choices will want you," said her mother, as she always did.

"You're going to go to Stanford," her dad added, beaming. "I *dreamed* of it happening."

Luna hated when they talked about this. "How long will you be in Taiwan again?"

"Only a week and a half," her mother said. "Don't worry. It'll go by so quickly. You should invite friends over to keep you company."

Luna knew her mother was thinking of Roxy, who had left for college and then dropped off the face of the earth. She hadn't returned a single one of Luna's calls or letters. Early on, Roxy had mailed a postcard of her school's campus with the words *Miss you!* scrawled on the back, and that was it. These days there was just one person who really fit in the box labeled *friend*. Friend... and something more.

It was also hilarious, Luna thought, that her parents had zero worries about her possibly throwing a wild, drunken party in their absence. They didn't understand American teenagers enough for the scenario to occur to them.

Her father mistook her silence for dismay. "We'll take you

with us the next time we go, Luna. It's too much right now, with your senior year wrapping up."

"All my college apps are about to be due, anyway."

"Yes, yes," her dad said quickly. "That, too. Obviously those are the priority."

"We would have skipped going this year," her mother added, "but the timing is too perfect—it happens to be the National Assembly elections. This might be the turning point we have been waiting for. Taiwan should be recognized as its own nation, with our own culture and politics."

"Next time will be easier," said her father. "Once you're a university student, you'll have longer breaks. And if you do have to miss class, it won't be a big deal. You can come with us then."

Luna uncrossed and recrossed her legs. "Yeah, it's okay. I'll be fine."

Her parents exchanged a glance, and she found herself struck by their symmetry, shoulders side by side, opposite hands dipping warm bread into shallow bowls. Her father's cheek glistening with an accidental brush of olive oil.

She felt a wave of fondness for them. Other kids at school complained about their families—annoying siblings, overbearing parents, disagreements and punishments—but her family was as close to perfect as she could have hoped for. The way her parents loved and supported each other inspired her. They'd struggled, as most immigrants did, with leaving Taiwan behind and building this life for themselves in the States.

She'd heard their stories. The beginning, when her mother's

English was nonexistent and she couldn't even ask a simple question about a coupon at the grocery store. When her father had worked into the late hours of the night, writing paper after paper to build his academic reputation. They'd been so determined to stay here in this country so that their American daughter could have this dream future.

Her parents had stumbled through the brush, climbed the impenetrable wall, and leapt down to the other side, where Luna's road would be paved. Easy peasy. The path was clear and she would follow it onward. She would grow up to become exactly what her parents wanted and needed.

The soup arrived and she popped the last piece of her bread into her mouth.

"Eat all the minestrone you want, Luna," said her father, winking, and her breath hitched. Next year, everything would be different. She would no longer live at home. She wouldn't be able to go out for dinner with her parents at a moment's notice. Visits would have to be planned. Her dad's cheesy jokes would have to come to her via the phone.

What was wrong with her? Most people couldn't *wait* to get away from their parents. But then, most people didn't seem to have parents as special as hers. As she stirred her soup, she reminded herself how lucky she was.

A small light flickered above her father as he ducked down to slurp.

Luna blinked, and the firefly was gone.

Hunter Yee

What a glorious gift from the universe, this early dismissal on the last day before winter break. Hunter got off with Luna at her stop, feeling shy and dreamlike. Were they *together* now? Dating? Was that what this was? He was almost afraid to ask, as if using words might shatter it.

How unreal that they were going to be alone together in her home, which was empty of parents. It turned out that she lived just on the opposite side of the woods from him. If they cut through the trees and hopped the creek, it would take no more than ten minutes to walk from one house to the other.

The Changs' residence was giant and beautiful. Two stories *and* a basement. It was painted sky blue, and decorative white shutters framed the windows. There was no mold on the side, nothing broken or stained. It looked crisp and well kept, like a house in a movie.

He took off his shoes and set them down right by the door, careful not to shed any dirt on the rug. The art on the walls, the furniture, the lush carpet beneath his feet—it all looked regal, expensive. Everything was pristine. Everything smelled like Luna.

Hunter felt like a rodent who had wandered into a high-ceilinged museum. He knew that it wasn't technically a mansion, but compared with the shabby one-story rental unit his family called home...

"I'm *starving*. You want something to eat?" Luna was already leading him into the kitchen.

"Sure." He pulled one of the stools out from under the counter.

They were so very alone in this house. Anything could happen. They might kiss again. They might do more than kiss. The thought simmered in his body.

"We can do instant noodles, grilled cheese sandwiches.... We can pop some mozzarella sticks in the oven. There's a tin of Christmas cookies. Ooh, and I think there are dumplings in the freezer."

"Wow," said Hunter. "Instant noodles sound great."

Luna filled the kettle with water and pulled two shiny ramen packages out of a drawer. He watched her movements, tried to memorize her grace. Here was Luna in her natural habitat. Long fingers turning a knob on the stove. Arms lengthening to draw bowls and plates from the cupboard. Thin wisps falling free of that ponytail. Her sweater rode up and he caught a glimpse of her midsection.

"Can I ask a question?" she said as she turned back around.

"Sure."

162

"Why *is* it that you had that reputation back at Stewart?"

Hunter tensed.

"I mean, I know what I've heard," Luna continued, "but I also know what you're like around me. And I just don't get it."

"It's complicated. I hate to think what you've heard." How was he supposed to explain? "Do you remember the last time we did basketball stuff in gym? And I made that backward shot?"

She laughed. "You mean, do I remember you showing off?"

He couldn't argue—he *had* kind of been showing off. "It's more than that. I sort of have a connection to the wind." He cringed. The words sounded ridiculous. "It helps me aim."

"When you made that shot . . . we were indoors."

Panic was beginning to stir in his veins. He hadn't realized how badly he needed her to believe him. "By wind I mean any movement of air. It's like, wherever I go, it's not far behind."

"Okay?"

"And it helps with other things, too. Though sometimes the wind . . . I don't know. It gets bored and stirs up trouble."

"Trouble," she repeated. "Like what?"

"Like, a teacher's desk getting knocked over. Or an alarm getting pulled. Things that look like pranks."

Luna narrowed her eyes. He could see how hard she was thinking. "So you're saying the *wind* is how you got expelled."

"Oh, no," said Hunter. "I did that myself. On purpose."

She blinked. *"Why?"*

Hunter sighed. "You know Stewart's a private school."

"Yeah?"

"The only reason I could afford to go was because of a grant.

I found out the policy was changing so that each family can only get one award per year. Meaning, one kid per household."

Luna caught on immediately. "You left so Cody could stay."

He nodded. "I hated it there. He actually likes Stewart."

"Why didn't you just tell your parents you wanted to switch schools?"

Hunter traced the swirls on the marble counter. "I tried that, and they were pissed. But also, with me being on the brink of graduation, I knew they would think it was more important for me to stay than for Cody. It seemed best to just get it all squared away before they got a notice about the grant."

Luna leaned forward on her elbows. "What exactly did you do to get kicked out?"

Hunter couldn't help grinning. "I paid one of the school geniuses to hack all the computers in the lab. She wrote some program so that when the teacher turned on the computers, the screens began endlessly looping the text *No one will believe that Hunter Yee didn't do this.*"

She laughed. "Which you didn't."

"Nope. It was meant to be commentary. I didn't do any of the other things I got in trouble for, either."

"What an epic prank. I can't believe I never heard about it," she said.

"I was relieved they kept it quiet. I'm not sure how many students even knew. Stewart hushed it up fast—it was embarrassing for them. And maybe they were worried about potential copycats."

There was a flicker, like the tiniest of lightbulbs turning on and off near her ear.

"Is that—a firefly?" He squinted to see it better.

"Where?" said Luna, whirling to look.

"It was by your head. I don't know where it went." Hunter tried to remember the last time he saw a firefly that wasn't during the summer.

Luna frowned. "If I tell you a secret, will you promise to believe me? I feel like, out of anybody, you would be the one to understand, but—you have to swear first."

"Of course," he said.

"There's something supernatural about the fireflies, and I don't really understand it. I mean, not like all fireflies to ever exist on this planet. But the ones that are hanging around me even though it's winter."

Hunter nodded. "I believe you." He wanted to ask questions, but she looked tense, hesitant. He waited to see if she would continue.

Instead, she passed him one of the packages of noodles. An illustration depicted a bowl of vegetables and a shrimp who looked ready to march away.

"This kind's the best." Luna tore into it. "My parents always bring back half a suitcase full of this stuff from Taiwan."

"How often do they go?"

"Every other year," said Luna, sliding the dried bricks of noodles into bowls. "I usually go, too—the school dates this year just aren't ideal. They didn't want to mess with anything that might stop me from graduating."

Every other year. Hunter couldn't wrap his mind around having enough money to comfortably do that. He didn't know how much plane tickets cost—but he knew it was definitely outside what his family could afford. He'd visited Taiwan only once, when he was three years old, to see grandparents. Cody had never been.

The kettle began to whistle, so similar to the cry of the wind that it sent his heart pounding.

Luna poured the water over the noodles. "Your family's Taiwanese, too, right?"

"Chinese," Hunter clarified.

"Oh, for some reason I thought they were born in Taiwan."

"They were," he said.

Luna looked confused.

He shrugged. "It's the same thing."

"No," Luna said slowly. "It's not."

"I mean, isn't that like saying a square's not a parallelogram?"

Luna fell silent, her brows furrowing.

Hunter's mood was slipping down a hill. How had they ended up in this conversation about their families? The sterile quiet made all their words especially loud and uncomfortable. He found himself longing for the usual roar of the wind in his ears.

Luna Chang

This rare, precious time alone in her house with Hunter
was not at all going the way she'd hoped. And now they were
having an argument. She hated it.

At the same time, she couldn't let it go.

Luna pressed her lips together, trying to think. Her parents had
always treated Taiwanese and Chinese as two distinct identities. A
memory crawled to the surface: dinner at Fortune Garden some
years ago, when her parents were talking to Mary about Taiwan
being independent, about preserving Taiwanese culture. Her parents
were so vocal about it, and she'd never met anyone who disagreed.

Hunter tilted his head, and she realized she'd been quiet for
too long. He looked uncertain. "I mean, that's just what my family's always said. That Chinese people and Taiwanese people are
all the same."

"Well, they're wrong," she said stiffly. She lifted the plate
covering one of the bowls and checked on the noodles. "That's
just . . . erasing an identity."

It was clear Hunter didn't know what to say. He tried to pivot, though not in the smoothest of ways. "Were you born here? In Fairbridge?"

Luna decided to go ahead and let him reroute. "Born and raised. You?"

"San Francisco. Annoying how I still get people telling me to 'go back to China' and stuff."

"It happens to me, too," she said. "It's disgusting."

"People are afraid of anyone who's different." Hunter's eyes had a faraway look. "It makes me worry about Cody."

"At least he has you." She was trying her best to help smooth over the conversation, but what he'd said was still nagging at her.

Hunter sighed heavily. "Yeah."

"What?"

"It's just—I want to get out of here. All I have to do is hang on long enough to graduate, and then I'll be gone." His voice stumbled on that last word.

She tried not to fixate on it—the idea of him being *gone.* "What colleges are you shooting for?"

"Ha. Screw college."

Luna laughed uncomfortably.

"I get that we need literacy, and basic math skills are useful. But I don't want to do more school. I don't *need* more school. I just need to get out of this place. It's suffocating." He lifted the plate off his bowl and poked aggressively at the noodles. She wasn't sure they were thoroughly cooked yet, but he was already digging in with chopsticks.

Luna had never thought that anybody in their community—

least of all anyone Asian—might consider not going to college. There was a rebelliousness in that kind of thinking that scared her.

"But you *have* to go to college. Your parents don't care about whether you get a degree?"

He snorted. "I didn't say that. They'll be furious. But what's it matter when they already have the biggest disappointment for a son? This'll just be one more hairline fracture on a shattered bone. Who cares? They probably wish I didn't exist. If I disappear, they can just write me out of the family history."

The resentment in those words was unbearable. Luna wasn't sure how to hold space for it. "Where will you go?"

"I don't know. Maybe Canada. Europe. Some big city, where there are people who get me."

"But how do you find those people?" she said.

"I don't know," he answered. "This is just a vague, big-picture plan."

"But isn't it a better plan to start with college?"

Hunter looked angry. "You sound like my parents."

"I'm just trying to understand. Like, how will you survive? You'll need to get a job and figure out where to live—how are you going to do all of that?"

"You're asking a lot of specific questions." His voice had gone cold. "Do you have a point?"

"I just think it's . . . a little bit cowardly," she said.

His laugh was sharp and sarcastic. "Are you serious?"

"You're planning to run away and leave your little brother behind to struggle in exactly the same way you have."

"Would you call it 'running away' if I were going to college on the other side of the country?"

She paused for a beat. "I don't know."

"So if I go do something privileged, with the Asian stamp of approval, but I do it as far from home as possible...it's not running away? But if I set out on my own with the support of nobody and try to make a life for myself—that's cowardly? *That's* running away?"

"I don't know," she said again.

"Herd mentality," he said. "Your transformation into an Asian sheep is just about complete."

At some point in the last couple minutes, the feeling flowing through Luna's veins had converted into something close to rage.

This was not what she had expected when she invited him over. She'd envisioned them side by side on the couch. Kissing again, like in the woods. Maybe stuff beyond kissing. What little time they had together, and here they were squandering it by fighting.

She wasn't sure how to fix the situation.

Hunter emptied his bowl, slurping up the last of the noodles. "Thanks for lunch," he said gruffly. He fiddled with his bracelet, then pulled his sleeves down. "I should head back before everyone gets home. See you later, I guess."

Luna didn't say anything. She just stood in the kitchen and listened to him gathering his coat, pulling his shoes on, the front door clicking shut.

Rodney Wong

Rodney Wong had always been a rule follower. At five years old, when his peers splashed and shrieked in the forbidden river, he'd remained on the bank, dry and scowling. He remembered studying calligraphy around eight or nine, looking on as another student not only brushed a stroke in the wrong direction but had the audacity to retrace it. Wong had been enraged, as if the act had been directed at him in a personal offense.

His father regularly reminded him that he was lucky. Born just as the war ended, and immediately given a Mandarin name, a Cantonese name, a Japanese name—and just a handful of years later, an English name, which would be the one to really stick. His father wanted him to be *known.*

Wong was also fortunate to be the son in a family that fell into exporting textiles at exactly the right time and then spied an opportunity to start up one of the first garment factories. Through these businesses, his father befriended members of the Lutheran Church who had traveled from the United States, and those men became Wong's tutors. His parents constantly reminded him that he was lucky to be receiving a *real* education. One day, they said, he would go abroad and make a life for himself.

Wong's strict adherence to all rules and his strong work ethic made him an excellent student. By the time he was studying at university he had grown into a proud and industrious young man.

He graduated number one in his class and was soon offered a spot in an American school for a postgraduate degree, complete with visa sponsorship. The future was a bright star he had plucked from the sky and wrapped in his palm, and he planned to carry it in his pocket and rise to the top. He strode through Kai Tak, Hong Kong's international airport, with a freshly tailored sport coat gracing his shoulders and a leather briefcase swinging at his side, both of them parting gifts from his mother. Soon he would be coasting among the clouds on a plane that would transport him to the land of dreams.

He was already at the gate, standing in line to board, when in between announcements he heard his name being shouted down the terminal.

"Huang Rongfu! *Huang Rongfu!*"

He turned, puzzled. Everyone mostly called him Rodney, or sometimes the Cantonese version of his name. But his mother's handmaiden—an older woman who had been a refugee from mainland China and never really learned English—she only ever called him by his Mandarin name. Always Huang instead of Wong. It was she who barreled down the wide hall now, weaving around travelers, her hand flapping in the air so that he would see her. He looked around, embarrassed. People were staring.

"Don't get on that plane," she said as she reached him, gasping for breath.

The words were so ridiculous he almost laughed. "Why not?"

"Your father's in trouble." Her distress made her Mandarin roll together, a bit more difficult for him to understand. "He needs you."

"What kind of trouble?" said Wong, baffled. His father, the businessman who was well respected not only locally but internationally. The one who had taught him the value of integrity, taught him to follow every given rule. There was no trouble Wong could imagine him getting into that he couldn't reason his way out of, with his charm and his promises and his reputation. Besides, his father was the very source of his family's wealth. What could money buy if not changed minds?

Ayi shook her head, glancing at the inquisitive faces nearby. "Not here."

Wong had no idea that in the next few hours, the pillars that held up everything he believed, everything he'd ever been told, would crumble to nothing.

On the way back home, Wong was given the picture in bits and pieces: It turned out his father was guilty of quite a lot. He'd been shaking hands on underground contracts for years. He'd been embezzling money for longer than that.

He was even cutting deals with a triad: running an illegal gambling ring, working a counterfeit operation, and he was double-dipping—the specifics of which Ayi did not understand—and it was a careless step in this that had finally given away his hand. Triad members had broken down the door, knocked him unconscious with a gun, and seized him.

The ransom they requested: Control over half his holdings. Double their original agreed-upon share of earnings. And his son.

Per their terms, the young Rodney Wong would work for the triad, indentured for the next five years, until current operations were concluded. At that time, Wong Sr. would be returned to his family, safe and sound. His fortune diminished, perhaps. But he would be alive.

It wasn't until Wong stepped through the door and saw his mother weeping on the floor, unable to stand, that he understood it was all real.

Rodney Wong had always been a rule follower, and now filial piety was calling, more insistent than ever before.

So it was that Wong found his path in life. The triad was so impressed with his work ethic that they quickly came to see him as a brother, for he had discovered that they weren't much more than an organization with its own laws and codes. Within that structure he did what he was best at and found himself thriving.

When the five years ended, he stayed on and became a true member in his own right. Three more years passed in a blink, and then by invitation he followed a triad officer across the ocean, finally setting foot on the land he'd always yearned to call home.

There, in a place named San Francisco, he learned the new rules. He honed his ability to smell out opportunities and bullshit. Soon enough, he became the master of a tong, overseeing his own band of sharp and brawny immigrants—at last his own king.

Hunter Yee

Days later, Hunter had grown sick of the questions wheeling around in his head, the echoes of his conversation with Luna. He kept trying to see it from different angles, like turning over a fake rock to find the seam where it would open and reveal the key inside.

During a lull at dinner he asked, "Are we Chinese or Taiwanese?"

His father frowned at him. "Chinese, of course."

"But our family is from Taiwan," said Hunter. "Right?"

"Isn't Taiwan part of China?" said Cody.

"Yes," their mom said. "It is. Though some people don't want it to be."

Cody poked at his slice of the pizza that had come frozen in a sealed box. "Why not?"

She considered this question for a long breath. "They don't understand that Taiwan needs China. It should not be its own country. The argument is ridiculous—we are all Chinese people. We should be united."

"United we stand, divided we fall," Cody quoted.

"Yes, exactly," said their father. "But the Minjindang don't believe that. They're fools."

Their mother made a derisive sound. "They're all terrible people," she said. "Like the Changs, you know? They support Minjindang. Evil people. They call themselves *Taiwanese* and pretend they're not Chinese. It's ridiculous."

Now Hunter understood: The enmity between his parents and Luna's was about politics, too. And if his parents—who were the quickest to condemn others for the tiniest things—thought the Changs were terrible, thought that Taiwanese people should not have their own cultural identity...

He felt guilty for what he'd said to Luna.

Late into the night, Hunter waited in his jeans for his parents to fall asleep, for stillness to descend over the house. He could hear his mother shuffling through papers, tapping away on the typewriter—she was often awake late, helping his father with some write-up or another.

At last it stopped. There was the click of a light turning off, the sound of her crawling into bed. Hunter stood up and pulled his coat on.

"Are you sneaking out?" Cody whispered, rubbing his eyes.

"Shhh. I'm just going to the bathroom. Go back to sleep."

Hunter went to his place in the woods. Clouds veiled the moon. It didn't matter; he didn't need to see in order to aim.

His muscles had been itching for this tension and release. These were the sounds that soothed him. The moment before he loosed an arrow—when he held his breath and waited for the pause between two heartbeats—was when he could find the clarity he needed.

He shouldn't have walked out of Luna's house and left their conversation where he did. Had her parents returned yet? He wished he knew. He wanted to knock on her front door and apologize.

The temperature dropped; his every inhale was ice in his lungs. Hunter stowed his bow and quiver and began to make his way back. He rehearsed his apology in his mind, the words looping and sharpening. He hoped it wasn't too late, that he hadn't ruined their friendship—or *whatever*ship—for good.

The next step he took, his foot found no purchase. His shoulder slammed into the twisting trunk of a tree—the only thing that stopped him from falling.

Clouds parted to let the moon pour down, and he could see where the ground gave way to black. Another breakage in the earth. Wind gusted and Hunter doubled over for a cough, wheezing hard. When he pulled himself back up—arm wrapped around the trunk—he forgot about the freeze of each breath, the throbbing in his shoulder.

All he saw was the light. He'd been wrong before: It wasn't from the moon. It was the fireflies, crowded en masse against a tree, sculpting their glow around its roots and trunk and branches, flashing their lanterns in unison.

Cody Yee

Cody opened the book, and the words it showed him told of the end of the world.

He reread the page three times to try to understand.

He pressed his fingers to the final sentences.

> *The darkness will rise from the ground and wrap its fingers around hearts, and in that squeeze the loudest thoughts will be of greed and cruelty and selfishness. That will be the end, unless everything is restored.*

Cody shivered.

The bedroom window unlatched itself and slid up, letting in a sharp gust. It wasn't like the miniature tornado that had hit the room last time, that had revealed the book hiding in Jadey's cage. No, it was a gentler wind. But it rattled the pages, flipping through them fast and hard.

When the wind died down, Cody tried to find the spot where he'd been reading before. But all of it had gone blank.

These latest words disturbed him. He didn't like what they had to say, didn't like this sense of *wrongness*.

What did it all mean?

Luna Chang

It was weird to go to the grocery store alone and wander the aisles looking for food just for herself. She supposed this was what living on her own would be like next year.

Luna zigzagged down the cereal aisle, swinging her basket at her side. As she was reaching for a box of Cap'n Crunch, a familiar voice called her name.

It was Joyce Chen, holding a gallon of milk and a bag of salt-and-vinegar chips. "Hey! I was thinking about calling you."

"Me?" Luna said, and then felt foolish.

"Yeah," said Joyce. "To see if you wanted to work on that social studies thing. Or even just hang out."

"Sure. That sounds great. Actually, you want to come over?"

"When?"

Luna shrugged. "How about now?"

In the kitchen, with Joyce perched on the very stool where Hunter sat just a week ago, Luna dumped mozzarella sticks onto a pan while the oven warmed up.

"So where are your parents?" Joyce asked.

"They're in Taiwan. They're actually flying back tomorrow night."

"Ooh," said Joyce. "I'm so jealous! The last time I went was in middle school. Every time I talk to my nainai she asks when we'll be back."

"Wait, so, I'm curious." Luna tried to think of the best way to ask her question. "Do you consider yourself Taiwanese or Chinese?"

Joyce tipped her stool back. "Both."

"Interesting," said Luna. "My parents say we're Taiwanese. Not Chinese."

"I know a lot of people who would agree. Taiwan is definitely its own place with its own specific culture. But some people who are Taiwanese identify as Chinese, too. Or instead. I mean, there are cultural differences, and there are things that overlap."

Luna frowned. She was getting a headache.

"It's not the most cut-and-dried," Joyce told her with a shrug. "People identify differently depending on how they were raised, and when their families moved to Taiwan, and what ideology they subscribe to, et cetera. I try to be objective because it's obvious some members of my family can be so biased. Like, there are people my aunts and uncles hate just because they identify differently."

The oven timer dinged, and the subject changed. Joyce told the story of how her older brother, who was away at college, had set off the smoke detector with his unsanctioned toaster oven. How he had a roommate who constantly left a rubber band around their doorknob to indicate that the room was not to be disturbed. Joyce called it *sexiling*.

This, too, made Luna think about Hunter. About his plans to escape. To skip even *applying* to college.

"What do you think of the general concept of going to college?" Luna asked.

Joyce made a face. "I don't know? It sounds fun? It also sounds like a lot of work?"

"I mean. What do you think of how people basically make it out to be some life requirement?"

"By people, you mean parents?" Joyce shrugged. "It makes sense, I guess. They want us to be the best we can be. Higher education leads to better opportunities, blah blah blah."

"But what if someone doesn't want to go to college?" Luna pressed. "What about them? What if they think they can go off on their own and make a better life than they have currently?"

Joyce raised an eyebrow. "You don't want to go to college?"

"Oh, no, it's not about me," said Luna. Though the question made her suddenly wonder: *Did* she want to go to college? She'd never actually considered the possibility of *not* going. "I'm just curious what you think about the concept of it."

"Well." Joyce chewed her way through an entire mozzarella stick and swallowed. "Not everyone can handle it. Like, say, financially. Or maybe health-wise, for example."

"Right," said Luna, though she had never considered any of these things before.

"*I'm* definitely going to college," said Joyce. "It'll be my excuse to move to a place where my parents are not. I applied to four safety schools just in case."

Luna sighed. "Do you worry at all about making the wrong choice?"

"Duh, we all make wrong choices. Doesn't mean I'm going to just sit here and do nothing."

Luna nodded. But what she feared wasn't sitting still. It was the possibility that she would spin so far in the wrong direction she'd fall off the map and lose sight of herself.

It was the question of whether she would ever become who she was meant to be.

Meihua Chang

Luna's mother

It felt like Meihua and her husband had only just gotten home from the airport, greeted their daughter, and stumbled into bed. But now she was awake again. Maybe it was the jet lag, or some jarring sound that had drawn her up through the layers of consciousness.

She walked out into the backyard, the grass cold against her bare feet. Nervousness tightened her stomach; it was that nagging fear of the dark that she'd had all her life.

"Luna?" she called out. "Where are you?"

The voice came bright and loud. "Here, Mama. Look up!"

Meihua angled her face toward the sky, but she could see nothing. There were only a few pinpricks of light, the purple smattering of clouds, and the bright shining coin of moon. "Where, baobei? Where are you?"

"I'm right here," Luna replied, but her voice was drifting away fast.

The light and the clouds and the moon swirled into nothing.

Meihua kicked off her blankets and rolled from the bed, sweaty and gasping. She hadn't been awake after all. It was the same recurring dream she'd had since Luna was old enough to speak, and it left her with a panic she'd never understood.

Sometimes she thought the dream was a residue on the surface of her brain that simply couldn't be scraped away, a scar from the years when little Luna was constantly in and out of the hospital, running a high temperature, contracting every virus, swelling with infection. But the dream had come before Luna was ever sick.

In fact, it was that dream that had first given Meihua the idea to carry toddler Luna out to absorb the light that fed down from the night sky.

Now she stepped into her slippers and made her way to her daughter's bedroom. Every day that she and Hsueh-Ting had been in Taiwan, she'd been anxious. It was a hum that never left her, vibrating softly in the back of her mind, this fear that something would happen to their child. What a relief it had been to return home.

Meihua turned the knob and pressed her eye to the crack. There was the shape of Luna, fast asleep with her hair spilled out over her pillow.

Meihua shut the door and exhaled. It was always the same: She had the dream, flung herself out of bed, and went to check that Luna was safe and sound. And there she was. Every time.

So what was Meihua so afraid of?

Hunter Yee

As if punishing him for fighting with Luna, the wind howled twice as loud all break long. It scraped at his eyes, yanked at his skin and hair, stinging with disapproval.

It had figured out how to open the window in Hunter and Cody's bedroom. The latch kept coming undone, the glass shoving up and ice pouring in.

Who had ever thought he could be so thrilled about school resuming after the break? At Luna's stop he sat up as tall as he could, watching people board the bus. She was the last one on. She paused next to him. Their eyes met.

"Sit down!" the bus driver shouted.

Luna sat.

"I'm sorry," Hunter said, at the same time that Luna blurted, "I didn't mean—"

"You can go first," he said.

"I'm sorry, too." She looked down. "I shouldn't have said what I did about college. I'd never given much thought to it before."

He sucked in a breath. "I'm sorry for what I said about being Chinese or Taiwanese and—I clearly just don't understand it enough. I don't want to be erasing anyone's identity."

"I also realized that...my family might be biased, too," said Luna. "Anyway. Apology accepted."

"Yours, too." He held out his open palm, an offering. She laced her fingers through his and kissed his knuckles. They watched the indigo blooms spilling across the peaks and valleys on the back of his hand.

"*Sit down!*" the bus driver was shouting at another student.

"What do you think *her* deal is?" Luna nodded toward the front.

He knew right away what she meant. "Ah, the driver. Her story is little known. She's a talented enchantress who sacrificed everything. Just before an evil wizard was about to murder her lover, our brave driver cast a spell that turned her beloved into a yellow school bus."

"Ooh, ooh!" Luna jumped in. "Now she spends her days ferrying students to school—and in the hours between, she goes off to her cave and tries to figure out the spell that will undo the bus, so that she can have her lover back."

"So many years have passed," Hunter continued. "She isn't sure her beloved will even recognize her."

"But when they first fell in love, they found a prophecy that said they would spend eternity together," said Luna. "So she has to have faith."

The bus pulled up to the front of the school.

"Hang on," Hunter said as she stood up. He drew her back down. He leaned in and she tipped her face up so that he could kiss her. "There. That's better."

"Anyone bring in current events for extra credit?" Mr. Amantia asked in the last ten minutes of Hunter's history class.

A girl with dark brown skin raised her hand. "I have an article."

"Great," said Mr. Amantia. "Let's hear it, Vanessa."

She cleared her throat and flipped through the loose-leaf pages in her binder. "We've probably all noticed by now how Route Four has been blocked off, as has the north end of Verona Street, and others. Um, according to the *Fairbridge Herald*, there are breakages expanding across those roads. In Medlar Borough there are power outages as a result. The township will be picking up fallen trees and stuff—in order to utilize this service, affected residents should call the Fairbridge Department of Public Works."

"Any update on what's causing it?" said Mr. Amantia.

Vanessa shook her head. "The township is still trying to figure it out, but—"

"It was obviously that earthquake back in the fall," someone interrupted.

Another student chimed in. "That wasn't an earthquake, Einstein. We don't get earthquakes over here."

"My dad was born in California and he said it felt exactly like an earthquake."

"All right, settle down," Mr. Amantia called. "Vanessa, anything else to add?"

"Yeah, so, a researcher at Fairbridge University found that the breakages—which actually are all connected to the same big crack—are resulting from some kind of upward pressure. The opposite of gravity, basically."

Hunter thought of the gaping blackness that had peered back at him. The way the ground was split, and how he encountered it again and again:

The earth setting its teeth into the wheels of that late bus.

His feet flying off the edge the day of the fire alarm.

The newly formed impostor of a creek dragging that little girl.

And just the other night, out among the trees, the forest floor disappearing from beneath his feet.

It seemed like at every turn a crack was waiting to swallow him up.

What was there in that darkness?

Sometimes he dreamed of the day he fell, wind whipping at him, luring him with those bills. The drop, his stomach flipping, gravity unspooling him. He'd been able to see nothing but pitch-black at first, so he thought he was going to fall forever. During the seconds he spent plummeting, a force had pressed up against him as if trying to find a way in through skin and muscle and bone.

Much later, he realized: Gazing into that darkness had been like peering into a mirror. That force had been the same as his mother gripping his arms, telling him to listen. The same as his father's anger ringing in his ears.

He was always listening. Always trying. But they would never believe that about him.

These were the thoughts that wound through him as he navigated the halls, sat through mathematical explanations and verb conjugations, walked down to the cafeteria. He settled into his seat at the usual table in the corner and watched Luna reach the end of the lunch line. Saw the tiniest bit of light against her dark hair as she fished for her wallet. A firefly. He thought of the other night, out in the woods, foot finding no ground, shoulder catching against the tree. The impossible light up above.

Luna finished paying and made her way toward him. On her tray there was an open Snapple bottle precariously balanced next to her meal.

"I was drinking the juice while I was in line," she said, shaking her head, "and then somehow I lost the cap. It's a miracle I didn't spill this."

"Listen," said Hunter. "There's something I've been wanting to tell you about."

She paused with a hand halfway to her fries, looking concerned.

"Nothing bad," he said. "Don't look so worried. It's just that, over the break, I went out by the creek?"

"Yeah?" said Luna.

"First—the ground is cracked again. I mean, *more* cracked. Like, the breakage keeps spreading. And then I saw all these fireflies—"

She spilled Snapple down her chin. Hunter handed her a napkin.

"It was weird. They were just covering an *entire tree*. At first I thought someone had put up Christmas lights."

"Do you remember where?" Luna's eyes were intense. "Can you show me after school?"

Dots had been connecting in his mind as he spoke the words out loud. "Yeah," said Hunter. "We'll go today."

Luna Chang

"Watch out." Hunter pointed at her feet.

Luna saw where the ground was fractured, where it had shifted out of alignment.

"It's moved," he said. "It didn't look like that the other night."

She tapped experimentally on the other side of the crack. The toe of her shoe found solid dirt. "Are you sure?"

"There was just empty space. I almost fell."

Luna froze, thinking of him lying in the broken earth that windy day after the fire alarm. "Weird," she made herself say, so that he wouldn't notice her moment of panic.

"It was right around here." Hunter stood between two trunks. "It might even have been this tree. It's kind of hard to tell. Everything looks so different in the daytime."

Luna ran her fingers over the bark of the one he pointed to. There were no signs of the fireflies, as far as she could see.

"Where were you walking? Do you remember the route?"

Hunter pointed. "This way. Careful where you step—there might be more cracks up ahead."

She followed him along the side of Lightning Creek. The stream was gentle and smooth, not like those rogue waves the day that girl nearly drowned. The day Hunter had revealed that secret and glittering facet of himself. That memory was a fresh flame in her mind: water gushing where it didn't belong, Hunter's arms moving the arrow into position, that fierce certainty in his eyes.

"Do you see that?" said Hunter.

Luna blinked. "See what?"

"Look at your feet. Look what the water does."

With each step she took, there was an ebb and flow, as if it were not a creek but an ocean, as if instead of a muddy bank there was a sandy shore. A tiny wave slid toward her ankle, and as she lifted her foot it melted back.

Luna crouched to graze the surface with a finger. Tiny fish darted toward her, drawn by some invisible force. She moved her hand away, and they hovered just under the surface, waiting.

"Do it again." Hunter's voice was reverent.

Luna dipped half her hand into the water. Other, larger forms rose from the depths. Nothing hurt her, but she thought there was the slightest tickle.

"It's like that fish tank, when we first met," said Hunter. "Remember?"

As if she could forget. Less fearful now, she sank her hand all the way in past her wrist. The water was ice; it was amazing that all these creatures lingered in the creek this time of year.

She reached deeper still. They surrounded her, like worshippers come to genuflect.

That was when she felt the pull.

Luna gasped and yanked her hand out. "Something's there."

"What do you mean? Are you hurt?"

She reached in again, lowering slowly until she felt it: a suction. The water, pulling with the insistent force of a whirlpool. Except it wasn't sucking her *down*, but to the side, in the same direction the creek flowed.

"It's trying to pull me over there somewhere," Luna said. "Come on. I think we should take a look."

They walked alongside the water and paused every several paces for Luna to check on the pull. Fish and tadpoles and geckos—and other creatures she didn't expect to see—followed along, as if she had beckoned them after her.

She knew when she had found the source. It felt dangerous. She drew her arm all the way out, unsettled.

"Whoa," said Hunter. He was gaping up at the trees. "Are those...*peaches?*"

He was right—Luna could smell them. The trees towered above, at least as tall as her house. The branches were empty of leaves yet full of those round fruits, rosy against the sky. You could almost forget it was the middle of winter. She wondered how they tasted.

"Look at these." He pointed at a bush flourishing with white blossoms that opened like sharp stars. They smelled like a floral tea. "I know what these are. They're used in traditional Chinese medicine to treat asthma. But I thought they only bloomed at night."

Luna's head was spinning. "How is all this possible? These flowers, and the peaches, and whatever is here in the water..."

Hunter crouched beside her to look into the creek. "What do you think it is?"

"I don't know." She knelt in the mud, trying to see beyond the reflections of the trees.

The afternoon sun drooped low. Its beams shifted through a gap in the branches, as if summoned. Now the water was clear as a pane of glass.

There were the creatures, some she could name and many more that she'd never seen in her life. There was the creek bottom, littered with rocks. And right there along the floor was a gaping crevice. A deep, dark crack where the earth had split open. It yawned wide, calling to her. She could almost hear her name bubbling up. Each breath she took brought a noxious scent: metallic and sharp, rotting and sickly sweet.

It wasn't a new smell. She had been catching vague wisps of this scent for months. But here in the water it was strong enough to trigger her awareness.

"It's connected, like the other cracks," she said, realizing what it was that she recognized. "And something's wrong with them."

"I can feel it, too," said Hunter. He shivered. "It's like...I don't know. Somehow awful."

The sun moved again, and the wind swept away the stink. She could no longer see that crack at the bottom of the water.

There was a different kind of light—twinkles that rippled with the surface. A mirror image. She looked up.

"The fireflies," she whispered.

How had she missed them before? In the gaps between the peaches, she could see them crowding together. Only a few winked; the rest were occupied. They were busy . . . weaving.

"They have *nests*," said Hunter. "Is this normal?"

The lightning bugs clustered around spheres made of threads as fine as spiderwebs, translucent and shimmering. Each woven orb was easily the size of a beach ball, strung up from the highest branches by a few precarious lines. A gust of wind swept by and the spheres bobbed horizontally, but the tethers held strong.

Where the treetops caught the glint of the sun, Luna noticed that the branches shined, coated in a silvery-gold dust. How strange. How magical.

Hsueh-Ting Chang

Luna's father

Hsueh-Ting blew gently on his hot chocolate, watched the foam skate across the surface. The first sip scalded all the way down. He cleared his throat.

"Is it good?" said Rodney Wong.

"Delicious." Hsueh-Ting's tongue prickled. "How about your coffee?"

Wong shrugged. "It's acceptable." Here in the back of this café the light was dim and orange, carving severe shadows in his face.

Hsueh-Ting straightened up to try to regain some sense of power. "I appreciate you coming all this way. I hope the cold isn't too unbearable."

Wong said nothing, only drank from his own cup.

Clearly there was little point in carrying on with niceties. "I didn't bring the item today," Hsueh-Ting said. "I thought we would first discuss."

"What is there to discuss?"

Hsueh-Ting studied this man. They'd had this mutually ben-
eficial partnership for years. Wong lent him the artifacts obtained
through his back-channel, underground, *whatever* ways. It wasn't
Hsueh-Ting's business to know about the legalities of the items'
ownership—or lack thereof. He simply analyzed the artifacts
that fell into his hands and wrote about them—cautiously, of
course, so that no one might catch on to just how it was that he
was able to draw such new conclusions from old history. As his
papers were published, each churning up exhilarating new conversations among historians and amateur enthusiasts, Wong
took said items back to the black market to be sold at a premium.

Wong boosted Hsueh-Ting's status as an academic within
the field, and Hsueh-Ting upped Wong's potential profit. It was
a safe enough arrangement—after all, the only person dealing
with any cash was Wong. And they'd done it with such success
for so long... this was the first time that Hsueh-Ting had thought
to question anything.

"I can't help but wonder if there are other people with whom
you have a... similar arrangement? Others in my field?"

Wong smiled for the first time since their meeting had begun,
and Hsueh-Ting wasn't sure whether he was being mocked.

"Now I understand," said Wong. "No. You don't have to
worry about that."

"You're sure?" Hsueh-Ting said.

"Yes." Wong looked amused, then thoughtful. "You made
your discovery via a colleague of yours, then?"

Hsueh-Ting picked up his hot chocolate again. It had gone
lukewarm, and now the sweetness was cloying.

"Someone who presents competition," Wong speculated.

"I want your help," Hsueh-Ting finally said, since he had lost the upper hand. "Eliminating the . . . competition, as you say."

Wong raised an eyebrow. "Eliminating as in . . . ?"

"Not death," Hsueh-Ting clarified quickly. "Just . . . gone. From my field. Discredited. If you can do that, then I'll give you the stone, and I'll tell you everything I know about it."

Wong leaned forward. "You're trying to negotiate, but all you're offering me is knowledge I already have. Not exactly a bargaining chip."

This startled Hsueh-Ting. "How could you know?"

"You obtained the artifact from Li Yubing," said Wong, his pronunciation of the Mandarin name slightly accented.

Hsueh-Ting blinked. "Who?"

Wong said nothing, only gazed at him expectantly.

"I don't know who that is."

"What kind of game are you playing?" said Wong. His face hadn't changed, but now his voice was a dangerous kind of quiet.

Hsueh-Ting understood him to be angry. "I've never heard that name before."

"She's your colleague," said Wong. "Don't lie to me."

"I'm not lying," said Hsueh-Ting. And because he'd clearly miscalculated, he gave up trying to keep it a mystery any longer. "It came from a man named David Yee."

"David Yee," Wong echoed, the way one might remember a line of poetry that had been long forgotten. "Yi Dawei. Of course." He began to laugh.

Rodney Wong

Rodney Wong had always believed in magic. Even before his adolescent years, when his tutor made a reference to witchcraft that nearly caused Wong to fall out of his chair. The man was a missionary of the Lutheran Church from America. He'd spent some years preaching the gospel in Sichuan before beginning his evangelical work in Hong Kong. From him, Wong received a Western education, with heavy emphasis on English and theology. It was during a lesson about the Scriptures that the tutor first mentioned that witchcraft was forbidden.

"Any practice of the occult, those wicked arts," he said, "takes one away from God and serves the evil spirits."

"But what if you do magic by accident?" a fellow student had asked, which Wong thought was quite a good question.

"Pray that it never happens. In the event that it does, you must repent and ask the Holy Spirit to help you fight against the desire to sin. In the past, there have been witch hunts, and those found guilty were executed."

That lesson had frightened the others, but it had the opposite effect on Wong, who found himself launched into a whole new universe of questions. For witchcraft to be punishable by death, it must have been truly a powerful thing. That, to him, was further evidence that it was real. Not that his belief had ever wavered.

He'd heard people talk about all sorts of things in Ancient and Imperial China: witches and shape-shifters, ritual poisons and alchemists. He hungrily absorbed every word. One day, he swore, he would touch real magic with his own hands—whatever that meant. And so it was that he was curious and eager and primed for what would fall into his lap many years later.

It was Wong's last year in Hong Kong before he moved to the States, though he didn't know it at the time, and he had gone to the wet market for a transaction.

"I'm purchasing four black hens for my uncle," he said, using the agreed-upon phrasing. "It was arranged in advance."

The merchant nodded his understanding. He gestured for his son to take over the stall and beckoned for Wong to follow. They wound through the city until they reached a shop selling dried and pickled fruits. In the back, from a space behind a loose brick, the man withdrew the four stacks of cash. Payment from a group operating across the water in Fujian, for a deal that had ended the day before.

The black-market banker cranked a fan up to its highest setting. Beneath the cycling hum of the blades, he said very quietly, "Some news."

Wong stepped closer. "From the mainland?"

"Farmers out in a village called Xiyang were digging a well, and they found something east of Qinshihuang's tomb."

"What kind of something?"

"A human figure made of terracotta. Other things, too. Treasures from the Qin dynasty. It's said that the farmers did not know what they'd found, but now archaeologists have begun to excavate."

Wong couldn't help checking over his shoulder to make sure they were alone. "And?"

"There's an entire army of these clay people. The archaeologists will be announcing their find to the rest of the world any day now. Xi'an is going to be famous."

"So, Hong Kong won't hear of it until the Western broadcasts," Wong said wryly. "And looters will have already gone in droves."

The banker smiled like a tiger.

At that point in his life, Wong had leveled up a couple rungs within the triad, and he had his own men beneath him. It was not a question of resources, especially if there was profit to be turned. Qin dynasty artifacts would fetch a lot in an underground sale. But the problem was how to get someone to the mainland and then up to Shaanxi Province. His mind was already trying to spin ways around the impossibility when the banker said, "There have been some acquisitions. They're looking for a buyer."

Aha. So the site had already been plundered. He shouldn't have been surprised. News traveled too slowly for his preferences.

"Your broker's fee?" Wong asked.

"The usual."

"If I then sell them in turn, with the transaction going through here, your commission—"

"You'd give me thirty percent," said the banker.

Wong smirked. "Ten."

"Twenty-five," said the banker.

"Fifteen," said Wong, and he braced himself for the counter. He would agree to 20 percent, if it came to that.

"Done," said the banker, much too eager. That meant the spoils were significant, or the circumstances around the exchange would be dangerous. Or both.

It took a month. Movement was slow, thanks to the Cultural Revolution. Smugglers had to stick to the inner roads, and each time the border of another province was crossed, the goods changed hands.

At last, a meeting was arranged. Wong found himself in the cabin of a fishing boat, gnawing on a joint of fresh ginger to fight the nausea.

They met the other boat in the waters just off Lamma Island. Code words were exchanged, and the fishermen from the mainland were invited aboard, and when Wong peered into the fish baskets, he saw first the terracotta head, so lifelike in the way the face had been shaped, and then the torso. The sculpture was broken—there were no legs, and one of the arms had been shattered—but still, it was a true marvel. Undamaged, the warrior would stand as tall as a real man. There were also bronze arrowheads, and other small weapons, and various broken pieces of terracotta.

But what interested Wong the most was a rectangular box the size of his foot, made from smooth wood. He had trouble getting the lid to budge, so a fisherman took it from him and wedged a gutting knife into the seam. Fumes hissed forth from the box. In a few blinks the man was no longer a man, but a corpse.

The other fishermen cried out, but Wong was fascinated. He pulled the collar of his tunic over his mouth and nose and used a rag to hold the box up for examination. It had contained some kind of poison gas, which had not leaked out in all these years. He could hear his American tutor saying with disgust, *Witchcraft*. Too bad the box was empty now, its value diminished.

When he moved to San Francisco, someone would teach him the phrase *Pandora's box*, and he would think: *Ah, I have held one of those.*

He sold the items from that first secret import. But years later, after he'd moved to California and established himself there, another opportunity presented itself, and he seized it.

Hunter Yee

Hunter stared up at the ceiling as he listened to his parents whispering in their room. They were bickering in either Mandarin or Taiwanese—too fast and too quiet for him to tell which it was. His parents' conversations were typically in English... unless they were trying to keep secrets from their sons.

They were so weird about language. He remembered being a child and speaking mostly Mandarin. They refused to teach him Taiwanese, said it was an ugly language. Then they'd moved across the country, to Fairbridge, and suddenly declared the new rule: In this house they would speak English, to help with assuming this new identity that would keep them hidden.

It was unfair of them to spend all those later years chiding him for being bad at Chinese school when he didn't even get to practice at home. But then, for as long as he could remember, his parents had never made any sense.

They'd stopped speaking, and now there was only the sound of Cody's steady inhales and exhales beside him.

In that silence, the weight descended.

It came to him more often these days: a sickening dread that twisted his gut. It wrapped around him and set his teeth chattering. Hunter wished he could give it a name, this thing that drained him and made it feel as though time were coming to an end. His head began to ache like there was a rope cinching tighter and tighter around his skull.

Doom. That was what it should be called. Once upon a time that word might have made him laugh. But right now it felt so very real and terrifying. He'd felt it on that late bus that got itself stuck in the ground. He'd felt it that time he tumbled off the edge where the earth broke away. And when he and Luna followed the creek to where everything was wrenched apart, where beneath the water was some kind of abyss, there had been the strongest, most urgent tug of dread. Like that dark, gaping crack down there was the very source.

He felt it in his core. An irrefutable truth.

Luna Chang

It snowed toward the end of January, and later on Luna would wonder if perhaps she should have taken those strangely gray snowflakes as a sign that everything was about to go to shit. The morning sky started out clear, but by second period all the students at Fairbridge High were staring out the windows at the dark clumps falling fast and thick. Luna glanced outside during AP Lit and thought she saw hints of her fireflies, gold confetti among the snowfall.

At the start of third period it was announced that there would be an early dismissal. Students buzzed with excitement. By the time Luna bid Hunter goodbye and stepped off the bus, the snow was high enough that it kept getting into her sneakers. Her feet were cold and wet; she couldn't wait to take off her socks.

She paused by the curb, where a red bird perched on the mailbox. It didn't seem to care about the snowflakes gathering on its feathers, sticking to its long tail.

"Hello," Luna said softly.

The bird cocked its head and blinked. An inky black tear fell from its eye.

Luna took a step forward, and the bird launched away, flapping and gliding. But that drop of the blackest black remained, a dot melted into the gray snow atop the mailbox. It had a vague stink, metallic and sweet.

"Weird," Luna muttered. It reminded her of the tree bleeding black, and the crack running through Fairbridge, fissuring out in every direction. It reminded her of that day by the creek, when she'd sensed something in that darkness. Something wrong, maybe dangerous.

Out of habit, she let herself into the house using her key, even though someone was bound to be home.

"Hello?" She kicked off her shoes.

She hadn't expected to come home in the middle of the day to such silence. No bustling sounds in the kitchen. No Chinese oldies playing from the stereo system. At the very least, her mother should be here.

No note on the counter, but then again Luna wasn't expected home for another few hours.

She slung her backpack to the floor and sank onto the couch, letting herself fall sideways. She stared at the empty television screen, at the remote controls lined up so perfectly on the coffee table. The one for the VCR was still covered in the protective plastic that had been part of its original packaging, the corners of the sticker rolling up from years of use.

It was a mistake to lie down. What she wanted was a glass of water, but it was too much effort to get up and go into the kitchen.

She was in the process of using her toes to peel off her wet socks when she heard it.

A giggle. High-pitched, girlish. Who the hell was in her house?

Luna sat up. It had come from upstairs, she was pretty sure. She paused at the bottom of the steps, listening intently. There was a noise. Enough to make her move cautiously, avoiding the squeaky railing and the steps that were likely to creak. What was she supposed to do when she found the intruder?

On the landing, she heard another voice. Maybe she was being silly. Were both her parents actually home? If she went any farther, was she going to find them in some kind of compromising position? She'd heard a couple stories from girls at school who had walked in on their parents having sex. . . . She definitely did not need to experience that ever.

But it was midafternoon—did adults even have sex when the sun was out and bright? And anyway, it sounded like they were just having a conversation in low, tender tones. Her heart swelled. She loved how much her parents loved each other.

They laughed again, both of them, except this time the sound confused her. Something was weird.

She wasn't sure what made her reach for the knob and push the door open without knocking.

At first her brain didn't quite register what she was seeing.

The comforter falling off the side of the bed. Clothing on the floor like it had been haphazardly tossed aside. Two naked bodies on the mattress, one rounded over the other, a head of short black hair bent close between two pale knees. Luna noticed first the spine, the little knots where the bones showed through the curving skin. Limbs positioned in inappropriate ways.

Her stomach churned. She meant to escape before they saw her, but an involuntary noise came out the back of her throat. The head snapped up to look at her from between her mother's legs.

It was a man who appeared as shocked as Luna felt. A man Luna did not recognize.

He was off the bed in an instant, fumbling for his clothes.

"Luna," said her mother, looking mortified. And naked. Extremely naked. She gathered the pillows in front of her body. "You're home early."

The sky turned the bruisey purple of evening. The man was long gone and Luna's father was home, and she could hear her parents speaking in normal voices down in the kitchen. When a voice traveled up the stairs to summon her for dinner, there was a slight falter in the words. Her mother was scared, Luna realized grimly.

She dragged her feet getting down to the dining room. It was her designated chore to put out plates, but tonight the table was already set with her favorite moon dishes, and food was already out. Scallion pancakes and chao mifen and tomato scrambled eggs—all Luna's favorites.

Her mother gave her a tentative smile, and Luna had a terrible urge to upend the table, let every last plate shatter against the walls and the windows. She wanted the entire room covered with the shards of her feelings.

Luna's father was rambling about work, about pressure from the dean, some new proposal he had to submit under a tight deadline. How did he fail to notice the tension strung across the dinner table, the heaviness in the air like a brewing storm? How was he so fucking oblivious?

A part of her wondered how her parents would react if she just casually mentioned her mother's paramour. The vision was seared into her mind—one sweaty body curled over another. The noises of mouths traversing skin. The expression on her mother's face. It made Luna want to throw up.

How long had it been going on?

"How was school today?" her father asked, shaking her from the thoughts.

She realized she was scowling and tried to smooth her forehead. "We had an early dismissal."

He looked surprised. "So you came home early?"

"That's what an early dismissal means," said Luna, then felt bad for snapping. He didn't have any idea why she was pissed. He was clueless.

Her father shrugged. "I didn't realize the snow was that bad."

She took a deep inhale and exhale. "I think they were

expecting it to be a lot worse." Luna had been avoiding looking in her mother's direction, but now their eyes connected. There was a silent plea: to keep quiet, preserve the secret.

"The weather this year," said her dad, shaking his head.

Luna took a scallion pancake and bit into it savagely. It tasted like dust.

Cody Yee

Sometimes late into the night, Cody woke to the soft noises of his brother sneaking out of the house. He was pretty sure Hunter was going into the woods to shoot arrows. Cody was always tempted to pull his own sneakers on and try to follow, but the fear of getting lost scared him into staying.

Besides, he had secrets of his own. Sometimes while Hunter was gone, Cody crept through the house, trying to find things that would help him understand what his parents were always whispering about. Like the white rock that had been hidden in his dad's car.

That day in the Fortune Garden parking lot, he'd gone to fetch his mother's scarf, and the yarn ended up catching on some bit of metal—a hook on a pouch that was fixed to the inside of the trunk. Its zipper yanked down as Cody worked to untangle the scarf. Naturally, he'd been curious, couldn't help stealing a peek.

An edge poked out, smooth and shiny, though not enough for him to see what it was. It left a shimmery residue on his fingers. Later, he'd gone and opened the trunk in the middle of the night, wanting to see the thing more clearly, but it was no longer there.

Tonight, Cody wormed his way under the bed he shared with Hunter, crawling to the place where he'd accidentally poked a hole in the bottom of the box spring. It had become the perfect spot to hide his collection of found things. Like Ariel the mermaid's treasure trove.

He reached a hand in and navigated by touch. There were the earrings he'd never seen his mother wear. A square of silk that had been under the driver's seat in his dad's car. A bouncy ball someone had lost at school. Past all these, he found the edges of that book.

Cody had been terrified to open it again since finding the sentences about the end of the world. He'd thought maybe it was made from a bad kind of magic, and so he'd stored it away and tried to forget about it. But nothing bad had happened since. Maybe it really was just a story.

He clicked a flashlight on and let the pages fall open.

> The moon was incomplete. There was a chip where
> the heart had broken away, and accompanying debris had
> crumbled free into the night. Some of those pieces became
> stars. Others fell until they ended up in places they didn't
> belong. Everywhere they went, they left dust and light
> where there should have been none.
>
> The dustlight learned to exist on its own, learned to
> drift and become what was needed.

Luna Chang

Luna wanted to tell Hunter about her mother's affair. But every time she tried to find the words, her eyes began to sting and her throat wrung itself shut.

The secret was the shape of a bitter pill slowly dissolving on her tongue.

Was she supposed to tell her father? She couldn't even begin to guess at the reaction he might have. Did such a thing deserve to be forgiven? Would they get a divorce? Luna wasn't sure what she wanted, except that she wished she could go back in time and unsee it.

Before the fateful night she met Hunter, she'd carefully fit all her actions and feelings into the spaces her mother carved. Luna had done everything expected of her. She worked to get the grades; she studied for the SATs; she applied to the schools her parents wanted.

She'd played her part in the family. Her mother had not.

Luna wanted to shake her mom by the shoulders. To scream at her: *Fuck you and everything you ever said to us.*

Those thoughts came in sharp, jagged pieces. They sliced at her.

The Lunar New Year arrived. Since it was a school night, plus her father had a class that ran late, the plan was to wait until the weekend to celebrate. Not like Luna could be bothered to care. On the festive mood scale of one to ten, she was at Burn Everything Down.

When she got out of bed Saturday morning, there was a new red sweater hanging on the back of her door. A gold box sat on her desk. The lid lifted away easily—perhaps her mom knew that Luna would not have opened it if it had been wrapped. Curiosity got the best of her, and inside it she found her mother's car keys neatly arranged on top of a folded note:

> Happy New Year. Even though it's not your birthday yet,
> your father and I agreed this car should be yours now,
> on the condition that you always tell us where you will be
> going and what time you will be home. Drive carefully.
> Avoid the roads with the cracks.

Out in the hall, her parents had hung the sparkling Chinese characters for *spring* and *fortune* upside down, to indicate that spring and fortune had arrived.

Her mother set a hongbao beside her as she ate a late breakfast. Luna ignored the red envelope. She didn't want that money.

If anything, it made her angrier. She was not someone who could be bought. The sweater continued to hang on the back of her door, untouched. She did, however, pocket the car keys.

Luna put on her headphones and hit play on her Walkman without even looking to see which cassette was inside. It was a mixtape of stuff she'd recorded off the radio. A Depeche Mode song blasted into her ears.

She picked up some bright nylon string and contemplated it for all of one minute before flinging it aside, too angry to make anything. She listened to that tape until she fell asleep, and reemerged only when her father summoned her for dinner. They were eating early so that they could head to the Chinese school for the Lunar New Year event.

Laid out on the table were all the usual suspects. Bamboo shoots and sliced pork. The sweet brown niangao. Dumplings, of course, because they looked like yuanbao. A whole steamed fish for that saying, "Nian nian youyu." A platter of noodles for longevity. Pineapple cakes and taro buns and peanut candies for dessert.

This was usually Luna's favorite meal of the year. She loved the ritual of it all. Listening to her parents describe the celebrations in Taiwan and tell the legend of the Nian monster. Calling grandparents and aunts and uncles long-distance to wish them xinnian kuaile.

Today it was unbearable. Her fury had peaked, and now she was sliding down, accelerating toward a deep depression. She couldn't even taste the pineapple cake. Her father poured another round of tea, and she went to the bathroom so that they wouldn't see her tears.

Hunter Yee

None of them wanted to attend the community's Chinese New Year festivities. His father was so stressed about work he'd been losing hair. Cody was anxious about the possibility of running into Mrs. Chang, who had been making his life hell in her Chinese language class. His mother seemed to be irritated and paranoid about multiple things.

As for Hunter: He didn't want to see Luna in the context of her whole family. She was this perfect human, and in his mind she wasn't even really a Chang. Like maybe she'd gotten switched at birth. To see her with her parents—would something shatter?

What about her seeing him in the context of *his* family? What was she going to think of *them*?

Plus, he worried that if they made eye contact, the air would sizzle and the volume would change, and everyone would immediately know that the two of them had been breaking the rules and sneaking around together.

Dread filled the quiet house. For about thirty seconds his

parents actually discussed skipping the event. But they were expected to be there. His mother argued that to be absent would be embarrassing, and she couldn't stand the thought of losing face.

His dad had been given usher duties, and his mom would be singing Chinese folk songs with the community chorus, even though she'd missed several recent rehearsals. All these were plans that had been made ages ago. A commitment was a commitment.

So the four of them piled into his father's car, and off they went to the Chinese school. They sat at the very back of the auditorium. There were the little kids reciting poems about three-wheeled cars and items in their backpacks, singing songs about tigers and dogs. There was the Chinese yo-yo team with their choreographed tosses. One group demonstrated the different styles of Tai Chi. Then came the older kids doing a traditional ribbon dance, a lion dance, a sword dance—Cody was in awe. Hunter loved seeing his little brother so enraptured.

The chorus came on stage, and there was their mother in the same emerald green as everyone else, standing on the second row of the risers.

Cody leaned over and whispered, "Mom's name isn't in here."

Hunter flipped to the page in the program that listed all the singers, and sure enough, she was nowhere to be found. Not her English name, not her Chinese name.

"I can't believe she forgot to put herself in," said Cody. "Didn't she make the programs?"

Only then did Hunter remember his mother complaining

about how cold it was in his father's office at the university, where she'd had to sit for hours to painstakingly design the layout using some software she'd just learned. It was obvious: She'd omitted herself on purpose.

She just wanted to be another voice up there, singing.

Hunter knew his mother was a soprano, which he was pretty sure meant she sang the high notes. Whenever the songs swelled in both volume and pitch, her face glowed with immense joy. Here, he understood, was a moment for her to be free, a creature emerged out of its shell and into the light. She could be seen, and at the same time, she could disappear into the bodies around her.

There were two soloists, both of their voices wobbly, one of them struggling with some of the pitches. His mother was clearly the superior vocalist. Hunter realized that she must have held back from auditioning for those parts. She couldn't risk standing out.

When would the Yees be allowed to really *live*?

The show ended with a standing ovation, and the audience poured into the lobby, and it was there that Hunter nearly crashed into Luna and her parents.

"Hi, David," said Dr. Chang, his voice falsely bright.

"Hsueh-Ting," said Hunter's father. "Meihua. Happy New Year. Wasn't that a fantastic show? Zhen bang."

Luna was very determinedly avoiding everyone's eyes.

"I didn't know your wife was a singer," said Mrs. Chang. She ignored Hunter and Cody as if they were invisible.

Hunter saw how his father tensed. "Yes. She sings beautifully."

Mrs. Chang gave him a thumbs-up and an exaggerated smile.

Cody was trying to disappear behind Hunter, and Hunter was trying to think of an excuse to get them out of the lobby, but then his dad cleared his throat.

"Hsueh-Ting, I meant to ask—I saw you outside my office the other day. Perhaps you thought I was there when I wasn't, and then you left just as I arrived. Did you need to speak with me?"

Dr. Chang blinked. "Oh, when was that? I must have been trying to find someone in your hall. I don't remember anymore." His laugh sounded forced.

"Well," said Hunter's father. "My door is always open, if you need to discuss anything."

"I appreciate it. Xinnian kuaile." Dr. Chang nodded, then guided his wife away. Luna followed without so much as a glance at any of the Yees.

"What was that?" said Hunter.

"That was office politics," his father replied. "Or maybe a chess game. Same thing."

Yvonne Yee

Hunter's mother

Yvonne walked out into the frozen night to soothe her rage.

How she detested the Changs. Chang Hsueh-Ting, that disgusting vulture—she'd hated him since before he started trying to tear her husband down. The thought of that man was enough to fill her face and ears with fire.

She hated his wife even more. The mere sight of Chu Meihua made Yvonne feel small, like a flower shriveling in the cold.

After the New Year show, she'd skipped the changing room and rushed into the lobby with all her things. Her pulse was racing from being on stage, standing so out in the open. Though she performed like this only once a year, she couldn't help but worry each time that Huang would be out in the audience, waiting. It was safer to hurry home. She could stay in her gown a little bit longer.

But in the lobby, she'd spied the Chang family, all three of them, speaking to her husband and sneering at her sons. She'd paused behind a column, close enough to hear their words. Meihua's clownish thumbs-up made her stomach churn. She watched the Changs stride away, their daughter rudely failing to make eye contact with anyone.

Yvonne would always remember standing in the bathroom at Zhang Taitai's house, directly next to the office where all the potluck guests had flung their coats. Her hand was on the tap, about to turn on the water, when she heard noises. Two women had stepped into the adjacent room for privacy, and though they spoke in low voices, Yvonne had been able to hear them clearly. She recognized only one of them: Chu Meihua—whom she'd first met just a couple hours earlier.

"Did you know David is interviewing for the same job as Hsueh-Ting?" Meihua said, in Mandarin that carried a wide-voweled Taiwanese accent.

The other woman made a sound of surprise. "At the university?" Her speech had the roundedness of someone from northern China.

"Where did that David come from, do you know? Where was he teaching before?"

"I can't remember," the other woman replied.

"You know Hsueh-Ting has been working very hard for this exact position," Meihua went on. "He really deserves it. He co-wrote four journal publications last year—*four*! He barely sleeps."

"He's truly outstanding," said the other woman. "I'm sure Hsueh-Ting is more qualified for the job."

"Of *course* he's more qualified," said Meihua. "Did you hear

David speak? He doesn't carry himself like a professor. And what publications does he have? Hsueh-Ting has never heard his name—and Hsueh-Ting knows most of the important people in the field. And look at the Yee boy. Can you believe the child of any respectable professor would be so unruly?"

"Hsueh-Ting is going to get it," the other woman assured her. "Didn't you say he interviews very well?"

"He does," Meihua agreed. "His English is excellent. You know he was top of his class? He used to be an English tutor in Taipei."

"Don't worry," the other woman said. "I'm sure Hsueh-Ting will get it."

"Anyway," Meihua continued, "there's just something odd about the Yee family."

"I think so, too," her friend murmured.

"That Yvonne—you see how strange she is? When Zhang Taitai asked if she was working, her whole face went red. I think she has a secret."

The two of them crept back down the stairs after that, and Yvonne counted to ten before finally washing her hands. She'd scrubbed for a long time, as if the water could rinse away the stain that Chu Meihua's voice had left on her skin.

She curled her nails into her palms to feel their bite. Chu Meihua would never know how Yvonne was so capable, so high-achieving back in her prime. How if Hunter had not been so sick as a child, if they had not needed to go to such lengths for him, their life would be entirely different. Yvonne would be doing great things—her name well known in her field, her publications numerous. In that parallel dimension, Yvonne would not be this half-faded shadow.

The fact that they would never see that made her hate the Changs even more. That family, with their tai du, with their belief that they were better than everyone else, their entitlement, their condescending words. A friend had said to her once that it wasn't worth expending such emotional energy, that it was like drinking poison and hoping someone else would die.

Well. She would go ahead and drink the poison. It hadn't killed her yet. She would develop an immunity. She and David would harden and steel themselves.

Her feet slowed. Absorbed in the remembering, she'd lost track of the present and walked so far that she'd come to one of those cracks in the ground. The nearby streetlamps made everything look dusty and yellow, but still she could see the lumpy edges where the grass had pulled apart and the roots had gotten yanked out. And various rocks—some the size of her fist, others the size of her head—peeking through the soil and gathered at the bottom of the split.

A delicious image formed in her mind: the Chang family tumbling into it, knocking their heads against something hard, bodies falling limp. Peering into that crack calmed her...and simultaneously set her hatred burning with renewed fervor.

She hoped that there would come a day when the Changs would regret treating the Yees so poorly. She crossed her fingers—a bit of superstition she'd learned from her youngest son—and stuck her hands in her pockets. Oh, how she hoped.

Luna Chang

Luna climbed onto the bus and sank into her seat, trying to shed the residual stress of a morning encounter with her mother. No words had been exchanged, only glances. The eye contact had been bad enough.

It was obvious that Luna was now expected to drive the car—*her car*—to school every day, which only made her determined to hold off. She refused to give the impression that she was offering a truce or taking a bribe. The choices a person made had consequences; wasn't her mother the one to teach her that?

Usually, Hunter was smiling when he greeted her, but this morning he looked serious.

"Hi," she said, trying to gather her energy.

"Hi," he returned, angling to face her. "You've been weird."

"I'm sorry," she began. "The other night—"

"No," said Hunter. "I mean. Obviously our parents make everything weird. But before that, even. I just wanted to say—are you okay? Is there a way I can help? Or if you need to talk about it…?"

His earnestness. It could almost make her cry.

She let him wrap his arms around her, let herself melt. It wasn't so long ago that they'd kissed for the first time, but already she knew there was a door in her heart that had gotten unlatched, and within that chamber she stored this precious feeling.

When she was with Hunter, the sky glowed a bit brighter, the wintry winds smelled all the sweeter, and she was energetic in a way she'd never known.

Her thoughts turned to the awful things her mother always said about the Yees. It made her boil. What right did her *mother* have to judge anyone? Her mother, slick and wild-haired and naked in bed with another man. Her mother, who had taught her the importance of doing what your family needs, who had pretended all this time to love her father.

Luna felt sick. Had it ever been real?

"What are you thinking so hard about?" Hunter said, pulling her out from the tangle of thoughts. He ran his thumb gently over her tightly drawn eyebrows.

"What a fucking hypocrite my mom is," Luna answered. She took in a breath to steady herself and began to tell him about the day of the snowstorm, about walking upstairs and opening that door.

He held her the whole time. He didn't offer any platitudes, any fixes, and for that she was glad. There was no way to fix this.

He touched his nose to hers, and she let her eyes shut, knowing what would come next. His thumb tipping her chin up, lips meeting lips, an urgency surging like a tide.

Here in this bubble of a moment, she was safe. She was okay.

She could spend forever like this, inhaling the smell of him, noticing every electric brush of his arm against hers, tingling as his exhales traveled across her skin. She wanted to press her hips against his, to line their bodies up and breathe in tandem.

They'd arrived at school. Slow and reluctant, Luna peeled herself away.

Hunter Yee

On the bus in the afternoon, he was intensely aware of the distance between their bodies. He laced his fingers through hers and she squeezed them.

All day Luna had been quiet and glum. As if she were grieving a death. The version of her mother she thought she knew.

He'd never had that kind of relationship with his parents, but still. He understood the devastation.

Hunter studied the edges of her face. The slope of her jaw. The slow shutter of her lashes. Outside their window the town rolled past. The bank, and the art store. Trees lining the sidewalks. Students with backpacks drooping low off their shoulders, heading for the library or the sweets shop. A few people crossing the parking lot of the shopping center, since the crack had split far enough up the sidewalk that the township had blocked it off.

Luna abruptly straightened as the bus slowed. "Let's get off here."

"Okay," he said. She merely had to say the word and he would follow. The realization of this truth was thrilling.

"I just—I need to get into a different headspace," she said.

They stepped off the bus and he saw they were a block away from Fudge Shack. The place was newly opened and already it was a regular spot for half the kids in their school. Luna led the way into the shop, which smelled overwhelmingly of chocolate.

He scanned the board, doing mental math as quick as he could, stacking prices up against the bills in his wallet.

In a blink, Luna had ordered and paid, and it was his turn at the counter. He was so flustered he bought the first thing his eyes found on the drinks menu, and followed her to a table.

"You didn't get any fudge?" she was saying. "That's kind of the point of this place."

Hunter shook his head.

"Are you okay?" she asked.

"Yeah," he said. "It's just that—I was supposed to pay for yours."

"Oh my god." She rolled her eyes. "No, you weren't."

"The guy's supposed to pay," he began. He didn't finish because the next words from his mouth were about to be *when it's a date*—but he didn't know if this actually counted as such.

"That's absurd," Luna said. "Why? The girl's not capable of paying for herself? What if she has a solid income? Or is it that the guy gets to demonstrate his ownership, like buying a treat for his pet dog? That's what it is—it's sexist. And what if the relationship isn't between a guy and a girl? What about if someone doesn't *feel* like a guy? *Then* what kinds of rules are there supposed to be? It's all just ridiculous."

Her voice had turned bossy, and Hunter found that he rather liked it. Her confidence. It lit a flame and sharpened her eyes.

"I'm sorry. You're right. I only said that because...I guess I wanted this to be an official date," he said.

"Strawberry milkshake? Excuse me, did you order a strawberry milkshake?"

Hunter turned to see the woman with the Fudge Shack apron peering at him over the counter, a tall cup of pastel pink sweating in her hand.

"Oh, yeah, sorry." He leapt out of his seat to grab it.

When he sat back down, there was a determined look on Luna's face.

"What?" said Hunter.

"This *is* an official date," she said, her voice firm and clear, almost fierce.

"Okay," Hunter said.

"It doesn't matter who paid for what," she said. "It's a date because we both want it to be. Because we like each other."

"You're right." A silly grin stretched his face wide.

"What?" she said.

"I do like you," he told her. "I like you a lot."

"I like you, too," Luna returned. "I *like* like you." Her eyes dropped to her marbled swirl of cookies 'n' cream fudge, to the corner she had been slowly and systematically flattening and tearing away. Hunter could see in the set of her jaw and the tightness of her shoulders that she was perhaps nervous after all, despite being the one to bring them here and to so clearly name this for what it was.

"So if this is an official date," he said, "then I guess that means...*we* are official? As in, together?"

"Is that what you want?" said Luna.

"Yes. Definitely."

"Okay," she said. "Me too. Though obviously I won't be telling my parents."

"I don't really tell my parents anything, so. Same."

How bright and intense she looked. He loved the loose hairs that had fallen from her ponytail to frame her face. He loved the way she dropped her eyes when she felt shy. Her fingers, long and sharp, poking at that square of fudge.

Luna looked up as if she could hear his thoughts. "Why are you smiling so much?"

He shook his head. "Just. Smiling at you."

"Weirdo," she said, but then she was grinning back. His skin went hot and buzzy.

She began to laugh, shoulders quaking silently, and that triggered the same in him. They were both laughing like fools, faces warm and eyes tearing up.

"Thanks," she said when they had quieted down.

"For what?"

"For letting me just be sad. And for... this."

Hunter nodded. "Are you feeling a bit better?"

"Much," she said, and leaned forward to kiss him.

Rodney Wong

The Terracotta Army had its first major exhibition outside China, in Melbourne—and a few items had been heisted. No warriors, but among the small artifacts collected was a box, and the burglars had heard that it was likely to be of particular interest to Wong.

Nobody had opened it yet; his pulse fluttered like a butterfly when he received it. It was a miniature chest, carved from a resinous wood with a heady scent. Smaller than he'd expected based on the description given, but Wong knew better than to judge anything on size, or to underestimate it. He took precautions. He wore a mask and protective glasses and gloves, and held his breath as he pried the lid off.

No poison spilled forth this time. Instead, there were two items neatly wrapped in ancient pieces of silk, which themselves were things of beauty and covered in faded calligraphy. The artifacts were the size of baoding balls, the little metal ones you rotated in your palm to improve dexterity. The first item he unwrapped looked like a fistful of dirt dried into a hard cake. He could see the various fibers and pieces rolled together, like herbs from a traditional Chinese medicine apothecary.

The best part was that some archaeologist had already done the work of interpreting the calligraphy accompanying each piece, and there were little cards labeling them, with English descriptions written in a neat hand. The one he was looking at was described as a panacea.

He thrummed with unadulterated joy. Emperor Qin had been paranoid and demanding, obsessed with the idea of living forever. His imperial alchemists had worked around the clock— it was likely that this precious herbal medicine had been among their results.

The other object was made of some pale stone. At first he thought there were characters carved on it. Wong's heart slammed in his chest, about to burst. No, there were no words. Just a trick of the light. He tucked the stone back into the box and pressed the lid shut.

Here at last was the magic he'd been waiting for.

Luna Chang

They traced each other's veins and kissed until their lips were swollen, until they thirsted for something unknown.

They talked more about the fireflies, and Luna marveled aloud at the strangeness and the magic. They talked about archery, and the wind, and Hunter tried to describe his aim. They talked about the people who worked the Fudge Shack counter, and invented stories about them as characters trapped in a castle, making candy under the spell of an evil prince.

Luna was a cloud beside the sun. A star dropped in the sky. She was a leaf drifting on a high wind.

She liked Hunter. *Like* liked him. And he liked her right back. He was *in like* with her, he'd said.

Their words had been like a spell muttered beneath the moon. It had transformed the air between them—they were breathing something different from the standard-issue oxygen that everyone else got.

After spending the afternoon at Fudge Shack, they walked

together to the street corner that was halfway between their houses. There wasn't even a kiss goodbye; they were too exposed on the sidewalk and didn't want to risk destroying this perfect snow globe of a secret. Still, Luna couldn't help smiling to herself the rest of the way, feeling light and lifted, the coldness of the winter air barely registering in her lungs.

It was convenient, how thinking of him could crunch down the stuff about her mom and shove those images into a dark corner.

Nobody was home yet when she unlocked the door—she could have invited Hunter over and her parents would never have known. Luna kicked off her shoes and climbed upstairs and fell backward onto her bed. They could be sinking down onto this mattress, his weight shifting into her side. Mouths colliding, bodies pulling close.

Her skin was hot and ticklish with want. She collected a pillow between her thighs and pressed her knees together, hungering for a touch and a crescendo, dreaming of a room tucked away from the world, a quiet place where she could hide with Hunter, where they could simply *be*.

In her release, Luna felt like her heart was being given the space to swell, to beat loud and hard, to grow wings.

Hours later the muscles below her belly button started to coil and ache. She stumbled into the bathroom and discovered that her period had begun.

Hunter Yee

At lunch they snuck into an empty classroom with the lights off. They found themselves horizontal on the thinly carpeted floor. Legs tangled, lips against lips. It was dizzying how Luna's breath became his, became hers again.

She rolled on top of him so that the weight of her body pinned him in place. Not that he had anything to complain about. Her kiss was like touching a flame to a wick; his body lit up.

Hunter held his breath. Did she feel it? He tried to relax. *Come on, Hunter. Relax.*

Luna shifted and his body responded. He went hot with embarrassment. She peeled herself away, giving him a devilish look.

"I did not plan to be seduced this year," said Hunter.

She giggled. "Neither did I. What do you think caused the actual seducing?"

"Let's see." He propped himself up on his elbows. "Well. You've got a very practical nose."

Luna snorted. "A practical nose!"

"See? It's even expressive. Very efficient use of your assets."

She rolled her eyes. "All right, what else?"

"Are you just fishing for compliments over there?"

Now she was batting her eyelashes.

"It was that sturdy neck," Hunter said decisively. "Your turn. What did it for you?"

"Obviously your porcelain face and luscious hair," said Luna, and leaned in to kiss his cheek.

He pretended to grimace.

"Tell me a story," she said, curling up on her side.

He settled back down, smiling up at the ceiling. "Once upon a time, there were two humans lost in the woods. Their names were...Lunar and Hunt."

Luna let out another snort.

"Using that nose again," said Hunter.

"Is that a part of the story, too?"

"Yes," he said. "Those were the words that Hunt spoke to Lunar. He said, 'Use your sharp nose to get us out of this place.'"

"And what did Lunar say?"

"She said to him, 'Why should we leave? Everything is wonderful in here.'"

The edges of Luna's mouth tugged up, but the smile was sad.

"I wish this didn't have to be a secret," said Hunter, serious now. "I wish our families didn't—"

"Shhh." Her voice dropped. "Let's not talk about them."

"All right," he whispered back.

239

"*I* wish we could—" Luna paused abruptly, as if swallowing the thought.

"What?" he said.

She took in a slow breath and winced.

"Are you okay?"

"Sorry, just—cramps."

Hunter sat up. "Do you need anything?"

"It's okay. It's not that bad right now. But thank you. I was *going* to say, I wish we could get some privacy. You know... where people might not suddenly walk in on us."

His brain was a firecracker of thoughts, little sparks bursting at the implication in her words.

"I wish we could, too," he said finally. "You're not allowed to date, right?"

Luna scoffed. "*Obviously* not. Are *you*?"

"No."

"I'm supposed to be focusing on my *academics*," she said bitterly. "I'm supposed to go to the school they choose for me, and major in the thing they want, so I can have the career they dream up and the life they pick for me."

"When do you get to pick for yourself?" he said.

Luna made a sound that was half groan, half sigh.

He didn't know what to say, so he settled for fixing his gaze on hers, studying the sweep of her short lashes, the little ledge just under each of her eyes, where the skin dipped down and there was a shadow.

She nestled her face in the spot between his chin and his shoulder. "I think I'm picking right now."

When he took out the trash that night there were dark clouds staining the sky, hiding the moon. The streetlamp on the corner cast its yellow glow on the yard. It turned the bushes menacing, made the house sag more. The place almost looked haunted.

Even before he got back to the door, he could hear the phone. It made a sharp bleating. When was the last time he'd heard that sound?

It was still ringing as he stepped out of his shoes. It stopped, hitting the answering machine, only to begin ringing again mere seconds later.

He found his parents in the kitchen, huddled around the phone, staring at it. Cody sat at the counter with an untouched bowl of clam chowder in front of him.

"What's going on?" said Hunter.

"Shh!" His mother held up a hand.

The call reached the answering machine again, and just as before, no one spoke. The machine beeped, and there was only the sound of a receiver clicking.

"That was six times," said Cody. "I counted. They called us six times."

"He found us?" said Hunter. He never spoke of *him*—as if it were simply a bedtime story he could ignore.

He couldn't decide if his parents were smart or cowardly for successfully hiding themselves all these years. There was no running away in life, not really. There was only the matter of facing your mistakes.

His father was shaking his head. "We don't know. Maybe not. We don't know anything for certain."

"We need to leave," his mother said. "We should have moved last year."

His dad went very still. "I'm up for tenure."

She shook her head. "If he's found us, does it even matter?"

"We almost have the full amount," he said. "If I get tenured, we can pay the rest of it off even sooner."

"Don't be ridiculous," said Hunter's mother, and it was like a slap to his father's face. "What about the interest? What about what's *gone*? And what if you *don't* get tenured—you really think the university is going to keep you?"

His dad straightened up and flipped on the light above the sink. "You have to have hope, Yubing."

"This life was always temporary," said his mother. "That's what we've always said. We were supposed to move somewhere better."

"Yubing," said Hunter's father in a quiet, pained voice, "this *is* better. That's why we've stayed for so long. Once we pay it off, life will be different."

"He'll always know where we are," she said. "His people will always be able to find us. We'll never be free."

Hunter's father picked up a mug and filled it from the teapot. The water that came out barely had any color to it; who knew how many times they'd brewed that tea. Without another word, he left the kitchen. Hunter watched his mother shut off the light above the sink, muttering about wasting electricity, about someone seeing the light on around the edges of the curtains. Then she, too, turned down the dark hallway.

Hunter looked at Cody, who looked back at Hunter.

"Are you hungry?" said Cody. "You can have my soup."

"I'm not hungry, either," said Hunter. "But thank you."

Rodney Wong

It happened in San Francisco. He'd had the artifacts with him that day, with plans to transfer half of them to an underground vault and sell the rest—but the man who was to meet him to coordinate both these things had gotten delayed and sent a messenger with apologies. The appointment would have to be rescheduled.

Wong was nervous about carrying the box out in the open, but experience had taught him to maintain an air of nonchalance. Guarding his briefcase would draw attention faster than anything. So he held it loosely, as he would any other day. It was the very case his mother had gifted him so many years ago, the leather grown old and patinated, its boxy edges scuffed. He ducked into the small room that he used for an office at the back of the tong hall and set his things down on the makeshift desk. There was some accounting to be done; plus, Yi Dawei was due with an update.

He hesitated for only a moment before popping up the latches of his briefcase. That was the way he always kept it, fully open to its ninety-degree angle, where the metal stays were locked in place so that he could easily sort papers between the accordion pocket and the folder he kept in the bottom. He slid the artifact box into the corner and began his work as usual.

Yi Dawei came running in over an hour late, stumbling against the doorway.

"Well?" said Wong.

The same excuses. The costs of taking their sickly child to the doctor, of buying him medicine. Their rent had just gone up, and Yi had not been invited back to teach, as he'd been hoping. It would take him at least a couple more months to find another adjunct position.

Wong sat there, silent and patient. He'd found that if he didn't speak, didn't nod, didn't move a single feature of his face, it made people nervous. It turned them more honest, usually, and he would sit there and watch as they dragged up the pieces of their shame one by one to be laid on the table.

What if they raised the interest by another percentage point, Yi suggested. A show of faith.

"We already agreed on the terms," Wong replied. "If you—"

He was cut off by a knock. It was the tong secretary, who only ever interrupted a closed-door conversation for urgent and sensitive matters.

"Just a moment," said Wong, and he stepped away to receive a report about a conflict. A crucial conversation indeed, for an almost done deal was about to go south. He stepped into the closet and picked up the phone as the call was transferred over.

His buyer did not believe that he had a true panacea, and wanted evidence of its effect. Nothing infuriated Wong more than when he was called a liar even as he told the truth. And really, was the man only trying to get a better price?

But at last the call ended, and Wong realized he was low on time. He had a flight to catch. Back in his office Yi Dawei was sitting on the rickety wooden stool by the door, looking harrowed and exhausted.

Wong felt tired himself. "Two weeks." He was feeling uncharacteristically generous, and anyway, that was the amount of time he would be away. "You have two weeks to collect the money, including interest. Now get out."

Had Yi been carrying a bag or a coat? It was difficult to recall. If the man had had a bulging pocket, Wong didn't notice. He clicked his briefcase shut and left.

It wasn't until he was touching down in New York City for a big transaction that he realized he was certain of the last time he'd seen the box.

He couldn't return to San Francisco right away; the New York deal would fall apart if he did, and that was a risk he wouldn't take. So he began to make phone calls. He had a suspicion, but surely Yi Dawei would never have been so rash.

And yet none of Wong's direct reports had any answers for him. Nobody had seen Yi.

When he made it back to San Francisco, he went straight from the airport to the address where the Yi family lived. The apartment was empty. The landlord reported that he'd woken up two weeks ago to find an envelope of cash slid under his door. It had contained only half the rent that was overdue for the previous month, and no note. The family was gone for good.

The search for the Yis—or, as he had yet to learn, the *Yees*—would span the next several years. It was no longer just the defaulted loan. Those artifacts belonged to Wong. He was going to get them back.

He would never forget the night—or rather, morning—that his phone rang while he was in the middle of a profitable interrogation. The call that had started this final leg of his journey.

"Yes?" he'd answered gruffly.

"Rodney?" the familiar voice had said. "This is Hsueh-Ting Chang. I found a piece that reminded me of some of the items in your collection. . . . I think you might want to see it for yourself."

And now he'd found the Yees. At last, this game of cat and mouse would come to an end. He would take their eldest son the way he himself had been taken. They would learn what it meant to pay their debts.

Luna Chang

The nausea ballooned up, as it always did, and then came that horrible tightening—like a screw being fixed in place somewhere deep in the soft part of her body just under her stomach. The stars filled the sky and the coil inside her sprang loose. It unleashed seismic waves of pain and an awful sensation that she was being wrenched apart.

Luna barely slept. The morning arrived with her lying on the floor, where she had fallen in the middle of the night, trying and failing to get outside to the fireflies. Her body was fire, was ice, one turning to the other and then back again faster than she could reach for any blankets or tear off any clothes. The sweat had drenched her hair, her shirt, her underwear.

That was where her mother found her when Luna ignored the shrill tone of her alarm clock. She whimpered as her mom scooped her off the floor and back into bed. Luna was only vaguely aware of the phone call to inform the school that she was home sick. It was around that time that she finally fell into a true sleep.

She woke to the sound of her mother sitting by her bed, stirring a bowl of ginger broth. Luna could smell the spices and medicinal sugar her mother had added; suddenly she was ravenous.

Her mother watched her eat in silence: first the sweet ginger soup, then the freshly steamed mantou, then the two squares of chocolate. She swallowed the painkillers last.

"Thanks," Luna said grudgingly.

"How are you feeling?" her mother asked.

"A little better," Luna answered, though her brain added, *for now*. Sometimes her body felt cursed.

"Good," her mom said.

Luna glanced at the clock. It was almost lunchtime, and she longed to be sitting beside Hunter, leaning into his shoulder. Stupid period. Roxy always used to say, "Hooray! You're not pregnant!"—as if that was supposed to help the fact that she felt like death.

"You've been mad at me," said her mother, calling her back to the present moment.

Luna tried her best to contain the fury that swelled. She worked hard to keep her voice even. "That's an understatement."

"You feel betrayed," said her mom. "I can explain—"

"You can explain why you were sixty-nining with a guy who wasn't Dad?" Luna said loudly. "Who even is he?"

It occurred to her that her mother might not even know that the act was *called* sixty-nining . . . but then she saw the wince.

"Luna, we've had misunderstandings before—"

249

"I know what I saw." She couldn't believe her mother was trying to lie her way out of this.

Her mom's face crumpled and she began to cry. "I'm sorry, baobei. I'm so sorry. I made a mistake."

"Why did you do it?" Luna hated how her voice scraped.

"It's a difficult thing to explain. I'm not ready to talk about it—but one day I will."

Luna didn't know what to say to that. Watching the tears roll down her mother's cheeks made her want to cry herself. There was the knot sliding into her throat, her sinuses tightening. She swallowed, searching for words to say.

She didn't want to be in the position of comforting her mother—because it *was* a terrible mistake. She almost felt ready to offer forgiveness if it could take her back to the time before any of this had happened, if it could erase her mother ever cheating.

But *it couldn't*, she reminded herself. Things had changed permanently. The only way was to see how they would move forward. It would be hard to earn the trust back, but Luna believed that if her mom was willing to put in the work, to be only honest and faithful from this point on, they could all get past this.

"You will forgive me, won't you, Luna?" her mother said tearfully.

Luna held her breath, willing herself not to cry.

"Did you tell anyone?" her mom asked.

Luna shook her head. Hunter didn't count as anyone.

Her mother let out a long breath of relief. Then she said, "Your father can never know."

It was like being transformed into a block of ice. The tears that had been hovering at the edges of Luna's eyes evaporated into the air. The knot in her throat smoothed away, and she was left with only a sour taste in her mouth.

"What are you talking about?" Luna heard herself say.

"You can't tell him," her mother said. "Please. I'll never do it again, but he can't know it happened."

"You want me to lie for you," said Luna, her voice hollow.

"No, no—"

"I'm not going to do that." Luna wanted to spit in her face. "I can't believe you would even *ask* me to do that."

"Luna, baobei, you know that—"

"I know that you're a liar, and that if you really loved us you would never have done any of this." She curled her fingers into her palms, pinching her skin with her nails. "Get out of my room. I don't want to look at you anymore."

To Luna's surprise, her mother stood, gathered up the tray with the empty dishes, and left without another word. Luna listened to the footsteps descending the stairs, the dishes clattering in the kitchen sink. At some point the garage door opened and closed—her mother must have gone out somewhere.

When Luna was finally alone in the house, she curled into her pillow and wept.

By the middle of the night, the cramps had faded, and she woke sticky with sweat, fighting off the blankets. Luna took in deep gulps of air, trying to keep her muscles loose. She knew her body. The racking pain wasn't done with her yet.

There was a *clack* against her window, too loud for a bug, too quiet to be a bird.

Clack.

Clack, clack.

She couldn't decide whether she was more curious or annoyed.

Clack as she pulled aside the curtain, and she saw a tiny pebble bounce off the glass.

Hunter stood in her backyard in a small patch of moonlight. He waved at her. Luna held up a finger for him to wait, then turned away to pull on a sweater and a coat. Downstairs she slipped into her boots and let herself out the back door.

The world was quiet in that way it only ever managed to achieve when it was cold and dark, night pressing down upon the earth. The winds were strong and now the moon was half-veiled by clouds. The occasional shard of light pierced through.

Hunter peeled himself out from the shadow of a tree.

"Hi," she breathed.

"Hi," he said back. She could hear the smile in his voice, though it was too dark to really see it.

Stepping into the cold was like cinching a belt across her midsection. It made her cramps so much worse. She could feel the wrenching in her pubic bone. She winced.

"Are you okay?" said Hunter.

"Cramps," Luna answered.

"I was wondering if that was it. I've heard my mom say that ginger helps."

"Yeah, I took some. Still hurts. But that'll be fixed soon.

Remember what I told you about the fireflies? Look." She pointed at the first of the lights, the tentative flash.

The lightning bugs spread out like flecks of glitter drifting in a snow globe. They landed in her hair, on Hunter's shoulders. The air lit up with them, and Luna could see the astonishment in his face.

They gathered around her navel, sent warmth into her body. They had a way of finding the knots inside her and loosening them, softening the muscles, dissolving the pain.

"How long will they stay?" Hunter asked softly.

Luna's eyes fluttered open. "Maybe five, ten minutes."

"Wait, I saw something," he said, and brought a hand to her elbow. "Take a step this way."

Luna let herself be guided, and together they moved under the tree, where darkness swallowed them. She gasped. "Where did they go?"

The fireflies had winked out—all but a few of them.

"Come back here," said Hunter, and they stepped out from under the tree.

This time Luna saw how they clung to her—they'd never really gone away.

"I think they need light," Hunter told her. "I think otherwise they're just...invisible."

Luna held up a palm, and two lightning bugs settled in the creases between her fingers. She passed her hand under the tree, watched her little friends disappear and reappear.

"I can't believe it. How have I never noticed that?"

Hunter shook his head. "It's only obvious to me because I'm seeing what they look like against you."

"What else do you see?" she asked.

He walked a slow circle around her and Luna's cheeks went hot. She shivered with pleasure.

It had never occurred to her that she would one day find someone who would make her feel so happy to be seen.

"There's some kind of residue they're leaving behind—or maybe. Well. It's more like a dust." Hunter traced a finger along her shoulder and showed it to Luna. It was just like the stuff that had glittered on those peach tree branches.

His chin was so very close to her. His mouth. She tilted her face up, and then he was kissing her. The air crackled. She wanted to stay right here beneath that fragment of moon.

The fireflies began to drift away. When the last of their lanterns winked out, Hunter smiled. His teeth were as bright as the stars.

Hunter Yee

"*What happens if* they *have* found us?" said Cody.

"I don't know," Hunter answered honestly. He wished it was a question they didn't have to think about. He wished he could give all the space in his head over to thoughts of Luna and the glow of those fireflies.

The brothers lay side by side under the blanket fort, with their heads grazing the wall and their feet sticking out the corner flap that made up the tent door. Well. Cody's feet stuck out—for Hunter, it was everything from the waist down.

His little brother wriggled closer and pressed his nose into Hunter's arm. "Who's *they*, anyway? Who's *he*?"

Hunter closed his eyes. "I don't know."

"You're supposed to know," Cody said unhappily. "You're older." There was the sound of him crawling out of the fort and over to the other corner of the room to unlatch the cage. A moment later, soft fur brushed against Hunter's elbow. When he opened his eyes, the rabbit was right at his cheek. She snuffled.

"Jadey's scared," said Cody.

Hunter stared up at the fort ceiling. It was an old patchwork quilt that his mother had bought at a yard sale for a few bucks. She'd washed the thing, of course, and every summer she hung it up outside so that the sun would disinfect it, but the splotchy yellow stains that covered several squares were a permanent reminder: This blanket had become theirs only after another person had used and saw fit to discard it. This was what they could afford. This life was the result of choices their parents had made—the same choices that forced them to hide, to pay for everything in cash only, to scrimp and save every penny in the hopes that one day they could buy back their freedom.

"Hunter? Did you hear me?"

"It's a good time for Jadey to practice being brave." It was hard not to sound as glum as he felt.

"What if Jadey doesn't understand how to do that?"

Hunter turned onto his side and bent his elbow to prop his head up. Cody lifted the rabbit and touched her nose to Hunter's.

"She could use some advice," his little brother said.

"Well, Jadey." Hunter saw one of her rare blinks and couldn't help but smile. "Sometimes it's about telling yourself a story that helps you to have courage. And sometimes it's about pushing yourself to try things that make you nervous. Or maybe being impulsive. You can experiment, you know."

"What's *impulsive*?" Cody asked.

"It means...doing something without planning it out first. Like, just making a decision a second before you do it."

"Oh. I like how it sounds."

"Like, just now, you impulsively decided to take Jadey out of her cage."

"But that wasn't scary." Cody stroked her back with one finger.

"Right. It's not scary *anymore*. But do you remember when you first got her? You were nervous that if you let her out, she might hurt herself, or she might run away."

Cody nodded.

"So, with practice, bigger things can get less scary, too. And you can start to be impulsive about them."

Cody held the rabbit up to his own ear. "Jadey says she'll try. I'll try, too."

"Good," said Hunter. "That's the best you can do."

Cody Yee

Cody opened his book, and this was the tale that hurried to make itself known:

> The ten suns who lived in the Eastern Sea took turns
> leaping from water to air, one lucky brother spinning with
> glee while the others looked on enviously. They delighted in
> flying around the world to marvel at the land, green and
> full, home to the creatures that lived on gulps of air and
> the sweets of the earth.
>
> But soon these playful sun-brothers grew restless and
> impatient. They disobeyed the rules of their father, the God
> of the Eastern Heaven, and tumbled together into the soft
> sky to play games and peer down at the world all at the
> same time.
>
> Their collective heat and light was unbearable.
> Sparkling rivers evaporated into dust as the suns danced

on clouds. Earth's beloved creatures began dying of heat exhaustion. Crops that had been so carefully nurtured shriveled to nothing. So distracted were the sun-brothers in their silly games, they didn't notice that they had scorched the precious earth.

The emperor begged for the gods to aid his people. Houyi, the God of Archery, was called upon to deal with the irresponsible suns.

You cannot behave in this manner, the archer said to them. You have burned up the land and wreaked havoc upon the earth's treasures.

The ten suns beamed brighter, stretching their rays defiantly, and skipped through the air. The land beneath turned charcoal black. The moans of the people, the whimpering of animals beneath dead trees—these glided up to the heavens in a dread-filled cacophony.

Angered by the sounds of suffering, Houyi drew out his bow, a curved piece of wood as thick as an elephant's leg. It looked thin and delicate in his hand. He gripped it as though it weighed no more than a chopstick. The archer plucked an arrow from his quiver and set it to his bow, one eye peering down the shaft. Listen to me, he shouted. The suns grinned at him; one even snickered.

Houyi loosed the arrow toward the heavens. It hissed through the thick air and pierced the westernmost sun in its center. The injured sphere turned red, then black, flame extinguished, and plunged from the sky. The remaining sun-brothers took no heed; they spread across the sky and lined up to form offensive shapes, taunting Houyi, for they did not believe he was capable of shooting them all.

Their impudence enraged him, and in quick succession he loosed eight more shots into the sky. His aim was true. Upon impact each arrow sent a loud pop reverberating through the air, followed by the sizzle of wood turning to ash.

There remained only one brother. Houyi glared up at the cowering sphere. He tightened his grip and drew the final arrow back, feeling the tension of the string against his fingers.

As he was about to release, he heard the emperor pleading for him to halt. Without any suns, the world would be permanently cold and dark. Nothing would flourish.

Leave us one sun, said the emperor.

Will you behave? Houyi bellowed to the sphere quaking in the sky.

Yes! the sun cried. I promise.

You accept your duty to provide light and warmth and cheer?

Yes, said the sun.

You swear to cease all mischief?

Yes! Yes.

Houyi lowered his arrow.

The emperor and his people regarded Houyi as their hero, but the God of the Eastern Heaven was furious: Nine of his children had been killed. Houyi had been asked only to punish them; he had taken his task too far. The god banished the archer.

Thus, Houyi was exiled from the heavens, sent to live on earth. His immortality was taken from him; he was forced to live as an ordinary mortal. And though the problem of too many suns had been solved, the earth continued to be plagued by the chaos of the universe.

Luna Chang

When Luna's father announced that they would all be taking a colleague out to dinner the next night, she stared blankly at him. Now did not seem like the time to be entertaining company. Hadn't he noticed the coldness between Luna and her mother? She wondered what he was thinking, whether her mom had fed him some invented reason for the silence.

The guest was an old friend and collaborator who was in town visiting, her father said. "Remember Uncle Rodney?"

Luna had the vague memory of a man in a suit who had come many years ago and gifted her some kind of carved toy that she'd promptly broken.

"He will be so thrilled to see us," her dad said.

They went to Fortune Garden, where the owner and waitstaff's adoration of Luna's father would make him look good. For his sake alone, Luna put on her best manners.

Uncle Rodney arrived just a couple minutes after them, wearing a fine long coat and carrying a briefcase. He spoke in English, full of jokes, with a hint of a British accent. At the sight of him a waitress was quick to bring out the restaurant's finest tea.

In the private dining room, where it smelled strongly of ginger and garlic, Luna's father was describing the fieldwork his colleagues had been doing in Xi'an. It seemed their guest had a special appreciation for this topic.

"Luna, has your father told you about the Terracotta Warriors?" said Uncle Rodney, probably because her eyes were glazing over.

"The Bingmayong," her father added, as if that helped.

"I don't really remember," she said.

"Qinshihuang ordered for them to be made to guard his mausoleum," said her mother. Luna ignored her.

"Qinshihuang," Rodney repeated. "The first emperor of China."

Luna's father continued on about some artifacts that had been unearthed a handful of years ago and somehow stolen before they could be thoroughly analyzed, and the speculation that a few relics that were now being examined by British researchers had been produced at the same time as those lost items. It was both interesting and tremendously boring, and Luna's attention drifted away.

Until Rodney began talking about planchette writing.

"Planchette, as in, the pointer thing that comes with, like, those Ouija things?" Luna interrupted. "The letter boards?"

"Ah, you mean a spirit board?" said Rodney. "Yes. However, planchettes were invented first, before anyone made any boards. Hundreds and hundreds of years ago, they were already being used in China."

Luna paused with her tea halfway to her mouth. "But what did they point to, then?"

"They were designed to hold a writing utensil, such as a brush. As the planchette moved, it would produce a mark, and these symbols or characters were then interpreted. Would you like to see an example?" Rodney asked in the kind of pleasant tone one would use to say, *Would you like some ice cream?*

"Right now?" said Luna.

"Oh, that's okay," her father said, and she could hear the tinge of nervousness in his voice. He looked around as if someone in the restaurant might notice.

Her parents were sometimes oddly superstitious. She looked at her mother, uneasy and squirming on the other side of the table. Luna took a vicious delight in it.

"It's no trouble at all," Rodney was saying. "I happen to be carrying one on me." From the pocket of his coat he pulled out a device that fit neatly in the palm of his hand. It looked like an overturned basket woven from plant fibers. He fed a hotel ballpoint pen through a hole and tied it in place with a leather thong.

"Did you make that?" said Luna.

"I did. I based it on an artifact from my Ming dynasty collection." He drew out a notebook and set the planchette on a blank page. "Do you have a question to ask?"

Luna considered for a few seconds. She wanted to make her question good. "What's coming from the crack in the ground? What does it mean?"

"Are you talking about the crack from the earthquake?" Her dad frowned.

Rodney gave her a look she couldn't read, and turned his attention to his hands.

Luna held herself very still, waiting to see what would come. When the planchette began to move, her mother jumped a little. It didn't look at all like Rodney was pushing the device around; he was simply connected via the tips of his fingers.

The pen dragged along the paper to create a circle so perfect it should have been drawn using a compass. No human hand could be so precise.

Rodney looked up, and the expression in his eyes was sharp and curious now, as if he were seeing Luna for the first time.

"Well, that was interesting." Luna's father laughed nervously.

"Yes," said Rodney. "Yes, it was."

David Yee

Hunter's father

When could the stone have gone missing? The pouch holding it had been unzipped, and he almost hadn't even noticed. David Yee massaged his temples, trying to think. When he first hid the stone in the trunk, after months of letting it float from one drawer to another, he'd been paranoid. He'd checked on it daily, in the beginning. Then weekly. After a while, feeling more secure, he let himself do it every month or so. Any time he cleaned the car or inspected the tires, he would duck down to look or palm the underside near the edge of the trunk's opening to make sure the pouch was still there, where he'd screwed it into the lip and then applied an entire tube of superglue for good measure.

He'd been proud of himself for that setup. The pencil case that he used was stiff and black, so it held its shape well and mostly disappeared into the shadows. You had to know where the zipper was in order to know to pull on it.

And the car was the most logical place to hide the piece. For the most part, it went wherever his family went. If they were home, the car and the stone were home, too. If they needed to make a run for it, the artifact would already be there with them. The car was such a beat-up piece of shit, he doubted any burglar would be tempted to break in. And if Huang ever found out where the Yees lived and sent someone to try to find the stone, they would most likely search the house, not the car.

But David had grown too comfortable. When had he last checked for the stone? Two months ago? Three?

He flipped through his calendar, trying to remember the places he'd driven, the things he'd done. His eyes froze on a square at the end of September.

That day had been so out of the norm—when had he last taken his family to a restaurant? A couple years, at least. The coupon had been tacked onto the bulletin board, and he'd gathered it up as he left work one evening, thinking that his wife deserved a show of appreciation for all that she was constantly doing.

But then there'd been the series of bad things: The coupon being expired; the buffet costing too much even after the discount; his son embarrassing him with that fistful of cash; his careless rear-ending with the Changs' car.

Where had Hunter gotten that money, anyway? David couldn't believe what his eldest child had become. Everything that he and Yvonne had sacrificed...and here they'd raised some kind of criminal.

He'd been in a foul mood all the rest of that day, as he went to photocopy some papers at his office, as he drove the car to a friend's house to get the latch of the trunk fixed. In his rage and humiliation he had forgotten all about the stone. How could he have failed to check for it? How would he even begin to search?

David cursed himself. He was the biggest fool.

Hunter Yee

Hunter and Luna wended their way through the woods, following the bubbling creek back to the fireflies and their nests. Back to the peach trees and those white flowers and that disturbing crack where the darkness gaped up at them.

There was the telltale whistling, the rustle near his ankles. Hunter looked down, and there they were: dollar bills of every denomination. The wind sent them skating toward him and he bent automatically.

"I'll never get over that happening," said Luna. "You didn't drop those, right?"

"No."

She was frowning. "Remember what happened last time? Aren't you worried about it, like, being cursed? Or like—my mom always talks about qian xian."

Hunter shrugged. "Last time was an outlier. I've picked up plenty of cash this way and been fine."

"How much money have you gotten like this?"

Hunter tidied the bills with practiced fingers until they looked like he could have just pulled them out of his wallet. "I actually don't know. I've never counted."

"Are you serious?"

He felt defensive as he stood up. "Look, if I don't know the full amount, then I can't waste energy imagining how I'd spend it. I'd rather pretend it's not there, you know? Then I have it if I need it. It's my emergency money."

Luna held up her hands. "Okay. Sorry."

He let out a breath and took his time catching up to her. "Why does it matter so much?"

"I just..." Luna seemed to be searching for the right words. "What if by taking that cash, you're racking up some kind of debt to the universe?"

Of all the concerns in the world. Hunter tried not to laugh. "Finders, keepers. What kind of debt could there possibly be in that?"

"I don't know. It just...it feels weird."

He was relieved when the wink of a firefly drew Luna's attention away.

"Oh, no, the nest—" She knelt down in the mud.

Hunter crouched to see better. "What's it doing all the way out here?" The woven sphere must have gotten blown away by the wind. It was deflating, the weblike filaments drooping inward. A few lightning bugs clung to the strands. Luna tried to gather up the nest, but her every poke and prod crushed the weave more.

He cupped her hands in his to try to soothe her fear. The

question that emanated from her face was the same one thudding in his chest: *What did it mean?* These fireflies with supernatural abilities, who defied so many rules of the natural world—how could one of their nests have fallen?

He was reminded of that sense of doom seeping from the crack. The feeling that everything was headed in the direction of *wrong*.

"Hang on a second. Look." Hunter picked up the thread that trailed off the end—the line that must have fastened the nest to the tree. He'd expected the strand to be sticky like spider silk, but instead it was cool and slippery between his thumb and finger.

"Don't break it," said Luna, her voice scratchy.

"It feels pretty tough," he replied. "Jeez, how long does this even go? You stay here, okay?"

It was nearly invisible; he could see it only in the glare of the sun. Hunter followed the line, moving palm under palm to keep ahold of it. He was several yards away from Luna when he confirmed that the strand was indeed unbroken, still connected to the peach trees, to the other nests bobbing high above.

"Well?" Luna called, still kneeling.

"I have an idea," said Hunter. "I'll be right back."

He pinned the filament under a rock and went running to the shed for his bow. He would need only one arrow.

"You trust me, right?" he said when he saw the hesitation in Luna's eyes.

She nodded.

"This is the part you're good at," said Hunter. "Can you tie this section of the thread to my arrow? It needs to be secure."

Luna was fast, her fingers doubling the strand against itself, then working through a series of loops. She tied it off. "I kind of combined a Chinese knot and a sailor's knot. It's probably overkill…"

"It's perfect." Hunter reached up a thumb to smooth the crease still tightening her forehead. "This is going to be okay."

He prepped the arrow. On the ground the woven sphere rolled slightly.

"Should we move closer?" she asked.

"I can make the shot," he said.

"But we can't even see the peach trees from here," Luna protested.

Hunter was already closing his eyes and slowing his breath. He didn't need to see. He knew exactly where they were and how the wind would guide the arrow. The bow was taut, his fingers attuned to every vibration that passed over the string, every whisper in the air. He visualized the arrow arcing high, sailing over a cluster of peaches to lodge itself in the thick knot of a high branch. He released.

"It's gone," Luna said quietly, and he opened his eyes.

"It went where it needed to go. Come on." He led the way, following the creek until he saw the bush of twisting white stars, again blooming at the wrong time. He gazed up at the peach trees. It took a moment of searching, but there it was: the arrow stuck firmly to the highest branch, the knot glistening around its shaft. He could just barely see the strand and the way it draped over neighboring stems, ending in that pendulous nest.

A breeze rose up, breathing into the sphere. Round and full once more, it caught a bit of the sun. Lights flickered—fireflies returning home.

Luna squeezed his hand, sighing with relief. She took a step forward and her foot splashed.

Hunter stared down at the water, at the way it tried to climb toward Luna, stretching up past the edges of the bank, clawing at her feet.

He shivered.

Beneath the ripples, he could sense that crack, the darkness fluttering there, reaching for him. When he looked directly at it, he felt faint, the air in his throat all ice.

Hunter swayed on his feet.

Luna steadied him, her free hand grasping his elbow. "Are you okay?" She looked pale. "I feel it, too."

He leaned against a trunk to steady himself. "What do you think it is?"

She knelt at the edge of the water and held her palm above the surface. Not touching, only hovering. Hunter was struck with the image of her falling in, the darkness sucking her under.

"Be careful," he said.

"I had a dream about the world ending. It felt exactly like this. This...wrongness." Luna stood up. "Have you noticed how it's expanding? I could feel it when we were at the edge of the trees. It didn't used to be that way."

"Yeah. And it's been getting colder." His teeth were chattering now. New winds were rolling in and the sky was dimming.

Luna stepped over and wrapped her arms around him. She pressed her forehead to his and offered her breath. The warmth poured through his body. The tightness in his chest melted.

She set her face against his shoulder. "Everything sucks. I hate my mom. I don't want to go home."

"So let's not," he said. "Let's go somewhere else."

"Like where?"

A boldness came over him. He took her hand and led her deeper into the trees and over to his shed.

In the corner was a cardboard box containing a comforter and a flashlight he'd unearthed a long time ago from the back of his closet. He turned on the light, grateful that it still had battery. Spreading the old comforter on the floor made his neck go warm. Luna knelt down to sit.

The walls around them seemed to both shrink and expand. Hunter looked at Luna, and she looked right back at him, her eyes like the pebbles that glittered in the creek.

Luna Chang

Luna rolled her anger toward her mother into a tight little knot and did her best to keep it tucked away. Instead, she focused on Hunter. There were no other sounds but the whistle of wind, the occasional pop or creak in the old wood.

He nudged down the hood of his sweatshirt, mussing his hair, making it poke out at a funny angle. Luna couldn't possibly have explained it: The way his black hair stood up was somehow incredibly sexy.

He was practically up against the other side of the shed. Why had he put so much distance between them? On the bus, he never hesitated to sit right beside her, knees bumping, hips touching, shoulder against shoulder.

"You're so far away," she said. "Why are you all the way over there?"

He shrugged. "You can move over this way, if you want."

She made an exasperated noise. "No, because I'm already in the middle, and that's a much more strategic position."

"Strategic? What do you mean?"

Luna rolled her eyes. "I guess you'll have to come over here if you want to find out."

Hunter shifted closer a few inches at a time, until they were side by side and Luna found herself leaning a little bit so as to have more space for her elbow.

"Hello." He wiggled his eyebrows.

The smirk on his face was too much for her to handle. She brought her hands up to his cheeks and drew him toward her until her lips found his. She kissed him so hard their teeth clacked, and they paused to laugh about it, but then they were kissing again and Luna's hands were reaching for the edges of his T-shirt. Her fingers found skin; he was hot to the touch.

She wrapped her arms around him and pulled. In movies, people moved so effortlessly, gracefully. But here in real life it was a bit awkward. Hunter gave up his full weight to her when she pulled, and together they fell horizontal. Their legs crammed against the wall in a jumble, and Luna couldn't move for fear of accidentally kneeing him. They were laughing again.

"Was that the strategic positioning?" said Hunter.

She laughed harder. "Shut up."

They rearranged themselves on the floor, and then their bodies pressed together, their noses and foreheads touched.

"Hi." Luna's eyes were almost crossing from trying to look into his. She squeezed one eye shut. That was a little better.

"Hi," he returned, his breath silky against her skin.

She slid her nose to his cheek so that her lips could reach his mouth.

In her waking dreams this had always happened on a bed in a dimly lit room. She certainly hadn't thought that it might happen in an old shed out in the woods, or that she might feel quite so nervous.

But the longer she kissed Hunter, the more confident they both grew, and she became very intensely aware of the parts of his body that were pressing against her.

An instinct took over. Luna was greedy for more touch. She let him be the one to tug her sweater off, and then rescued him when he fumbled for too long with the clasp on the back of her bra. They were down to pants.

The thought crossed her mind: Was her period absolutely over? She was pretty sure it was, but sometimes there was a bit of spotting for an extra day or so.

Any other time, that would have been enough to make her intensely self-conscious. But right now there was that same boldness that had seized her when she first met Hunter.

She broke away from a kiss. "Do you have a condom?"

"I—uh." He looked like he'd been caught with a hand in the cookie jar. "Not with me? I'm sorry."

"It's okay," she said. "Can you get up?"

Hunter looked like he'd been reprimanded. His face was tight with embarrassment.

"I don't mean—" But she broke off because it was easier to just show him. Luna stretched for her backpack and unzipped the outer pocket. She pulled out the box just as Hunter stood up. "What are you doing?" she said.

"I was. Um." He sat down again. "Where did you get those?"

She smirked. "I stole them from my mom."

Luna had gone rooting through her mother's things, unsure what she was looking for but determined to find *something*. She needed evidence if she was going to tell her father about the affair. She hadn't yet decided if she would.

The box had been jammed into the very back of her mother's underwear drawer, tipped on its side with one of the corners crushed. Inside were five condoms connected by perforated edges, like a roll of tickets at a fair.

She *would* show her father. She would bring him this box, tell him what she'd seen. Her perfect family would be ruined. But then again, they had never been perfect to begin with. It was all a lie.

This was the anger that churned in her gut as she kicked off her jeans. Hunter was the escape she needed; she wanted to drown herself in his touch. The taste of him, the sizzle of his skin as it slid against hers, the twining of his legs beneath the undersides of her knees—she let all these things cloud the hurt.

She let the fire in her gut burn upward and take over. She let the rage and the want swallow her whole.

Yvonne Yee

Hunter's mother

In case the stone could have somehow made its way back into the house, Yvonne and David searched everywhere. In the walk-in closet. All the drawers. The kitchen cupboards. The laundry basket, even. How could David have lost it?

He told her he would search the car again. He drove to Fortune Garden and back. Yvonne traced the perimeter of the house, in case the stone had fallen.

It was simply gone. Did this spell their doom? Was this the reason why they'd gotten those mysterious phone calls? She hadn't believed in that ridiculous little hexagon... until she did.

Yvonne was so very tired. Sapped and withered, like a piece of malnourished grass bent in the wind. David, too. He'd worked himself into the ground trying to get his job into a stable place, trying to make things better for his family. Yvonne wasn't sure either of them had the energy to run away again. To start over.

They were beyond tired. They were deeply afraid.

She remembered the whispers they'd heard, the consequences they'd seen with their own eyes. How their friend Guo Xiansheng had been disappeared in the night. Connie Ng, that sweet woman who couldn't have been much younger than Yvonne, whose face was permanently scarred. The man named Cai, who had lost two teeth and a thumb by the time Huang was through with him.

"We must be prepared," said David.

"For what?" said Yvonne, though she already knew what he would say.

He closed his eyes. "Disaster."

Hunter Yee

When they had finished, happiness radiated from Hunter like sunlight. Here was everything in the world that he needed. The tension between his ribs had melted. A block of ice and hurt, dissolved. What a wonder Luna was, lying there with her eyelashes fluttering against her cheeks.

He huffed the quietest of laughs.

"What?" Luna opened her eyes.

"I can't believe you stole condoms from your mom," he said. "That's kind of amazing."

Her face tightened and he immediately regretted bringing it up. "She's a fucking liar. I hate her."

"I'm sorry. I shouldn't have said anything."

Luna softened again. "No, it's okay. I don't mean to complain about her all the time. Let's talk about something else."

"Like what?" said Hunter.

"Once upon a time," she began, "Hunt and Lunar found a

little wooden house out in the middle of the woods. It looked old and forgotten, and it turned out to be made of magic."

"I thought we were supposed to be un-Disney," he said teasingly.

"It is un-Disney, because they did unnameable things in it."

"Ah, right—how could I forget." He buried his face in her neck. "Do you think this is what it feels like to be in love?" he said without quite meaning to.

When he pulled away to look at her, she was smiling.

Hunter could tell from the stillness of the air and the quiet in the street: It was very late. In all likelihood, he had missed dinner, and he was about to be in deep shit.

Whatever. It had been worth it.

He was so distracted by the memory of Luna—the dip of her navel, the ridge of her collarbone—he didn't notice until he was walking up the path to his house that his dad was standing there in the dark doorway, waiting for him.

"Did you take it?" his father said.

"Take what?" said Hunter, immediately wary.

His dad grabbed him by the cartilage of his ear, dragged him into the house, yanked him past the living room and into the kitchen.

The shouting began then. "You're always up to no good. I *know* you stole from me."

Hunter felt like he was trapped in an angry ocean of a dream, where he was a piece of driftwood being tossed about. It was hard to believe that only a couple hours ago he and Luna had been twined together on the floor of that shed.

"What are you talking about?"

The blow came unexpectedly. Hunter fell against the fridge, registering only that his mother was shrieking for his father to stop. His dad had punched him in the ear. His head was a clash of thunder.

"You idiot—did you know it was keeping us *safe*? What have you done with it? You give us nothing to be proud of, and you put us in danger."

It was Cody's scream that stopped the fist from coming again. Cody, who burst into tears as Jadey leapt out of his arms and scrambled under the counter to hide.

Their mother dragged their father away down the hall. Eventually, when Cody was done crying, Hunter followed him to their bedroom, where they locked the door for good measure and returned the rabbit to her cage.

Hunter tucked his little brother into bed and sank down to the floor, where he lay staring at the ceiling, unable to sleep.

Luna Chang

Luna had expected to feel changed after sex, but for the most part she didn't. There *was* a feeling between her legs like she'd discovered a new part of herself. *Sore* was the wrong word, because it implied some kind of hurt—it was more like having worked and become aware of a muscle.

There had been the soft, uncertain fumbles. There had been her body and Hunter's figuring it all out. She peeled away her shirt and saw the purple blooms where his lips had found her skin. The marks were already fading. They weren't hickeys— what an ugly word, and equally ugly on the skin, like some kind of injury. No, these were more of that same magic they'd discovered on the bus. Their bodies in conversation.

Luna wanted to be with him again. To learn all the different ways their bodies could speak to each other.

She wondered if this same feeling was what drove her mother to be unfaithful to her father—and then immediately squashed the thought.

She would *never* be like her mom.

Luna sat up. Her mother would go out to run Saturday errands, and that was when she would tell her dad what she knew. He was probably still mad at her for coming home so late the night before. But he wouldn't stay annoyed for long. He never did.

And when he heard what Luna had to say...

Well. He would side with her. Her mother—his wife—had betrayed them in the worst way. Together they would decide what was supposed to happen next.

She could hear her parents chatting over their breakfast. It sounded disgustingly normal.

Another thing that bothered Luna: Yesterday she'd felt herself lose control. Her anger toward her mother and her wish to be with Hunter had blurred together, until she knew only her body's firecracker desire. Why did those two have to be mingled? If she was being perfectly honest, a part of her had *wanted* to do it to spite her mother.

She pulled her sweatshirt on and went down the stairs. Perfect timing: Through the window, she saw her mom's new car drive off.

Her father was at the dining table, working his way through a pot of tea, reading his students' assignments. She sat down in front of him and yanked a banana off the bunch.

"You shouldn't eat a banana on an empty stomach," he said without looking up.

Luna pushed it away with a sigh and went to grab a box of cereal. She watched the flakes tumbling into the bowl, watched the milk filling the gaps. She sat down again, spoon in hand, and tried to make herself eat.

She had no appetite.

"You shouldn't have cold milk, either," he said. "You know what traditional Chinese medicine says."

Luna didn't respond.

Her father noticed her expression. He took off his glasses and pushed the papers aside.

"I have to tell you something," she said.

His shoulders seemed to droop. He nodded. "Okay?"

"I caught Mom cheating," said Luna.

Her dad didn't blink. He said nothing.

"Remember that snow day, when I had an early dismissal? She didn't know I was going to be home from school early. I went upstairs, and she was with another man." Luna's voice broke on the word *another*. Her throat was swelling into a knot. "She told me not to tell you."

Her father's eyes took on a glassy, distant look. Luna wondered if he believed her.

"I found this." She drew the flattened condom box from the pocket of her hoodie.

He swallowed, and that was the only sound she heard.

"Dad. Say something."

Finally, he looked up at her. "I'm so sorry you had to find out about this, Luna."

The words stopped her heart. "What? You *knew*?"

"Yes." His eyes dropped to the table.

"How long have you known?" she demanded.

He sighed heavily. "About a year. I suspected for a long time before I confirmed it."

"You've known for a whole fucking *year*?" she said.

Her father narrowed his eyes. "Don't speak like that."

Luna stood up because she couldn't bear to sit any longer. "You've known for a year and you haven't done anything about it?"

"There's nothing to be done."

She was going to lose her shit. "I can't believe this. You're just letting our family fall apart?"

"No, Luna," he said very gently. "I'm keeping us together."

"Well, *news flash*: It's not fucking working." She fought the urge to smash her cereal bowl against the window and instead stomped her way back up the stairs to her room. She slammed the door so hard the framed family portrait fell off her bookcase and broke.

"Good riddance," she said to the frame, and threw herself back in bed.

At night Luna tossed and turned. When she finally passed out in the early hours of the morning, she slept fitfully. She dreamed of a breezy afternoon at a white beach. A day from real life, from the past, when she and her mother had walked barefoot over hot sand in search of shells. They were sharing a joke and Luna was laughing, but then her mother's voice began to warp. It turned garbled and loud and monstrous.

When she woke up, her face was wet.

Hunter Yee

Hunter didn't go to school on Monday. Or on Tuesday. Cody did, because he did not have a hideous bruise on the side of his face that would draw questions.

Both evenings, Cody crawled into their bed and carefully traced his fingers from Hunter's temple to his earlobe.

"Does it hurt?"

Hunter shook his head, even though the real answer was yes.

"How are we supposed to be brave now?" Cody whispered.

"It takes practice," Hunter said. "Maybe when you need an extra bit of courage, hold Jadey. She'll give you what you need."

He watched as his little brother went to the rabbit's cage and carefully pulled her out. Cody pressed his cheek to the soft white fur.

"Better?" said Hunter.

"A little."

While Cody slept, Hunter stared at the night sky through the gap in the curtains. He tried not to think about his father's knuckles making contact with the side of his head, tried to forget the sting of his father's words.

Luna. He would think about her instead. Her breaths in his ear. The smoothness of her thighs. His face against her neck.

On Wednesday, the bruise was still there, a storm cloud blown across his temple. Hunter could tell from his mother's expression that it probably looked worse. Oh well. There was a calculus test; his parents would never let him skip that.

He was glad to go. He missed Luna in an aching way, as if someone had wrenched off a piece of him.

She wasn't on the bus, but she was waiting at his locker. She playfully lifted away the beanie he'd yanked down around his ears, and gasped.

"Shhh." He brought his finger to her lips. "I'm okay."

"Who—?"

Hunter shook his head. "Later." The last thing he needed was for a teacher or someone to overhear that his dad had punched him, and for them to call child protective services. Hunter would soon be of legal age—but Cody wouldn't.

"Will I see you after school?"

He hesitated. It was risky. His mother expected him to go home right away, but he knew that nobody would be around for an extra couple of hours.

"I haven't seen you in ages," Luna begged. "And I finally started taking my car to school. I can drive you home."

All he wanted was to disappear with her somewhere, to hold her and feel like all was right again.

"Yeah," said Hunter. "Okay."

The homeroom bell rang. He turned toward his hall, but she caught him by the wrist. "Let me take that bruise away first."

After school they went directly to the shed. On top of the comforter, Luna curled into his side. She traced the knots of his bracelet for a while, then reached up to thread her fingers through his.

"Tell me what happened?"

What happened. It was a good question, and he didn't even have the complete picture. But he had the wisps he'd heard through the vents when his parents thought he was sleeping. He had his fuzzy memories, pulled to the surface like a net of things drawn up out of the sea.

He'd turned all those pieces over and over in his head until they spun into a thread that he could understand. Hunter drew in a deep breath and began to tell her. Not a fairy tale. Just what he knew of the sad truth, starting from before he was born.

Yvonne Yee

Hunter's mother

Yvonne often thought back to the very beginning of it all. Meeting young Dawei, who was so cheerful, so handsome. The friends who set them up had explained—bragging for him so that he could be modest and embarrassed—how he'd gathered up a healthy pot of savings and dreams of a very specific kind of future. How he'd bought himself a one-way ticket to the States for the exact master's degree they were both pursuing. She'd thought to herself: This was a man who knew how to make his life do what he wanted.

A month after graduating, the two of them made a trip back to Taiwan to get married. The following year, they were both on to their PhDs, and she was pregnant. She found Hunter's name in a baby guide on the discount shelf of a bookstore and wrote it down on the back of a crumpled receipt in her purse. *Hunter* sounded like a name for strength and survival. For resourcefulness.

In the graduate student dorms, Yvonne and David watched

their funds dribble away, converted cent by cent into textbooks and diapers and cans of food. By the time David was putting the finishing touches on his dissertation, Hunter was five years old and their money was gone. Yvonne would finish her PhD later. She swore it.

Renting a home outside the university was so much more expensive that they often found themselves digging fingers into every crevice in search of dropped coins that might help them reach what they owed for the month. On top of that, Hunter was chronically ill. He complained of pain in his chest. He often had trouble breathing. He couldn't stand the cold.

Yvonne took him to a friend of a friend, a San Francisco doctor who practiced traditional Chinese medicine at a grimy office in Chinatown. Unsmiling but kind, the woman examined Hunter as a favor. But when it came time for her to prescribe herbs, Yvonne had to tell her, shamefaced, that they couldn't afford to purchase any of the medicines. Could the acupuncture be enough to help him?

The doctor was already shaking her head, and years later Yvonne would wonder how well Hunter remembered the next part. The door had been left ajar because it didn't quite fit into its frame, and at that moment a young man ducked his head in. He explained that he'd accidentally overheard their situation, and he was happy to pay for the first round of treatment. It was such a terrible thing for a child to be so sick—he wanted to help. He insisted.

The doctor wrapped the herbs and wrote down instructions for preparation and dosage, and Yvonne was embarrassed but grateful. She asked the name of this generous man.

Huang Rongfu, he'd answered, smiling.

The herbs were bitter, and Yvonne watched how her son gagged at the taste. She sat beside him to ensure he swallowed every last mouthful.

They didn't do anything.

At the next visit, the doctor closed her eyes to take Hunter's pulse and shook her head. The bizarre thing, she told Yvonne, was that his meridians were ever-shifting. The air whooshing in and out of his lungs did not sound like anything she'd ever heard. She wanted to try other treatments—but she couldn't continue seeing Hunter free of charge. She ducked her head, apologetic.

Sometimes Yvonne wondered if there was a parallel universe in which she'd never gotten pregnant. They would never have had to hide. She would have finished her doctorate and been far more successful than her husband. All those late nights she spent toiling away over notes, pouring her heart into writing papers... Instead of letting his name claim the byline at the top of all those publications, the credits would have been rightfully hers. *By Yubing Li.* Her own name, nothing disguised.

Hunter Yee

Hunter didn't know how it was that his parents found that man Huang again. Or how the first loan came to be arranged. He knew only that there had been a time when he'd slept beside his parents on the stained carpet of their apartment, sandwiched between ratty blankets. There had been a time when for every meal he would scrape his bowl clean and still be hungry.

Then the three of them had gone to meet Huang, who took them out to a dim sum restaurant where Hunter had eaten until he felt sick. That day was a dividing line: After that, Hunter's parents bought their first pieces of used furniture. What a luxury to have a couch.

They took Hunter to a white doctor, in a facility that glowed with fluorescent lights and smelled chemically clean, where he was given his first prescription for an inhaler. They took Hunter back to the Chinese doctor. Neither Western nor Eastern medicines worked, but at least now they could afford to buy syrups that suppressed some of Hunter's coughs, and thicker blankets to keep him warm.

He stopped being so hungry all the time. Occasionally, his parents would even buy a package of Little Debbie Nutty Bars, if they were on sale, and Hunter would break the wafers into tiny pieces to melt in his mouth, making them last as long as possible.

He was seven years old the first time Huang came to visit them at their apartment, expecting the money back. They welcomed him in as an old friend. But when Hunter's father began to explain that he needed more time to find a job that would pay enough, Huang's expression changed. It took on the sharpness of a wild animal, a predator observing its prey.

Hunter's family reassured Huang: Of course they would pay back the money. They had made the promise and signed a contract. They would pay it back with interest. Of course.

Huang summoned Hunter's father to his office once a month to inform him that the interest had risen by another percentage point, making sure the Yees felt the squeeze of his power. It was after one of these meetings that Hunter's dad rushed home with wild eyes and announced that they had to move.

So they made their way across the country, taking very few worldly possessions. They changed the spelling of their name from *Yi* to *Yee*, hoping it would buy them some more time before they were followed. As all that was happening, Cody was only the size of a mango, suspended in their mother's womb, happily oblivious to the world and its bleak corners.

Weeks after they moved, cramming into a tiny apartment,

they received word that Hunter's grandmother was in poor health and badly suffering. They wired her money to cover her medical care. A waste, he would hear his parents say years later. She passed away days after the transfer had gone through.

Then Cody was born. With another mouth to feed, money was tighter than ever. Hunter was sharply reminded of how to live while treading through the hunger and the cold. There were no Nutty Bars to be had. The blankets were never thick enough for the ice that wormed between his ribs.

Luna Chang

"*But we got* by," Hunter told her. "Just barely. My dad took every odd job he could get, every adjunct position he was offered. Two years after we moved here, he finally got a full-time position at Fairbridge University, so that gave us a bit of stability. I remember them saying to each other that in six months they would call up Huang and explain the situation, and send him whatever cash they had. But I'm pretty sure they never did. It was just so easy to hide. For a while there it actually felt like...maybe we were okay."

"And now?" said Luna.

"Now we're obviously not. Or maybe it was always an illusion. I guess my parents thought that we could live like this for a while longer."

"This is why you ran away after you saved that little girl," said Luna, the pieces clicking into place. "This is why you were afraid."

He nodded. "Yeah."

"Huang Rongfu," she echoed. "Why does that name sound familiar? Maybe my brain is just making it up."

"I hope so," said Hunter. "It's not someone you want to know."

"So is the goal just to hide forever?" she asked.

"I don't really know what the endgame was, except that they hoped they would be able to pay back what they owed, and I guess whatever interest. And somehow find a way to mollify him." He laughed bitterly. "They're delusional. We'll never be free."

He fell silent, and so she listened to him breathing. It made her think of the sea, those waves and crests. She took on his sadness, slipped into those feelings herself, as if together in that ocean she could keep him afloat.

"Are you better now?" she asked.

"Better?"

"Not as sick as when you were a kid?"

"I guess. When we first moved here, my parents made me eat these weird herbs. My mom said they were some kind of panacea, and she was really mad when I told her they were disgusting."

"So they didn't work?"

"They sort of did, and they sort of didn't. My fevers went away, but breathing is still a problem. The cold is still a problem. And, you saw—it's a lot worse these days. Although...this is going to sound ridiculous."

Luna shifted so she could see him better. "What?"

"I think those herbs are maybe what gave me my aim, because the wind felt different after that. See? Ridiculous."

Luna smiled. "Almost as ridiculous as having perfect aim in the first place."

He laughed again, and this time it actually reached his eyes.

"I was sick a lot as a kid, too," said Luna. "I'd actually nearly forgotten about that. It was the same thing for me—doctors couldn't figure it out."

"Weird," said Hunter. "Maybe we're superhuman. Maybe the day we were born was special."

"Well, that's not fair, though," Luna said. "You've got your aim—what's my power?"

He kissed her on the nose. "Your power is being you, with your wonderful nose and your sturdy neck. That's far better."

It began to rain, and they focused on its pitter-patter as a way to escape the world for a little while longer.

Rodney Wong

Rodney Wong had managed to dig up quite a lot in the time he'd spent in Fairbridge. The house where the Yees lived and the amount they paid in rent. The university that accounted for their entire household income. The bus route that ferried their eldest son to and from Fairbridge High School. The private school where they'd enrolled their youngest. They had no other children, he confirmed. He hadn't yet managed to get a look at Hunter—his timing was always wrong.

But then he'd met with the Chang family for dinner and discovered that Chang Hsueh-Ting's daughter was most fascinating. A girl in the same school and graduating class as Hunter Yee.

In the days since, he'd begun to wonder if he should reexamine his plan. If it was meant to be adjusted. Expanded. There at that table, with his planchette between his hands, Luna Chang had brought about a perfect circle.

A circle could represent so many things. An infinite number of possibilities.

But the thought Wong returned to again and again was the image of a target, with its concentric rings and a bull's-eye at the center.

So he began to investigate Luna Chang.

She really was quite fascinating.

Hunter Yee

Hunter noticed that his little brother was being secretive. It was weird—usually Cody wanted to share everything and couldn't get Hunter's attention fast enough. But now he was being cagey. Sometimes he would hide away under the blanket fort, and if Hunter came into the room without warning, there would be frantic shuffling sounds before Cody emerged.

One afternoon the door of their bedroom was open just a sliver, and from out in the hallway, Hunter pressed an eye to look. Cody sat cross-legged in the fort, reading a book, turning the pages as if they were fragile. His eyebrows were drawn together like he was trying to solve a puzzle.

What was he up to?

Hunter took a step and accidentally shifted right onto the loudest creak in the floor.

Cody snapped the book shut and tucked it away. Hunter really hoped it wasn't porn. *Way* too young for that.

"What do you want?" Cody said brusquely, lifting the blanket corner that made up the door of his little fort.

Hunter blinked. That, too, was unlike his brother. This was a tone that sweet and sensitive Cody had never used before.

"Nothing," said Hunter. "Am I not allowed in my own room? Anyway, I was going to see if you wanted to play a game of wrestle-ball."

"Nah," said Cody. "I don't feel like it right now." Jadey the rabbit crawled into view, her nose twitching.

"Are you feeling okay?"

"I'm fine." Cody's voice was falsely bright. "Just have a lot of homework."

"Sure." Hunter turned away, feeling stung.

He supposed his little brother had to start growing up at some point.

Luna Chang

Sleep refused to come for Luna. Deep in the night, light flickered at the edge of her window. It glowed brighter and brighter, until she stood up and yanked aside the curtain.

There was a whole patch of lightning bugs crowding against another window—the one in her father's study. What were they doing?

Her room was adjacent to the office, so it was easy to sneak over. But as Luna drew near the fireflies they flitted away.

"Come *back*," she whispered, hurrying to maneuver the window open. Not quick enough—they were gone. She was left with only the low moon and the night air that wafted in. As Luna slid the window shut again, her heel knocked the recycling bin. Papers spilled to the floor. She froze, listening for signs of her parents waking. There was the sound of blankets moving, someone turning over. Then, stillness.

She gathered up the recycling, careful not to let anything thump against the bottom. She was nearly done when she saw her name in the moonlight. There was a large piece of mail addressed to her, and it was torn open. It was from a college she'd applied to. Based on the size of the envelope, it was likely an acceptance letter. What was this doing in the trash? Why hadn't she seen it?

Luna had been so distracted by everything—Hunter, the fireflies, her cheating mother, the crack—she hadn't given much thought to the timeline for notifications. She wasn't particularly invested, but obviously she was still curious to know which schools would accept her and which would reject her. Her mind worked backward to when she'd mailed in her applications, and the list of dates for when she should expect to hear back. It was odd, now that she thought about it, that she hadn't seen a single reply. At the very least, the two that her guidance counselor had called *safety schools* had rolling admissions, and she should have gotten responses from them a long time ago.

She pawed through the rest of the pile, and sure enough there were more. She couldn't believe she'd missed all these. Why would her father have trashed acceptances without showing her?

Luna wasn't exactly sure what drove her to open the filing cabinet, but then there was a familiar smell. Instinct made her reach for the folders in the back.

She almost laughed when her knuckles grazed the edges of the cold stone, balanced on top of the folders. It was the white hexagon that her father had tried to tell her was a dream. He'd hidden it here all this time.

And behind it: an acceptance packet from Stanford University.

The date on there made no sense. How the hell could she

have gotten an acceptance in the middle of December when she hadn't even mailed out her application yet? Unless—

She thumbed through the papers until she found the actual letter. Her eyes scanned the sentence that began with *You have been selected* and skimmed until she saw the words *under our Early Decision program.*

The day she'd shown her father her essays—which she had slowly and agonizingly typed out on his computer, hunting and pecking each letter one by one—he'd insisted on transferring them to a floppy disk and taking them to his office so that he could print them for her. It was a much better way to edit, he'd said. But now she knew the truth. He'd done that in order to get his hands on her essays.

She remembered that dinner at Giuseppe's. She could hear her father saying, *You're going to go to Stanford,* could remember his gleeful expression the whole night.

It was just after five in the morning. Luna banged on her parents' bedroom door and threw it open without waiting for an answer.

Her mother and father each slept at their respective edges, a wide ocean of bed between them. The fact that they had two separate comforters made Luna even angrier.

"What the *fuck* is this?" said Luna, waving the letter.

Her father sat up and reached for his glasses, immediately furious. "What did you say?"

"You applied to Stanford *early decision* for me? What is *wrong* with you? That's—is that even *legal*?"

He blinked at her. "You should be happy. You got in. It was your first choice."

Her mother was sitting up, too, now. She looked shocked.

"It was *your* first choice," Luna spat. "I don't give a fuck about any of this. I don't want what you want. But who cares, right? It doesn't matter what I think!"

He started to speak but she was done listening to him. She stormed into her bedroom to change her clothes and grab her stuff for school. On her way out, Luna kicked aside the neat row of shoes and made sure to slam the front door extra hard.

Hsueh-Ting Chang

Luna's father

It was barely six o'clock when Hsueh-Ting pulled into the empty parking lot in front of his office building. He wasn't expected anywhere for another four hours, but he would rather be here than in that house, where everything was a reminder of Luna's anger and Meihua's coldness.

How had things come to be this way? He remembered when Luna was first born, when the nurse handed her to him, a mere six pounds, a full head of hair that was oddly silver and wouldn't turn black for weeks. Her soft little fingers had curled like flowers, and Hsueh-Ting had the thought that he would do anything for this child.

He would never forget how Luna had been sick constantly in those early years, how he would cry in the shower where Meihua couldn't see, wondering what he had done to bring such misfortune upon his family. He had heard that in some religions there was a practice of setting water out beneath the night sky to absorb the lunar energies, and so he thought to try it. In the days of his daughter's infancy, he set out a bottle whenever the moon was visible and the temperature low enough that the milk wouldn't sour. He didn't tell his wife, for he wasn't sure how she would respond. But he saw that when Luna drank from the moon-charged bottle, her energy was refreshed, and so was the color in her cheeks.

They loved her so much and so hard. It was a want that became a habit, that became a life and an instinct: for Luna to be happy. That was all that truly mattered. It was why, when he discovered that Meihua was otherwise occupied, he did every-thing possible to hide the fact from Luna. It was why he sent that application to Stanford, so convinced that if she were admit-ted, it would guarantee a baseline of happiness. If she had been rejected, at least then he would've bought himself some time to find another solution.

She would succeed in life; he would make sure of it. She would have the best career, and money and stability. She would not have to suffer as he and Meihua had suffered, immigrants who had had to learn to fly in a place where everyone else seemed determined that they should have no wings.

Yes, Hsueh-Ting had done his absolute best for Luna. And once the acceptance from Stanford had come in, he'd begun day-dreaming about a new life. If Meihua wanted to be free of him, well, that could be easily arranged. Luna would graduate, and he would move to California to be near her. Perhaps he could even teach in Palo Alto—there were plenty of schools in the area. He was willing to start over, to begin from scratch and work toward tenure again.

That December day when he took them out to Giuseppe's, he'd been bursting to share the news. It had taken every ounce of energy to sit on it, to remember that it was supposed to be a surprise. He would tell Luna—when? In March? He would figure out the best time later. He couldn't very well tell her right then, while she was still working on her applications. She wouldn't believe him. Or she would think he'd lost his mind.

There in Giuseppe's he'd watched his sharp, beautiful daughter sipping at her minestrone, utterly unaware of how amazing she was. He swelled with pride to think of her so young, so full of potential. A rising college student who would soon call Stanford her home.

Even now, even with her rage, her inability to understand, Hsueh-Ting still felt the same. He loved her the way one loved a goddess; he was honored to worship at her feet. The feeling was at once intoxicating and heavy, a weight that perched on his shoulders. He would gladly bear it for all his days.

Hunter Yee

Something was wrong. Luna's eyes were bloodshot when she picked him up for school.

He reached over the center console, and she let herself be pulled into him. They listened to the *click-click, click-click* of the blinker.

"What's wrong?" he said into her hair. "Do you want to talk about it?"

A shudder went through her body. He was pretty sure she was trying not to cry.

She shook her head.

"Okay," he said.

Luna sucked in a thick breath. "We gotta go. Someone's going to see us."

He craned his head around to check out the window. They'd taken the precaution of meeting two blocks away from his bus stop, but she was right. They were exposed here on this shoulder, and he wasn't sure when his father would be driving out.

He sat back and buckled his seat belt. "Are you okay to drive?"

"I'm fine."

She was quiet all day, and he spent each class period trying to think of what might cheer her up, or at least offer a distraction.

When the school day finally ended and they were walking toward the parking lot, he had an idea. "What if we go to my house?"

That got her attention. "Right now?"

Hunter nodded. "Nobody will be there for a few hours. Cody has an after-school program, and I just remembered that my parents are both at my dad's office today."

She threaded her fingers through his and said, "Okay."

She parked the car at her house; it was less suspicious that way. It wasn't that cold, but as they cut through the trees, Hunter curled his fingers around hers and tucked her hand into his pocket. She was close enough for him to smell her shampoo.

As the back of the townhouse came into view, his embarrassment set in. His family's home was a third the size of Luna's. She was going to see the cluttered living room, the kitchen with all its stains. He unlocked the door and realized his heart was pounding.

"Sorry it's so . . ." He waved his hand around at the general state of the place.

"It's where you live," she said, as if that simple fact swept everything else aside.

He led her to his room, relieved that he and Cody had tidied it up the other day. Luna wanted to go into the blanket fort, so they crawled in on their bellies, headfirst, smiling at how cramped it was. Luna tapped Hunter's foot with hers, starting up their silly game. They laughed, and they kissed, and then Luna's fingers were working at the button of his jeans, and his hands were sliding under her sweatshirt.

He was ravenous. This time he had a condom ready.

"Wait," she said, once he'd gotten it on. "Is this the correct angle? Should I...reposition?"

He grinned into her hair. "You make it sound like trigonometry. The *correct angle* is whatever makes you feel good."

"Stop laughing at me," she said, smiling.

"We can find you a textbook on it if you want."

He tried to memorize the music of her bubbling laughter.

This time they were slow and tender. They experimented with lips traversing skin, their touches drawing little violet petals. He drank in that honey-sweet smell. This was the safest place he'd ever been.

His favorite part was afterward, when they curled together like two perfect seashells, when he could press his nose into the back of her neck and be tickled by her hair as he inhaled.

The window was beginning to darken. In another hour his parents would come home. Hunter wished he had a way of stopping time, stretching this moment out into an eternity.

Luna stiffened. "What was that sound?"

He froze, straining to hear.

There was a rustle and a light thump—at first he thought it was the wind. Then he laughed in relief. "It's my brother's pet rabbit." He pointed to the cage, where Jadey was grooming herself. "She must have just woken up."

"That startled me," said Luna. "It's so quiet in here. In the whole house, I mean."

Hunter was sleepy and sated. "It's a house full of secrets."

She propped her head up on her palm. "They're not so secret if you know about them."

"I know *of* them." He couldn't help the bitterness in his voice. "It doesn't mean I have any answers. I'd have to go digging to find those."

"So what's stopping you?"

"My parents are always around." Hunter shrugged. "There's no good time to do it." He thought of his father spitting the accusation at him, *I know* you *stole from me.*

"What about right now?" She sat up and dragged her fingers through her hair, retying her ponytail.

A part of him had always been afraid to look. He knew that there must be things to be found in the walk-in closet of his parents' bedroom. He'd listened to their whispers for so many years.

She pulled him to his feet.

"Okay," he said.

There was more junk crammed into that space than he would ever have guessed. Piles upon piles, boxes tucked behind other boxes and drawers packed with trinkets. The closet was a time capsule of the eight years the Yees had spent here, shrinking themselves down as small as they could.

There was no clear system of organization. They found paperwork, some of it in English, some in Chinese. His parents' diplomas. Photographs, which Luna paused to look at while Hunter moved on.

There were tiny bottles of powders and pastes, one of which he recognized as the tinted vial of Yunnan baiyao gao that his mother had once applied to an infected scrape on his knee. There was stuff she had purchased at garage sales for a quarter, or fifty or seventy-five cents. She never spent more than that. Costume jewelry, fake pearls, a hatpin.

What were they even looking for? Hunter was about to call it quits when Luna stood on her toes to get at a shoebox deep in the back. The box slid farther out of reach, but a yellowed piece of parchment came fluttering down.

"Hunter..." she began to say.

It smelled old and dusty, like it had been pulled right out of the earth. It made him want to sneeze. In clear, handwritten letters, the scrap said:

UNIDENTIFIED, UNABLE TO BE DATED,
FOUND AMONG ITEMS ESTIMATED 218 BCE

There were creases where the paper must have once been wrapped around a geometrical object.

"I know what this is," said Luna, tracing the folds. They drew the imprint of a hexagon.

He heard the familiar sound of a car engine cutting out. In a matter of minutes, his parents would be unlocking the front door. "You have to leave through my window."

She held the paper out to him, her eyes wide and her skin ghostlike.

"Take it with you," he told her.

"Are you sure?"

"Come on, hurry!" He yanked the closet door shut.

Luna folded the paper and jammed it into her pocket, and they rushed back to his room. He heard the key turning in the doorknob.

"See you tomorrow," he whispered as she swung one leg over the ledge and hopped the rest of the way down.

She gave him the thumbs-up, and he passed her backpack through. Then she was running into the dimness, and he was closing the window.

By the time his mother opened his door and Cody shuffled in, Hunter was at his desk, pretending to be immersed in homework, grateful that nobody could see how fast his blood was racing.

Rodney Wong

Wong stood in the trees behind 7 Belladonna Court and watched Luna Chang drop down out of the window. The sun was gone and so the only source of light was a small desk lamp in the room from which she'd emerged, but Wong had excellent vision, thanks to his good genes. No one in his family had needed glasses until very late in life.

So it was rather curious that he saw her backpack slide through the opening of its own accord. He saw the window slamming shut as she sprinted off, heard its latch clicking into place, but there were no hands to be seen. There was a blur of movement; that was all.

Strange indeed.

By now Wong had managed to catch glimpses: Li Yubing during her solitary nighttime strolls. Yi Dawei as he entered and left the university that employed him under this fake name, that probably had been served fake documents of identification. And their youngest, little Cody Yee, who was rather pathetic from what Wong had observed.

But there'd been no sign of the eldest son. Not on the campus of Fairbridge High School. Not at home. Not anywhere.

Where in the world was Hunter Yee? How was he managing to keep himself hidden?

Meihua Chang

Luna's mother

Meihua put the kettle on to boil and sat down at the kitchen counter with a sigh. It was difficult to be hated by one's child.

She heard Luna up in her room, slamming drawers, throwing textbooks. Heard Luna storm down one flight of stairs and then another, into the basement. Meihua had never loudly exhibited such anger in her teenage years. Like other parents of that generation, hers would have beaten her for it. No, she'd learned to swallow such feelings, let them travel down to the gut and be passed out of the body like food.

But she remembered what it was like to be that age. Of course she did. She'd felt everything with such sharpness. Such weight. The fear when her grandfather fell ill. The grief when the neighbor's youngest child drowned in a rain-swollen stream.

And the love—her first romance. It had sent her heart flying. How would she even try to explain to Luna? Would she start at the beginning? How a boy in her year at the university had started walking with her after their shared English class?

He would often bring her wildflowers, or the most perfect guava. His name was Lin Guangming. She marveled at how perfectly his name matched him. *Guangming*. Shining bright.

Her English was much better than his, and so they began to study together. Soon they were finishing each other's sentences. Guangming understood what she wanted and needed before she could even think to give voice to it. One day he opened his palm in a question, and she let him take her hand. That became their new habit, and at night she would think about their interwoven fingers, the brush of his thumb beneath hers.

He left abruptly. The rumors would fly afterward, but nobody knew for sure why it was that Lin Guangming had packed up his things and vanished in the night. Some said he suffered from secret health problems; others said his family's fortune was swallowed in one vicious gulp by unforeseen events.

All Meihua knew was that one day he'd been there, squeezing her fingers, and the next day he had been replaced by wind. She waited for him to return, for him to appear around the corner. She checked her mailbox obsessively for a letter, a token, anything at all. How could he disappear without a final word?

A year passed, then two, and then Meihua was preparing to finish her undergraduate degree. She'd thrown herself into studying, but it was exhausting and joyless. When there was no exam to cram for, she let herself sleep for long, endless hours.

Meihua's parents had been paired up through a matchmaker,

and their marriage worked like a perfectly oiled machine. They were partners; they supported each other. More like best friends than lovers. That was ideal. Meihua told herself to forget Guangming and that fleeting passion. Her parents had always emphasized that a good match should offer stability.

They wanted her to meet with the same matchmaker who had brought them together—the woman was old and bent over and walked with a cane, and she was still working. It was there in that auntie's house, drinking her best tea, that Meihua met Chang Hsueh-Ting for the first time. He was sweet and funny and attractive. He had integrity and felt like someone she could trust.

They met several more times, their conversation always spinning into philosophical debates. It soothed some of the hurt of Lin Guangming leaving. There wasn't that same spark for her—but Meihua realized that Hsueh-Ting had quickly come to adore her. He was thoughtful, considerate beyond anyone else she knew. He remembered every detail she shared. This, she decided, was a man she could grow old with.

Chang Hsueh-Ting wanted to marry her. He consulted with Meihua's parents, and then she said yes. Not long after that they moved to the States, and not long after *that* Meihua discovered she was pregnant. Here was a life, she thought. The kind of future she'd always wanted.

Over the years she would occasionally think of Lin Guangming with the glimmer of nostalgia. That was an interesting time, she would tell herself. Ah, to be young.

Two decades after that heartbreak, the last thing she'd expected was to hear a knock and find Lin Guangming standing on her doorstep, looking just the same as she remembered, though somehow handsomer. She'd invited him in for tea.

He had found her because of a Mother's Day article in the Chinese American newspaper, which had included a photograph of her with her daughter.

They spoke for hours, retracing all the years since they'd last seen each other. He explained that there'd been a disagreement in his family; they'd forced him to go south to take up his grandfather's business. He regretted never having the chance to say goodbye to Meihua. He'd never married.

That day was transformative. Guangming left before Luna was done with school, before Hsueh-Ting came home. Meihua meant to tell them about him at dinner—but then it felt almost too precious to be shared. She wanted to keep it to herself just a little longer. A secret, like a prized jewel. And so she kept it… and kept it some more. Guangming was in New York City for an extended period of work; the thought of his proximity made her restless. He'd left behind a slip of paper bearing a number. A few weeks later, she picked up the phone and shyly dialed it.

He took the train and a car and came to visit again. It became a regular occurrence, and they struck up their same old friendship. One day, as she pulled a tin of tea leaves from the cabinet, he kissed her.

That had been nearly two years ago. Every single day since, Meihua had been racked with overwhelming guilt. She still loved Hsueh-Ting—truly, she did. It was just a different sort of affection. But if she was being perfectly honest with herself, she'd never stopped loving Guangming. All these years he'd waited to find her. Why had she not done the same?

She felt herself fracturing in every direction. She should stop seeing Lin Guangming. She should bid him goodbye and turn him away.

And yet, she couldn't.

Luna Chang

The world was gauzy with light. It turned everything silver. She could feel it on her skin, in her hair. This was a dream,
but also not. This was real.

Her feet carried her through the house and she felt nothing
in her muscles, none of the impact of feet against floor.

No longer floor but grass. Dirt. Nothingness. She went gliding over clouds and between stars. Was she headed for the creek?

The moment she had the thought, she was there, standing
in the woods, at the edge of that place where she could feel the
wrongness vibrating from the crack. The rushing water obscured
it from view, but it tugged at her. She was a marionette and that
thing beneath the water held the strings. They were knotted
around her heart, across her throat.

Luna dug her heels into the mud, clung tightly to the side of a
tree. She would not let herself be yanked down into those depths.

As she looked on, she noticed how the world around her was

changing. The wind was ice and it tore at everything. There were those white flowers, doubling and tripling in number, snaking upward. Peaches began to fall, *thud, thud*, some rolling toward the water and others smashing open.

Trees bent, branches snapped and fell, roots ripped free of the ground. It was still night but the sky was brown, the moon was nowhere to be seen, and the earth beneath her issued a toxic glow. Everything was wrong. The smell of the flowers was masked by other scents now ... the oily sweetness of rot, and something coppery and sharp.

Everything wrong, wrong, wrong.

The water dried up and there was that gaping crack. It stretched as far as she could see. Pale and wispy figures made of smoke were climbing up and out of it, their fingers long and greedy. They grabbed at everything. The roots, the blooms. And coins that had fallen in the grass. So many coins, gleaming like ancient treasure.

Everything those hands touched turned to ash and reeked of sulfur. Two of the figures stood up and Luna saw that they were her parents. They were destroying everything.

Make it stop, she thought, squeezing her eyes shut. *Fix it.*

Now she stood in a field. The stink was gone, and so was the crack in the ground. The air smelled of fresh grass and overturned earth. All around her were the shadows of men digging and scraping. The ground opened like a gift being unwrapped. Out came shards of clay; broken pieces were gathered up by stained hands.

The moment slowed and Luna noticed a silvery light. Just a seed at first, turning in the dirt like a cocoon beginning to wake. She held her breath as it emerged.

The glowing speck was expanding, rising. It rocketed into the sky, and there it bloomed. A brightly burning star. Luna could see so clearly: the arms and legs unfurling, hair tumbling free, mouth opening to gasp for air.

It was a girl. She arced through the universe.

The image should have been surprising. But as Luna gazed on, she felt only a sense of the vision being *right*.

Luna woke in her bed, shivering on top of the twisted lump of blankets. A sliver of morning sun showed her feet to be a collection of tiny cuts and scrapes, and caked with dirt. In her palm: the white hexagon. She had no memory of picking up the stone. It left a delectable smell on her skin.

She'd nearly forgotten about that piece of paper from Hunter's house. Her jeans were in the laundry basket, and that old parchment still in the pocket, warped and wrinkled. Pulse hammering, she unfolded it. The stone and all its faceted edges lined up perfectly against the yellowed creases.

218 BCE. It was hard to hold the span of time in her head, to fully grasp the age of this hexagonal thing.

Tearing through her drawers, Luna found a red pouch embroidered with gold thread. It had once housed a gift of beads from her grandparents when she visited them in Taiwan. The mala lived in her jewelry box now, and its empty pouch was the perfect size. She slid the stone and the paper in and pulled the drawstring shut.

Luna stuck the pouch into the bottom tier of a pencil box, just in case.

She didn't trust anyone anymore.

Hunter Yee

The stone, *Hunter's* parents hissed at each other on the other side of the wall. This was an obsession. He had figured out a long time ago that it was an object they kept hidden in their home, though he had no idea why. He'd tried to find it a couple times, to no avail.

Their voices rose and fell. It sounded like they were flinging around blame, or scheming, or complaining about their eldest. Maybe all of the above. Through the thin curtains he could see the pale moon grazing the tops of the trees.

At last there was silence. Hunter pushed aside his quilt—slowly, so as not to wake his little brother—and crept into their closet. He reached into the very back, in the dark corner beneath all the jackets and coats dangling from hangers. The duffel bag was old and worn, and when unzipped, it looked to be full of junk. Broken pens and old homework assignments, half-used school supplies, a tool kit missing a screwdriver. But all those sat on top of a bundle he'd wrapped in a T-shirt and placed at the bottom, hiding the important contents. His hopes, and his future. His escape.

Thick stacks of dollar bills that he kept carefully sorted and rubber-banded together. Most of them were smaller denominations. And underneath those a heavy collection of coins, stored in a plastic package that had once contained Halloween candy.

Here was all the money he'd ever been lucky enough to find on the ground, swept his way by that tricky wind. He thought of Luna's wide-eyed concern. *Aren't you worried?*

The way he saw it, bad luck had already latched on to him. It had taken up residence years ago in this tiny little townhouse. Hunter knew bad luck well, and it didn't scare him anymore.

The money took him a long time to count.

Twenty-nine thousand eighty-three dollars.

He'd always known that one day he would run away from home. These were the funds on which he'd planned to survive, until he got himself a job, until he built his own stability. He would change his name so that he could be his own person, free of the net his parents had knotted around all of them.

But what had always stopped him from leaving was Cody. His darling little brother, who was so determined to never be angry. If Hunter left, would Cody ever forgive him?

Would his parents be happier without him? Their disappointment had dug such a deep groove. He wasn't sure they could repair it even if they tried.

Hunter had realized in the last few months: Their feelings

about him were a familiar habit. They reached for it the way a smoker lit a cigarette for comfort.

He separated out the eighty-three dollars. He would use it to take Luna out to dinner on a *real* date. They would go somewhere and eat delicious things. They would pretend, for an evening, like they were two carefree people whose lives were not crumbling.

That left $29,000.

Hunter had spent years listening through the vents to his parents making their calculations, trimming costs every way they could. An additional $29,000 would be a balm. It wouldn't cover all the debt, but it would put them *significantly* closer to the finish line.

He returned the bag to the shadowed corner of the closet and clicked the flashlight off, waiting for his eyes to adjust to the darkness.

If he were a good son, he would give that money to his parents. He would do what he could to free them of their debt.

But had they been good parents? Did they deserve a good son?

Even after he returned to his bed and pulled the quilt up to his chin, he still couldn't sleep.

Hunter lay awake until dawn.

Luna Chang

The moment Hunter buckled his seat belt, Luna peeled away from the curb.

"In a rush?" he said.

"I need to talk to you." She turned off the main road and brought them to the edge of the woods. Next to the split tree, she put the car in park. "I had a dream. But...that makes it sound silly. It was much more than that."

"Okay?" said Hunter.

She described it to him, her fingers rubbing at an obstinate smudge on the steering wheel. It was still there when she finished. She dug through her backpack for her pencil case, then passed the red pouch to him, watching as he unfolded the parchment, as he weighed the stone in his palm.

Luna was unprepared for the way her pulse surged, seeing the hexagon in someone else's possession. The impulse to snatch it back. That strange hunger that had gnawed at her for months.

She had to remind herself that it was only Hunter.

"So this is what my parents lost," he said very quietly. "I've heard them whispering about it."

For a moment she worried that he wasn't going to give it back. But then he put everything as he'd found it and returned the pouch to her.

As soon as she held it again, her body uncoiled. It was ridiculous to have worried.

"Somehow my dad was the one who had it. Do you know what it does?"

Hunter shook his head. "It was supposed to be protecting us, somehow. Helping to keep us hidden."

"Everything feels wrong," said Luna, pressing her palms against her temples. "Everything *is* wrong."

Hunter sighed. "Yeah."

"What if we left this place?" said Luna. "You said you used to imagine yourself running away. What if we left together?"

It was an age before he answered. "I wish we could. But I think we have to do something. We have to stay here and figure it out." Hunter tipped back against the headrest and closed his eyes.

"Tell me what you're thinking about?" Luna said, her voice soft.

He smiled sadly. "You know, I just would really love to be a normal teenage guy for one day. *One day*. Is that so much to ask?"

"Describe *normal* to me," she said.

"Normal, like, I get to stress about bombing a math test. Or how to surprise you for your birthday—*our* birthday. Or, I don't know. How to ask you to be my date to prom."

Luna tipped her head back. "You never struck me as the kind of guy who would want to go to prom."

"To be honest, I had zero interest until now. Until we had this." He gestured between the two of them.

She took his hand.

He squeezed back. "Can we just have one night? I want to take you out on a real date. And I want to pay for it. Please?"

"We've talked about this," she said. "I don't want you to pay for things for me. We can split it."

"Listen, I've saved up the money. Just let me do it this once. You can get it the next time. Plus, it evens out because we need your car. You'll be the one driving. You can pay for gas."

He looked so earnest and so desperate—there was a fire in his eyes, and she realized what he meant. It wasn't about formalities or anything like that.

It was about seizing control of their own lives.

So she agreed. One night as normal, lovestruck teenagers.

Then they would figure out what needed to be done.

Cody Yee

Inside his blanket fort, the world was smaller and quieter. Safer. Cody curled up with Jadey snuggled in the crook of his elbow. He ran his index finger over the spot between her ears and down her back, watched that twitching nose. He had once heard people on TV talk about meditating; he wasn't sure what exactly meditation was, but he closed his eyes and pretended that petting Jadey was one way of doing it.

Things were changing somehow. He could feel it in the air. He could sense it in Hunter's behavior, in the set of his father's shoulders.

Cody wished someone would explain what was happening and what they were all supposed to do.

He opened his eyes and Jadey had her gaze fixed on him, staring intently, as though she agreed.

"Sometimes I think you're the only one who understands me," Cody said, and she touched her nose to his. "If only you knew how to talk."

Jadey hopped around his head, her little feet kicking up

against his hair and making him giggle. There was a soft thump. She'd knocked over the book.

"What? You want to see what's in it today?"

Cody slid the book around and Jadey eagerly followed. When he thumbed it open to a blank page, she set her front feet on the corner. These were the words that appeared:

This is my book.

He stared at it.

"*Your* book," he said, dropping his voice to a whisper, for he didn't want to be overheard. This felt more secret than ever. "Who is . . . who are *you?*"

More words shaped themselves out of nothing:

I am the keeper of these stories. They are the records of the universe and its past. They are the truth of what is to come. You gave me a name: Jadey.

Cody blinked at the rabbit. "Jadey?" He looked down at the page again.

Didn't you know? You chose me, after all.

The words from before cleared themselves away, and new ones were forming.

You were meant to find me. You were meant to find this book.

David Yee

Hunter's father

David regretted taking that box. All for the sake of some stupid herbs he'd believed to be a panacea. And what happened? Nothing. Hunter's sickness remained. They'd watched him closely for a year, thinking perhaps the panacea needed time to work. Eventually, they'd realized what fools they were.

Now they were living this life of debt and hiding, and for what? A scam.

In his anger and shame he'd flung the box to the ground. It was a miracle it didn't break. But then something else came rolling free. A hexagonal white stone wrapped in paper. He'd nearly forgotten there was a second artifact in there.

It made him think of an object he'd once read about. A round disc made of some pale stone, with three characters in the center—遁地符—surrounded by a hexagonal design.

A disc to keep its owner safe and hidden. The idea was absurd, and yet. David wondered. Could this hexagonal thing serve some similar purpose? What was the harm in keeping it around, just in case?

So the theft continued to haunt him.

On some days, he thought he should take the stone into the lab, get some fresh eyes on it, let it be shared with fellow researchers. Other days, he thought about dropping it into the ocean.

Some fear or instinct—or both—always stayed his hand.

Was it too good to be true, that all this time had passed and Huang had not found them? This man with connections in every corner of the world, who had eyes everywhere? Perhaps the white stone was doing its job.

Or perhaps it was a coincidence. Nothing more.

In those early days, when it had first come into his possession, the mere sight of it had been a balm on his nerves. It was, after all, a beautiful ancient object. He couldn't exactly mark when he began to believe in it.

David told himself there were other reasons that he kept the thing around. What if it came in useful one day? What if he sold it? The artifact could potentially fetch enough money to pay off his family's debts.

(But that made him nervous. If he *did* sell it, whatever money he received would be dirty, cursed. He'd be no better than Huang Rongfu.)

He told himself he would think on it some more. He would come up with the best course of action. In the meantime, he planned to study the piece. To photograph and examine it. Who knew what more there was to be discovered?

At last, months after he moved it to the trunk of the car, he realized he'd committed himself to guarding it—and, in turn, would be guarded.

Except now that the stone had vanished, they'd lost its protection.

All sense of safety and security was gone. Not only because of the external factors. A few days ago, he'd returned home to discover the light in the closet left on. His wife would never have done such a thing, which meant it had been one of his sons. How could there even be any question?

The more he considered it, the more certain he was: Hunter must have gone digging in the trunk. Hunter must have taken the stone. Was there any chance he still had it?

The rage burned behind his eyes. He began to watch his eldest son more closely. And he noticed that Hunter was secretive. Sneaky. How sometimes, when David pretended to be asleep, his son crept out of bed and into the woods.

It became a matter of duty: David decided to start following Hunter, to see the places he went and the things he did.

Hunter Yee

Hunter would get in trouble later for sneaking out, but what were his parents going to do? Disown him?

His mother was running an errand, his father in the bedroom grading papers. Cody was in the blanket fort, probably reading whatever secret book he had.

Hunter walked right out through the front door, straightening his jacket, smoothing his hair. The wind whipped at him and he breathed in its sharpness. *Let it come*, he thought. *Let it be wild.* Tonight he would not be ruled by fear.

It didn't take long to get to Luna's house, and she emerged wearing his favorite parka of hers. Her hair was free of its ponytail for once, streaming down her shoulders, full of moonlight. He wanted to run his fingers through it. He wanted to feel it against his skin.

Luna tossed him the car keys; he'd asked to drive so it could feel like an actual surprise. When he leaned in for a kiss, she pressed her fingers to his mouth.

"Let's get out of here first," she said, giggling. "So that we're not seen."

"Okay, okay." He tried not to show how nervous he was behind the wheel.

In the parking lot they held hands and walked toward the cheery lights that decorated the entrance. The sign said GIUSEPPE'S in glowing red cursive. A firefly winked nearby.

"This is where I always go with my parents." Her voice was quiet.

"Oh." Hunter stopped. "I had no idea. I just picked it because—do you want to go somewhere else?"

Luna pulled him closer and shook her head, smiling. "No. It's okay. I still like it here. It's one of my happy places."

Their waiter seated them at a table in the back corner, for which Hunter was grateful. It was more private there. They ordered gnocchi and one of the specials of the day.

"Would you like the bottomless soup?" the waiter asked. "The minestrone is our most popular."

Luna shook her head before Hunter could answer. "No, thanks."

"Well, let's get some other appetizer, then," he suggested. "How about the fried zucchini?"

"Sure. I've never tried it."

"Fried zucchini it is," said the waiter, whisking away their menus. He returned in the next blink with a basket of warm bread.

When Hunter looked back at her, Luna was chewing on the skin around her thumb. She seemed anxious.

"What are you thinking about?" he asked.

She set her hand down. "That stone, actually."

"Yeah? What about it?"

"It's got to be valuable. It's labeled as an artifact."

A new thought struck him. Was there more to his parents' debt than he realized? Was it also about that hexagonal rock?

"Hunter," Luna was saying. "You could sell it. It might give you enough money. Then your family would be free. Right?"

Her face was so earnest, so sweet. When she shined her light on him, he felt safe and protected. He felt loved. "Maybe."

"Also," Luna said haltingly, "I think the stone gives me those dreams. I had another one."

The words made him tense. He sipped at his water and crunched a piece of ice between his teeth until his gums ached.

She continued. "Remember that night we met? That whole Seven Minutes in Heaven thing? In my dream, I saw these silhouettes that I'm pretty sure were us. And when the silhouettes touched—that was when this huge beam of light exploded. That was what caused the cracks."

"A beam of light from where?" said Hunter. "Like a thunderstorm?"

"No," said Luna. "It came from us."

His head spun, and he thought he heard a rustle of wind.

"It means something," she said.

Hunter reached for her fingers and sandwiched them between his. "I don't want to think about that stuff right now. I just want this to be a regular date." He curled her knuckles and brought them to his lips.

Luna Chang

It was different sitting in Giuseppe's with Hunter instead of her parents. She'd had a flutter of panic at first and debated hiding it from him. But they promised each other to be honest, and as soon as she told him that this was where her parents always took her, weight lifted from her shoulders.

That was the beautiful thing about being with Hunter. Luna lived her life like a tightly wound coil, and he was the one who helped her to release and be fully herself.

They used the pointiest pieces of bread to draw shapes in the oil and vinegar. They shared bites of the gnocchi, so soft it melted on their tongues. They took forkfuls of spaghetti into their mouths at the same time, to see if they might end up serendipitously connected by one long noodle, like in an old animated film about two dogs falling in love.

"I thought we were supposed to be *un*-Disney," said Luna.

"Shhhh," said Hunter. "Don't ruin it."

As they ordered tiramisu and cheesecake, Luna heard the laugh. The low-in-the-belly, head-thrown-back laugh. She knew it well.

"What are you doing?" Hunter said.

She was already on her feet, turning to look.

There on the other side of the room was her father. The candle on his table danced. Across from him was a woman with light hair—a woman who was obviously not her mother.

Her father was on a date. He was supposed to be at the university tonight. What was he thinking?

"Luna," Hunter was saying, but she was already halfway to her dad.

There was a bottle of wine on the table. Luna could not remember the last time she saw her father drink.

"Eat all the minestrone you want," he said to the woman, smiling.

The words were a knife.

She reached her dad, and time slowed. He saw her and his face twisted with surprise. Luna's fury had seized control of her body. He spoke to her but she didn't hear it; in her head there was only a roaring static. Her limbs were heavy and carbonated.

The pace of time changed, and she wasn't sure if it was faster or slower.

Her fingers wrapped around a glass, and she was flinging the wine at her father. The woman gasped, and Luna realized she was just a fellow professor, one of her dad's colleagues.

Another glance, and Luna saw that the table was in fact set for three people. It was a work event.

Then Hunter was at her elbow, and there was the look of recognition on her father's face—

"What's this?" said a familiar voice. When she looked up, there was Rodney Wong arriving at the table, setting his hand on the third chair. She should have noticed the fine long coat that was draped on the back of it.

Hunter let out a sharp gasp and Luna thought she heard him whisper, "*Huang.*" Something lurched in her chest.

"Well," said Wong. "The young Mr. Yee." He smiled with all his teeth and lunged at Hunter.

Except he missed, or something got in his way and made him trip. It was hard to tell what happened. The next moment, he was on the floor, nose bleeding.

Luna was caught in a fog, still trying to process. Hunter pulled her out the door and to the car, digging into her coat pocket for the keys.

He sped out of the parking lot, and everything in her vision went blurry with tears.

Hunter Yee

Hunter stopped Luna's car at the corner that was his bus stop. She climbed out of the passenger side and there in the middle of the road he gathered her into his arms, thumbing away the tears on her face.

"We'll figure out what to do," he said.

Luna nodded and put herself in the driver's seat.

He turned to walk the rest of the way, their usual strategy so nobody would see who had dropped him off. But he'd only taken a few steps when a different car screeched to a stop beside him, and the window rolled down.

"Get in." His father's voice rang like a blade against a sharpening block.

Hunter obeyed.

There was only silence for the couple of minutes it took to arrive home and pull into their parking spot. The door of the house flung open.

"Where were you two?" his mother said tensely. She was

little more than a shadow in the dark entryway. "Do you know how worried I've been?"

Inside, his father locked the door and checked all the windows. It was in the kitchen that he seized Hunter by the arm.

"How *dare you?*" his father said.

Hunter tried to pull back but the fingers were claws.

The rage in his dad's expression. The disgust. "You will never speak to Luna Chang again, or you will regret what happens."

His mother gasped. "Luna Chang?"

"It's worse than that, Yubing. Huang Rongfu was there. He recognized Hunter."

She swayed on her feet, and for the first time in years, Hunter felt truly guilty.

"Dad," he said. "I have a question."

His dad stared at him. "What?"

"If we had the money..." He thought of his duffel bag, his stacks of bills. "Would all our problems really be fixed? Like *actually?*"

His father backhanded Hunter in the shoulder. "How dare you speak to me with this attitude?"

The look on his face. Like Hunter was a pile of dog shit.

Then his father was charging down the hallway, bursting into the bedroom the brothers shared.

"What's going on?" said Cody from the blanket fort.

Their father did not respond; he was busy yanking on drawers, tearing into any pocket or bag or compartment. He banged open the closet door and Hunter froze. His dad found the duffel tucked deep into the corner and tore at the zipper. Junk spilled out; he made a noise of disgust before kicking the bag aside.

He grabbed Hunter by the shoulders. "Where is it?"

"Where's what?" said Hunter. By now the words had grown robotic. He was exhausted. Nothing he said or did would ever be enough.

"The *stone*. I know you stole it," his dad snarled.

Hunter thought of the white hexagon Luna had shown him, the weight of it in his hands. "I don't have a stone."

His father took a step forward, fists clenched. He might have thrown a punch if not for Cody calling out, *"Dad."*

That one syllable ended the spell.

"Pack everything essential," their father said. "We leave tonight. Our lives depend on it."

Luna Chang

"*Is this true?*" her mother demanded.

Her father had rushed home from Giuseppe's and reported the events to his wife. Of all that had happened—throwing wine, humiliating him, lying about where she had been—it was apparently the worst crime to have been associating with Hunter Yee.

Her parents stood side by side, looking at her as if she'd murdered someone. How ironic that this was the thing to unite them again.

"So what?" Luna said. "Are *you two* going to lecture me on what I've done wrong? Please, go on. I have *so much* to learn from you."

"Watch your mouth," her father said, his voice all ice.

Her mother was shaking her head. "When did you learn to tell so many lies?"

"Hunter's my boyfriend." She'd never said the word out loud before, and the shape of it felt odd. He was so much more than that. He was a home and a haven. "Is that what you want to hear? That's the truth. He's the best person in my life right now."

Her mom looked sick. "Stay away from that family, or you will be sorry."

Luna couldn't decide if she wanted to laugh or throw up. What could her parents do that would be any worse than the things they'd already done?

"You'll *never* speak to Hunter Yee again," said her father.

She raised her eyebrows. As if her parents could control her every waking moment.

"I'm going to file for a restraining order," he continued. "We'll make it illegal for there to be any other interactions."

Luna felt like she was swallowing a rock. "You can't do that."

"You think so? I've been gathering evidence against that family for the last several months. A little side project."

Never before had her father's laughter sounded cruel.

"That's an empty threat," she said, though she had no way of telling whether it was. Her throat was dry.

He continued on as if she hadn't spoken: "When you graduate, we'll move to Palo Alto. We'll sell this house. You'll never come back here, and you will forget he ever existed."

Sometime after four in the morning, Luna crept out the front door. It was too cold to walk through the trees; she drove instead, parked the car a block away from the entrance to Belladonna Court.

The Yees' house was completely dark. She went around the back, to the window she'd leapt out of just the other day.

Luna tapped a finger against the glass. When that did nothing, she rapped with her knuckles, then pounded with her fists. By the time she was calling Hunter's name, she'd already figured it out. Nobody would answer her, because nobody was there.

Where could they have gone?

Cody Yee

The book had warned him to be prepared. Or rather, *Jadey*, with her impossible words, had warned him.

He wasn't prepared. There were a million other words that more accurately described how he was feeling: angry, scared, disbelieving, tired, sad.

Also, he was way too hot. His mother had forced him to layer up in order to save space in the suitcases, so here he was, a marshmallow in the back of the car.

Jadey wriggled in his sweatshirt pocket. He'd hidden a piece of carrot in there and she must have found it. He could feel her nibbling. At least *someone* was happy.

It was the middle of the night. Not a single lit window in any of the houses they passed.

"Where are we going?" he'd asked. Nobody had answered.

His father pulled the car into the first gas station they saw.

"I need to use the bathroom," Hunter announced, flinging

his door open before anybody could respond. He disappeared into the shadows beyond the lamplight.

Cody heard his mother make a noise of frustration. She clutched a strand of little wooden spheres, her thumb pushing down bead after bead. Cody could hear them making contact, *clack, clack, clack,* like they were telling time.

He thought he saw a lightning bug near his dad's headrest, but that didn't make any sense. Did lightning bugs come out in the winter? Then his attention turned elsewhere, because Hunter had left a folded piece of paper in the back seat. It said FOR CODY in thick marker.

He opened it. His brother's red bracelet, neatly snipped, fell out from between the creases. The sight of it made him shiver with fear. Why had Hunter taken this off? He was supposed to wear it forever. The feeling of wrongness screamed in Cody's ears. And scrawled on the paper:

> Cody—
> I'm sorry I couldn't stay, and that I couldn't take
> you with me. One day we'll meet again.
> I love you.
> —Hunter

He looked out the window, craning his neck. His brother was nowhere to be seen.

He thought of Hunter telling him to be brave. To take a deep breath if he was feeling nervous. He remembered Hunter explaining the word *impulsive.*

"I have to go to the bathroom, too." Cody opened his own door.

"I'll take you," said his mother, reaching to unbuckle her seat belt.

"No, it's okay. I can see Hunter right over there." He hopped out, and then he ran.

Hunter Yee

The air was ice in his throat, each breath stabbing the shards deeper. Hunter was wearing so many layers, it should have been more than enough to keep him warm. Clearly the wind wanted him to suffer.

He knew how to get back, but the night sky pressed close and his teeth chattered, and that made the journey feel so much longer. When his inhales turned to gasps, he slowed to a walk. He would get there. He would. One step at a time. He tightened the straps of his backpack to trap in a bit more heat.

Hunter thought about the note he'd left for his parents in the trunk, tied around the careful stacks.

> Here's $28,000 I saved. Use it to pay off the debt.
> (No, I didn't steal it.)
> —Hunter

Would they even appreciate it? It was impossible to say.

Probably not. But at least he felt better knowing that they were that much closer to freedom.

And the note for Cody—the memory of it stung Hunter's eyes. He wouldn't think about that. Not now. Later, when it was safe to pause and grieve, he would let himself curl up in some dark hollow somewhere and weep. Later.

The sun was beginning to rise. Out of habit, he walked first to 7 Belladonna Court. Home. Against all his best efforts, that was what it was.

The front door was gaping open, hinges creaking slightly. All the lights in his house were on, and all the curtains pulled aside. The windows cast a warm yellow glow out into the world. He could see clearly into the living room.

A man walked in front of the television. Huang.

Hunter ducked. He should have noticed the unfamiliar sedan parked across two spaces. His parents had been right to leave.

Hunter crept around the side of the house, checking over his shoulder to be sure no one was following. He ran for the woods.

Rodney Wong

The Yees were gone; he could tell by the way it smelled. The eldest son must have warned them.

Wong stood in the house, marveling at how pathetic it truly was. All these years he'd imagined that Yi or at least his wife—she always had been the smarter one—would have had the sense to sell the artifacts, make a small fortune, move their family somewhere comfortable. They were more foolish than he'd believed possible.

Sitting down on the couch with a lit cigarette dripping from the corner of his mouth, Wong took out his planchette and pen. He leaned over the coffee table and closed his eyes, humming tunelessly.

The planchette drew a crude arrow, pointing toward the back of the house.

He followed it and chose a room at random. By the look of things, this was where the two brothers slept. What a disaster. Wong's father would have beaten him for leaving such a mess.

He stepped over a pile of clothing to throw the curtains aside.

There, darting into the trees, was Hunter Yee.

Luna Chang

There was a note under his window. If she'd been moving any faster she would have missed it. Pinned to the ground with a rock:

Meet me by the shed.

Luna needed to think. Hunter's family was gone. Her own family had carved out the shape of a life she didn't want, and now they were angry that she didn't fit.

She had a sudden memory of her father telling her about her great-grandmother's feet. How they'd been conical, like a cross between zongzi and the hooves of an animal. He'd described the process of it: Cutting the toenails as short as possible, soaking the feet in warm pig's blood and herbs to soften the tissue. Curling each toe—except for the big one—and pressing down until the knuckles had broken in enough places that they could be folded under. Bending the middle arches of both feet until those, too, snapped. Finally, the long bandages wrapping around and around so that the toes stayed folded underneath, pulling tighter on each loop, until the balls of the feet pressed against the heels.

"That's horrific," Luna had said.

"Yes," her father agreed. "Then your great-grandmother was made to walk around to flatten out the bones and ensure they healed that way."

Luna remembered cringing. "I don't understand why."

Her father's reply was so matter-of-fact. "At the time, that was believed to be the best thing to do. She dealt with the pain for the rest of her life."

Outside Hunter's window, grasping his note in her hand, Luna couldn't help but think that what her parents were doing to her now was also a kind of binding. She could choose to walk around with those bonds forever. Or she could break free of them.

Her choice was clear.

She made her way back to the car, back to her house. Nobody had noticed her sneaking out. As quietly as possible, Luna gathered up spare clothes and cans of food, cramming them into her backpack.

When she started high school, her father had given her the combination to unlock their safe. *Just in case*, he'd said. The envelope full of emergency cash was sitting right in front. She wrapped it in a coat and stuffed it into the very bottom of her bag.

At the front door, pulling her boots on, she hesitated for just a moment. There was a portrait of the three of them there, between the windows. Her father seated on a high-backed chair.

Her mother standing to his left. Luna to his right, squeezing a plush lion beneath her chin. She must have been four or five. They looked so happy.

That was the thing about time: It changed people.

One day, maybe, she could see herself coming back. Once she had become fully her own person. Then she would be ready to forgive them, and maybe they would forgive her.

One day.

Luna stepped into the world, and let the door close.

Hunter Yee

Hunter didn't realize he was holding his breath until he saw Luna under the trees. Her backpack slammed to the ground; it had to weigh a ton. She flung her arms around him and tucked her face into his neck.

He breathed deep, tried to forget the fear that he would never see her again. His heart had pounded *gone gone gone* as his parents drove away. But he was back now, and here she was. Her warm exhalations and her cold little nose. The smell of her hair, the silk of her skin.

"I packed everything," she said. "I'm ready to go."

He had a thousand dollars zipped into his coat pockets, and he'd just retrieved his bow and arrows. The rest of his stuff was stowed in the trunk of his parents' car. But it didn't matter. All he needed was Luna. The important thing was that they were together.

"I can carry your backpack," he said.

She snorted and hauled it onto her shoulders. "Don't be ridiculous. You're the one who has trouble breathing."

Hunter knew better than to argue. She led the way through the trees until they reached the nests. Fireflies drifted down to hover around them.

"I guess this is the last time we'll be here," said Luna, with a sadness that mirrored his own.

He'd spent so many years waiting until the day he could leave Fairbridge, and now that it was here, he was full of an unexpected grief. This was where he'd first discovered his aim, and met that strange wind, and become a brother. So many hours spent in these woods, showing Cody the tadpoles, loosing arrows into the trees. It had never occurred to him how the memories of this place could one day feel so precious.

He took in a breath. "Once upon a time, Hunt and Lunar left the fair land where they'd found each other, and walked hand in hand to a new place to become who they were meant to be."

Luna tightened her backpack straps. They were ready. They would embark on this journey together. The thought comforted him. He threaded his fingers through hers and looked to the sun to help him choose a direction.

West, he suggested with a tip of his head, and Luna nodded. But as they took the first few steps the fireflies swept around the trees and came down to gather near the bottom of her coat.

"What—?" she began to say, and then Hunter saw the drawstring ties of the red pouch hanging from her pocket.

Luna pulled it out, and the fireflies began to flash their lanterns, winking faster than he'd thought possible.

"Maybe they want to see it," he suggested.

She loosened the ties and poured the stone into her palm.

Hunter backed away to let the fireflies crowd in close. When they lifted into the air once more, the hexagon was glowing. Luna's hand was luminescent with dust.

"Do you smell that?" she said. "It's coming from the stone."

Hunter took one step toward her and the earth sank. He fell to his knees in front of a newly formed section of the crack. It brought that gut-squeezing twist of nausea, a dread that froze him in place. He could feel the darkness staring up at him.

Luna Chang

There was that smell. The rot, and the tang of metal. The crack was full of it, stronger than ever. The temperature dropped; cold soaked through her skin. She felt herself hardening with ice.

Not her hand, though—the one that held the hexagon. That stayed warm and glowing. It made her stomach rumble.

There was something she was supposed to do. The fireflies had made that clear. But what?

Hunter was beginning to wheeze. His quiver and bow had slid off his shoulder, the arrows fallen free. He was on all fours, gasping for breath.

"Are you okay?" she said.

Her ankle was somehow caught, locking her in place.

She looked in the crack and saw shadowy figures. They clawed at the earth, hauling themselves up by the exposed roots of trees. They had the faces of people she recognized. Classmates, teachers. Her parents. Hunter's parents. All of them moving like monsters and climbing fast. Their eyes were milky and full of greed. It was just like the dream she'd had—except she knew that she was very much awake, and these were as real as anything could be.

"I'll just take that, thank you."

The voice broke the spell. The stone was snatched from Luna's hand and its absence was immediately sharp in her stomach.

Rodney Wong held the hexagon up to the sky and squinted at it. He spat his cigarette out to the side. "Such a curious thing. You would never know it was an immortality elixir. How did you make it light up like this?"

"That's mine. Give it back." She didn't mean for her voice to sound so small, but she'd noticed the gleam of a blade in his other hand.

"Actually," he said pleasantly, "it belongs to an emperor who died a couple thousand years ago. But then it became *mine*, and it was stolen from me."

Hunter started to cough, a soupy noise that came scraping up from low in his chest. Luna bent toward him.

"Don't move," said Wong, his voice sharp. "Don't try anything."

"He needs my help," she said, hating how it sounded like she was begging.

Wong laughed and stepped around her. She thought for a second that he was going to offer assistance. Instead, Wong set his foot down on Hunter's knuckles.

"What did you change?" he asked.

Hunter's eyebrows drew together. Luna couldn't tell whether he was wincing or actually trying to respond.

"I couldn't see you before," Wong continued, speaking more to himself. "I couldn't focus on you. I saw you in that restaurant for the briefest moment, and then you disappeared. But I see you now, crystal clear. What did you do?"

In his fall, Hunter's sleeves had shoved up his arms, and Luna saw that his bracelet was gone. The red knots he'd worn the entire time she knew him. Had he lost it?

"Answer me when I ask you a question." Wong leaned his weight onto the fingers. "Or your parents might never see you again."

Hunter began to laugh. He laughed so hard he set his forehead down in the dirt. "My parents," he said in between coughs, "don't give a shit."

The ground trembled. A gust of wind brought the smell of smoke, resinous and bitter. Luna searched for its source and saw how dead grass and twigs on the ground were alive with orange. When she blinked again, she saw flames.

Hunter Yee

Hunter had tried to build a fire from scratch once, during some school nature trip. All he remembered was that it was difficult, even with matches. It took forever for the flame to catch, for the kindling to burn the right way.

This wasn't like that. He heard Luna shout her warning, then flames were rushing up trees. One of the firefly nests lit up, became a comet. With the wind shrill and fast, the fire began to jump. The ground shook and everything rattled. Huang stepped aside just in time. Hunter rolled out of the way as a tree slammed down.

"Luna!" he shouted. He couldn't see her. It was no longer a tree; it was a wall of fire. Was Huang over by Luna? Hunter appeared to be alone on this side of the flames. Unbearable heat pressed against him.

"I'm okay," she called from the other side, her voice tight. "The nests—shoot them down! We have to stop them from burning!"

He wanted to find his way over to her, but the nests were aflame and she was right. They knew the fireflies were important just as surely as they knew that the crack was very wrong. But it scared him that she was out of his sight and so was Huang.

It scared him that he didn't understand what was happening. That they might not survive.

"I'm okay," she said again, as though she knew he needed the reassurance.

Hunter grabbed his bow off the ground. A few fireflies had taken to the air, but most of them were trapped. He raised his bow, brought up an arrow. It hurt his eyes to look at the spheres; they burned brighter than anything he'd ever seen. They were ten suns hanging low in the sky.

He tried to slow his breath, but it was so difficult to breathe. He needed stillness and precision.

And he had it, Hunter reminded himself. He *had* precision.

Stop thinking. Just feel.

He closed his eyes, let the instinct take over.

The wind obeyed and parted for him. He heard the first nest fall into the creek, the flames hissing in the water. He pulled another arrow from his quiver and aimed for the second sphere.

It was a meditation. All the sounds of the world muted. His worry and anger—even his hope—suspended in the split second before he'd begun to shoot. There was just Hunter and his breath and his aim. He shot the nests down until just one was left. The last sun, scorching everything.

He reached for a new arrow, but a hand was at his elbow, stopping him.

"Cody!" he exclaimed in a wash of surprise and fear.

"That one's not burning," his little brother said.

Hunter looked again. The final sphere wasn't glowing with fire but with the light of the fireflies. They were brilliant. They were dazzling.

"How did you get here?" Hunter demanded. But Cody was already gone.

Cody Yee

Jadey leapt out of his pocket. Cody yelped in alarm and dove after her, through clouds of smoke and tangles of brush. Then he realized she was showing him the way around the fallen tree.

On the other side, he saw two bodies wrestling on the ground and tried to figure out how he was meant to help.

A man Cody didn't recognize grunted with pain as Luna kneed him somewhere questionable. He had a hand wrapped under her throat while she clawed at an object in his other fist. Cody watched her fight to bring her teeth to his knuckles and bite down hard. The man snarled, his fingers loosened, and the thing went flying.

It was a stone, shining bright. Something about it was very familiar, but Cody didn't have time to think about it. He gathered it up from the dirt and cupped it in his palms for safekeeping. There was a flash white as snow at the edge of his vision.

Jadey. She bounded through the air and landed on the man's face. It bought Luna the chance she needed to scramble away.

The man tore the rabbit from his head and flung her aside. Then he was lunging for Cody, for that warm and brilliant stone.

Luna Chang

The rabbit slammed into Luna's chest and fell to the ground, limp. There was no time to check if she was okay. Cody tossed the hexagon into the air and Luna caught it by the tips of her fingers.

She gasped with immediate relief. The stone's absence had gnawed at her, and now it gave her a fresh surge of energy. It felt right. Irresistible. There was some scent that it had: buttery and sweet, floral and earthy. Like pastries about to come out of the oven. Like fruit turned ripe in a garden. All of those things.

"Where is it?" Wong roared, knocking Cody off his feet.

"Over here," Luna shouted before the man could land another blow. "I have it."

There was a perfect clarity, sun piercing clouds: She knew what she had to do.

Luna fed the stone between her lips, let its weight settle on her tongue. As her mouth closed over it, the texture changed. It melted like honey, like cream. It tasted just as sweet.

She chewed fast. Swallowed.

The stone was gone.

Hunter Yee

The world tilted. Rocks and branches and other debris slid fast as the ground rumbled. Somewhere underneath him, a fresh crack was developing. Hunter could hear the clicks and pops as things broke under the dirt. He threw himself backward as a gaping maw opened in the earth. It swallowed the fallen tree, fire and all.

The smoke and dust thinned, and Hunter saw Huang take two steps in the wrong direction. Everything shook fiercely.

"Wait!" Hunter called in warning. "Stop!"

Huang teetered at the edge. He was silent as he tipped back, the expression on his face one of absolute surprise. He seemed to smile uncertainly, with more curiosity than fear. His hand reached up as if some invisible person might grab ahold of him. Then he fell out of sight.

Hunter leaned as far as he dared to try to look, wondering if it was like the time that he himself had fallen, if he would see the man crumpled at the bottom. But this was different. There was only darkness. Huang was gone.

Hunter was uncertain how to feel. Relief, exhaustion, regret...they all rolled together. He wondered if he could have done something to save the man—but at the same time, he felt a hollow sort of satisfaction. This shadow that had haunted his family was no more.

He waved his hands to clear the smoke faster. Beyond it he could see the shape of Luna, of his brother. "Are you okay?" he called out to them.

Cody nodded, but Luna clutched at her throat.

"Is something wrong?" said Hunter.

Her eyes were wide as she looked at him. "I swallowed it."

"What?" He was slow to understand her words and even slower to process what he was seeing.

As if a hot-air balloon had taken hold of her, Luna's feet left the ground. She drifted up, gaining speed.

"What's happening?" said Cody.

The fireflies rose from the remaining nest. Their lanterns didn't flicker; they were like new bulbs, incandescent and unwavering. They gathered around Luna, helped her turn in the air like a leaf riding on a breeze.

"Hunter." She reached for him, but she was already too far away.

"Come back," he said. Panic churned in his gut.

"I don't think I can." Her voice was so distant. Jadey leapt off the ground, hind legs kicking at nothing, pumping upward all the same. Luna caught the rabbit in her arms and floated higher still.

He looked around, tried to think fast. A branch caught his attention—the limb of a peach tree that had once swayed high above the woods. An arrow was stuck to it. A thin filament that was knotted to the shaft glistened where it caught sunlight. He remembered watching her tie that knot.

"Do you trust me?" Hunter said, yanking the arrow free of the branch. Could she even hear him?

"Yes," replied Luna, "of course."

Hunter watched how her clothes billowed out around her like wings. He ignored the way his blood pounded in his ears, the tightness settling into his chest. It would work. He would aim for the fabric. The arrow would catch, and he would reel her back down to earth.

He anchored the tail end of the filament around his waist, then looped it around his hand. He wound it over his knuckles a few times for good measure.

Set the arrow to the bow. It was just a matter of sending it into the edge of her coat. The fabric of that thing was strong enough, he was sure.

Hunter blew out a breath and took aim.

The arrow shot into the air. He watched it draw the filament up after it. The binds tightened around his hand, his midsection. Gravity released its hold on him, and he felt himself becoming weightless. His own feet left the ground. He could hear Cody's voice down below, but none of the words.

Hunter rose up into the sky behind Luna, and her face twisted with dismay. Memories came—the other times he'd aimed at her: The dodgeball. The acorn.

He'd missed, because he couldn't hit Luna.

Of course. He'd forgotten. She was the only one immune to his aim.

Hsueh-Ting Chang

Luna's father

Hsueh-Ting was the first to see it. It was the light that caught his attention, made him lean closer to the wheel so he could look up through the windshield. They'd been driving around Fairbridge for hours, trying to figure out where their daughter had gone.

"Turn here," Meihua was saying, pointing to the upcoming intersection.

But Hsueh-Ting pulled over to the side of the road and parked the car right by the woods. "Do you see that?"

There was the shape of a girl, turning and turning as she drifted across the sky, beaming an impossible light.

He saw another celestial shape, bright as a star. When he squinted he could make out a figure, following her like the tail of a kite.

There was an awful feeling in his chest, a splinter wedging into his heart. The glowing shapes disappeared between clouds. He was remembering a night long ago, when his daughter was small enough to be held. Watching her sit in the grass with her head angled toward the heavens, babbling with delight.

"Luna," Hsueh-Ting said, and began to cry.

Luna Chang

All along, she'd been meant for *this*.

The night sky wrapped around her like a blanket. It was cold, but she didn't feel it. Her body had dropped the mask of being human. She was not flesh and bone.

She was cast from the silver of moonbeams.

Luna hugged Jadey close. Together they watched Hunter trailing behind. He would never reach them.

The rabbit began to weep. Luna had never seen such a thing, silent tears streaming down Jadey's face, staining her fur and falling away in shimmering specks. Her little body trembling.

Luna couldn't help herself. She, too, began to cry. How could things be so wrong and so right all at the same time? Her eyes leaked the warning drops of rain. Soon it became a quiet storm. Gray clouds swirled below them.

As they neared the moon, she saw that the fireflies were not actually Lampyridae, or any other species that an entomologist could have recognized. They were particles of moonlight. They had followed her to the earth, and now they followed her back. They sparkled like other pieces of the galaxy.

She landed in a crater. It caught her the way a mother wraps a child in a hug.

Hunter passed overhead, still drifting. He said something she couldn't hear, but she could see the shape of the syllables on his lips. Three simple words.

Yvonne Yee

Hunter's mother

It began to rain. Yvonne's eyes were fixed out the window, praying she would see a sign of her boys and dreading the moment that Huang might appear in the rearview mirror.

Her husband pulled the car over to the shoulder.

"Why did you stop?" she asked tensely, then saw what had caught his attention.

There, out of the dense woods, emerged their youngest son. He walked with a slow, stumbling gait, hair wet and face smudged with dirt. His shirt was torn.

He opened the back door and slid into his seat.

"Where's your brother?" David asked.

"He's gone," Cody whispered. "He's not coming back."

The words were ice, and she began to shiver. It was hard to breathe. The memory that flashed across her mind was of her arms cradling a newborn Hunter, with tiny fists and a full head of hair, opening his eyes for the first time.

She'd gazed down into those two inky droplets, and he'd stared right back up at her, unblinking, while she silently offered all her promises and all her love.

Hunter Yee

Hunter drifted higher and higher, trailing Luna, then passing her. After a while he began to hear words, like an old friend speaking into his ear. Not a friend... but in fact his brother. He heard Cody's voice, loud and clear, telling a story:

Once upon a time, there was an archer who lived in the sky. From his perch beside the moon, he kept the world shining with stars. He nocked sparks against his crescent bow and launched them into the night. It was his divine duty to keep the world in balance.

One otherwise unremarkable day in the middle of eternity, the moon fell. Not the whole thing, but the most important piece of it. The archer made his choice: He dove through the sky, chasing the being he'd always loved.

The wind warned him that down on Earth he would have to be human, and he would remember nothing.

Everything would tilt and stick for as long as that
crucial piece of the moon was missing. But the archer
would help find her. Together, they would return to the sky.

Hunter orbited the moon, attached to his arrow and forever aiming for a target he would not hit. He inhaled the air that Luna exhaled, and so never again did his chest tighten.

In time, he learned to conduct the stars. It was a gift and a curse, to oversee the shooting of the sparks. He chose where to aim them. He watched them go where he could not.

Luna Chang

Luna belonged on the moon. She was its heart and its breath.

Her tears were necessary, she knew. They caught the light as they dropped. They would rinse away the wrongness. And so she wept for days.

It wasn't *all* grief, though she was sad to leave her parents, and to know that they wouldn't remember her. Sad to clearly see the awfulness that seeped from the cracks in the earth and tainted the hearts of people who were fundamentally good.

Sad to be kept forever this distance away from the one she loved.

Hunter arced past, licked gold by the sun, and she called out the three precious words she'd never had the chance to return.

The tears continued to fall, many of them for the sense of peace that overwhelmed her. She would fix those cracks with her ocean of care and nudge the earth back into its rightful place.

For the rest of time, she would gaze upon all that was precious to her. She marveled at her duty. From up here she would do the most extraordinary thing she was capable of: She would love.

Cody Yee

Cody stuck out his tongue and found that the rain tasted of salt. There was no thunder, no lightning. Just water, pouring down for a week straight, filling the cracks in the ground and flooding the roads. There was a rumor that if it kept up, if any more trees and power lines fell, the schools would have to close for a couple days. But the storm ended just as suddenly as it had begun.

He woke up to bright sun, the world washed new.

He discovered that his parents had forgotten everything. The hexagonal stone that had once been the object of their obsession. The terrifying man named Huang.

His parents didn't even remember Hunter.

At school, it was the same. Everyone had forgotten the way the earth had been broken before the rain fell. Cody found a copy of the Fairbridge High School directory and ran his fingers down the line of names. There was no Hunter. There was no Luna.

Everything had changed.

Except for Cody—he alone remembered. He tied Hunter's bracelet around his wrist. He kept Jadey's cage in his room and the special book under his pillow.

He would never forget.

Full Moon

Strange things had been happening in Fairbridge since the beginning of time. People acknowledged such events the same way they regarded a sprinkling of bright meteors expected to pass annually: There was a wonder and appreciation for the phenomenon, but also the certainty that something like it would happen again. They would rather sleep than stand by the window, vigilant.

Decades later, though, some would boast that they'd been paying attention all along. Because who in their right mind would dare to brush aside the divine?

And because it was hard to resist a good love story—especially one that had so shaken the universe, like a pair of dice between cupped hands, watched by invisible eyes to see how they would tumble and land.

Some years, when the moon swelled in preparation for the fall harvest, an old uncle would visit the local language schools where kids studied Mandarin on the weekends. He would teach the children to tie traditional knots, fashion them into bracelets just like the two red ones he wore on his own wrists. And as their hands worked, he would tell them his version of the story of Houyi and Chang'e.

"That's so sad," the kids often said when he reached the end.

"Sad?" Mr. Cody echoed, thoughtfully tapping the book in his lap. "Perhaps. But also how beautiful, that these star-crossed lovers will spend all of eternity up there. One of them a guardian, the other forever in orbit around her. If you gaze long enough, you can see the two of them, and their friend, the jade rabbit. Try it. The next time the moon is full, look up."

Acknowledgments

It feels as though I have as many people to thank as there are stars in the sky. I will do my best to count them all, but I know I'm certain to miss a few.

The very first thanks must go to my beloved agent, Michael Bourret, one of the kindest and sharpest humans I know, and the brightest of moonbeams.

Thank you to my brilliant editor, Alvina Ling, who was the perfect champion for this story, and so patient in helping me carve it into its final form.

My Little, Brown publishing family is a constellation of phenomenal people: Danielle Cantarella, Ruqayyah Daud, Olivia Davis, Janelle DeLuise, Jackie Engel, Shawn Foster, Nikki Garcia, Bill Grace, Stefanie Hoffman, Patrick Hulse, Sasha Illingworth, Savannah Kennelly, Siena Koncsol, Annie McDonnell, Amber Mercado, Christie Michel, Emilie Polster, Marisa Russell, Victoria Stapleton, Megan Tingley, and everyone who worked to make this book glow—I owe you my endless thanks.

The astonishingly talented David Curtis brought the cover to life. And Anna Dobbin was a copyediting genius and guardian angel.

Across the pond there's my wonderful UK team at Orion Children's Books, including Nazima Abdillahi, Naomi Berwin, Hannah Bradridge, Helen Hughes, Alison Padley, and Minnie Tindall—and likely others whose names I have yet to learn—thank you all so much.

I'm the absolute luckiest to have the Dystel, Goderich & Bourret agency behind me, and I must wave extra sparklers for my foreign rights fairy godmother Lauren Abramo, and the kind and glittering Michaela Whatnall. A million thanks also to Mary Pender-Coplan, my very magical film agent over at United Talent Agency.

In 2019, Caldera Arts in Oregon awarded me a much-needed residency. My cabin was nestled in snowdrifts that were higher than I am tall, and occasionally I looked up from my desk to see an eagle pluck a fish from the creek. Those weeks offered me crucial breakthroughs as I rewrote this book.

So many people generously gave me their time and thoughts as I assembled and disassembled and reassembled this story. My earliest readers included such stars as Shenwei Chang, Preeti Chhibber, Sarah Nicole Lemon, Emily Ritter, Marie Rutkoski, and Alexa Wejko.

I'm lucky to have many friends to lean on, and in particular I must thank Dani Bennett, Mia García, Jaida Jones, Delilah Kwong, David Lee, Tiff Liao, Erica Sergott, and Fiona Yu, for always cheering me on and keeping me together.

There are a few MVPs who gamely read *multiple* drafts of this book and offered very smart feedback in addition to emotional support, to whom I definitely owe all the hugs and ice cream: Melissa Albert, Bri Lockhart, Britt Lockhart, and Aisha Saeed. And Joanna Truman, my razor-sharp critique partner who somehow always knows exactly what's missing and what I need to hear.

Special shouts and extended hugs for the Mice & Uteruses: A-M McLemore, Anica Mrose Rissi, Nova Ren Suma—I adore you to the moon and back. The cards say we were meant to be.

My amazing parents dealt with so many late-night phone calls in which I asked for help translating or parsing some new piece of research I'd come across. They also put a giant foam board poster of *The Astonishing Color of After* on their altar, and are always the first to remind me to celebrate.

My nesting partner and constant source of light, Loren Rogers—how did I get so absurdly lucky? Thank you for every minute of every day.

Emily X.R. Pan

Emily X.R. Pan

lives on Lenape land in Brooklyn, New York, but was originally born in the Midwestern United States to immigrant parents from Taiwan. Her debut novel, *The Astonishing Color of After*, was a *New York Times* bestseller, winner of the APALA Honor and Walter Honor awards, a finalist for the *Los Angeles Times* Book Prize, longlisted for the Carnegie Medal, and featured on over a dozen best-of-the-year lists. She received her MFA in fiction from the NYU creative writing program, where she was a Goldwater Fellow and editor-in-chief of *Washington Square*. She was the founding editor-in-chief of *Bodega Magazine*, and went on to co-create the *FORESHADOW* platform and anthology. *An Arrow to the Moon* is her second novel. Visit Emily online at exrpan.com, and find her on Twitter and Instagram: @exrpan.

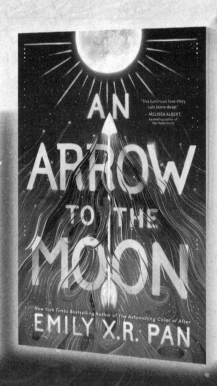